Mary,

Hope you enjoy!

Mark

The
Trophy
Wife
Divorce

The Trophy Wife Divorce

by

John D. Mills

Pono

www.PonoPubs.com

Library of Congress Control Number: TBA ISBN -13: 978-1519404398
ISBN -10: 1519404395

Printed in the United States, Third Printing, October 2019

Editor: Megan Parker
Layout and editing: Inge Heyer

Cover art and map of Pine Island Sound: Cameron Graphics

Pono Publishing
Laramie, Wyoming
Hilo, Hawai`i

www.PonoPubs.com

Acknowledgements

I am grateful to the following people who read my original manuscript and offered ideas for improvement:

Clinton Busbee Chana Busbee Kerry Empson Libby French Lisa Hansen Jack Lurie Anna McDaniel Karrie Miles Bill Mills Jackie Mills Joy Mills
Shara Ray Angela Savko Kami Ward Megan Parker
Stephanie J. Slater Timothy F. Slater Inge Heyer

Pine Island

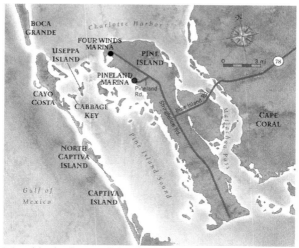

Pine Island is the largest island off Florida's Gulf Coast, located in Lee County in southwest Florida.

Prologue

On a warm sunny afternoon in October, Dr. Stan Jacoby walked to his rented limousine at the Ft. Myers, Florida airport. Stan had come home a day early from a golfing vacation at Hilton Head with three of his country club buddies. Stan's wife, Karen, was a school teacher and had stayed home to teach, so they talked on the phone every night before he went to bed. Stan and Karen had been married for seven years, but the last year had been dismal because Karen had found out about Stan's two affairs.

On Stan's fifth day away from Karen, he realized how much he missed her and felt guilty about his affairs. He went to a jewelry store and bought her a $200,000 diamond and emerald necklace. He called the airline and arranged to come home a day early to surprise Karen and give her the necklace. Karen had always complained that he wasn't spontaneous, so he was certain his early return and generous gift would make her happy.

During the thirty-minute limousine ride to Stan's estate on the Caloosahatchee River, he tried to think of all their happy times together. When Karen was off for summer break, they traveled to Europe every year. During the winters, they would fly to Aspen for weekend ski trips at Stan's condo. However, Karen was always happiest when they were at their beach cottage on the island of Cayo Costa, which was an hour drive from Stan's estate. Stan had bought it for Karen on their one-year anniversary, and it became a frequent weekend getaway.

When the limousine pulled into Stan's driveway at five in the afternoon, he saw an old white Bronco parked at the back of the driveway. He assumed there was something wrong with the sprinklers or pool, and someone was fixing it. The uniformed limousine driver helped him inside the front door with his luggage and golf clubs, and Stan gave him a hundred-dollar tip because he was in a good mood. After the limousine driver left, Stan pulled the jewelry box from his luggage and anticipated a passionate welcome home from Karen. He heard some music coming from their bedroom and figured she was showering or dressing. As he walked down the hallway to their bedroom with his gift, he realized it was Marvin Gaye's *Greatest Hits* CD playing. It was Karen's favorite CD to play while they were making love. She must be missing him.

When Stan was at the door's edge, he heard Karen yell, "Yes! Yes! Yes! It's been so long since someone was that deep!"

Stan walked into the bedroom and saw a muscular Hispanic man having sex with Karen, whose feet were up in the air. Stan tightened his hand on the jewelry box and growled as he ran and jumped on the startled man's back, beating the back of his head with the jewelry box. The muscular man wrestled him to the ground and ended the fight with a right cross to Stan's face. Stan felt the blood explode from his nose, and he passed out.

When he woke up, a female paramedic was waving smelling salts under his nose, and Karen was standing behind her, fully dressed and crying. The ambulance took Stan to the hospital where he was treated for a broken nose, but there was nothing that could soothe his damaged ego. Karen drove him home from the hospital and confessed about her monthlong affair with a fireman. She apologized repeatedly while sobbing, but Stan was silent until they stopped at Walgreen's 24-hour drive through pharmacy so he could fill his prescription for pain killers. When they went through, Stan leaned over from the passenger seat and talked to the pharmacist through the rolled down window. The pharmacist observed Stan's bandages over his nose, Karen's puffy eyes filled with tears, and the lack of communication between the couple.

He quickly filled the prescription and gave it to the distressed couple before a fight broke out in the drive-thru.

Stan and Karen drove home in deafening silence, but Stan knew he was filing for divorce the next day.

Chapter 1

Beth Mancini was sitting at her antique polished mahogany desk at eight in the morning and looking at her court schedule on her laptop while she waited for her divorce client, Mrs. Karen Jacoby. Beth was sipping coffee and trying to figure out when she could take some time off for a long romantic weekend with her boyfriend. The divorce mediation started at nine, and Beth wanted to meet with Karen first to discuss strategy before they walked over to the mediation office. However, Karen was always late, so Beth had set the appointment early, fully expecting her to show up at least twenty minutes late. It was a ten-minute walk to the mediation office, so there'd be time to talk on the way over.

Beth was a young-looking forty-eight-year-old in pretty good shape, but no one had ever called her beautiful. She always had fruit for breakfast and salads for lunch, but her creamy pasta addiction was her major downfall for dinners. She power walked five days a week for two miles around her neighborhood with pink rubber barbells and ankle weights. She walked the stairs to her third-floor office every day, but couldn't get rid of the twenty-five pounds she'd been trying to lose for fifteen years. She dyed her hair the shade of brown closest to her natural color to keep out the gray. When she was younger, she stayed out of the sun, so her fair skin was aging better than all the tanning salon queens she'd grown up with. She got her teeth brightened every year, so she looked younger than she was and was often told her smile was her best trait. However, she was a perfectionist and fretted over her minor flaws.

The Jacoby divorce was full of clichés—a young, gorgeous blond wife, a rich, controlling husband that was eighteen years older than his wife, a pre-nuptial agreement, and the classic seven-year itch. However, when you looked closer at the marriage, the clichés didn't hold true. Karen was a third-grade schoolteacher who chose to continue working after she married and didn't overspend her allowance. In fact, she'd saved some of her allowance in her own savings account over the seven years, and it totaled a little over $100,000. Stan was older, but he was in good shape for his age, and according to Karen, he never needed Viagra. The seven-year itch struck Stan first, and it was his affairs that started the downfall the marriage. However, Karen's retaliation affair with the fireman caused Stan to file for divorce. Karen had hired Beth to defend her in the divorce, and Beth found a way to possibly have the pre-nup voided.

Beth proudly reflected on how she'd discovered a defense to the pre-nup. On the one-year anniversary of the marriage, Stan bought Karen a beach cottage on Cayo Costa, a barrier island on the Gulf of Mexico only accessible by boat. The cottage was worth about 1.3 million and was jointly titled in both of their names. While reviewing the financial disclosure from the husband, Beth saw the beach cottage had a mortgage of $700,000 on it. Beth was curious why a mortgage was placed on the cottage when Stan had plenty of stocks and bonds that he could've sold to pay for it. Beth knew from past divorce cases that people always try to show their financial strength on loan applications. She subpoenaed the mortgage application from the bank and saw five hundred Krugerrands listed as an asset that he had owned since 2001, two years before the marriage.

During Stan's deposition, Beth asked him why he didn't sell some stocks or bonds to pay for the beach cottage. Stan replied smugly that because his stocks and bonds were increasing in value, it made more financial sense to get a mortgage and pay the interest and fees. He lectured to Beth that he would've lost the profits from the increase in value of the stocks and bonds, so he got the mortgage. Beth could feel Stan's confidence in answering her questions, so she threw in the unexpected question—*where are the five hundred Krugerrands currently located?* Stan admitted they were in his safety deposit box at his bank without considering his answer or consulting his attorney. Beth had been worried that Stan would claim he had sold the Krugerrands before the pre-nup and there would be no way to prove otherwise. Beth had carefully set the trap for Stan, and he'd fallen right into it.

Beth promptly filed a motion to set aside the pre-nup because Stan had not disclosed the Krugerrands in his financial affidavit when the pre-nup was signed, as required by Florida law. The pre-nup stated if the marriage ended in divorce, the husband would pay the wife $250,000 as lump sum alimony, and she'd be entitled to no other money, even though Stan was worth fifty million. Karen had been ecstatic that it might be possible to have the pre-nup thrown out by a judge.

Beth walked over to her window and looked down at everyone scurrying about on the sidewalks. She saw Karen come out of a Starbucks across the street from her office, carrying a large coffee. Karen was wearing a tight, dark blue skirt with a white buttoned blouse and red four-inch heels. Karen was 5'2" and had a stunning hour-glass figure with wavy blond hair that fell half-way down her back.

Karen had confided to Beth that Stan always insisted on picking out her outfits whenever they went out together, and that was Stan's favorite combination. Beth was amused at Karen's choice of outfits for mediation. On the day of Stan's deposition, Beth had worn her dark purple business suit with a white camisole and black pumps. She had intentionally worn the same outfit today, a gentle taunt of Stan that she was certain he'd notice because of his obsession over his wife's outfits.

Chapter 2

Beth and Karen were sitting in the warm mediation room waiting for the mediator to return. The room was fifteen square feet with a window facing east. The morning sun was heating up the room. The walls were covered with cheap tan wallpaper, and the room's overhead lights were fluorescent bulbs that quietly buzzed. The mediator, Mrs. Michelle Barnes, had gone down the hall to bring Karen's husband, Stan, and his attorney, Ralph Purvey, to their room for a joint session.

Beth noticed that Karen was tapping her perfectly manicured red nails on the Formica table, so she reached out and touched Karen's arm. "Don't worry, it'll only last a few minutes, and then they'll go back down the hall to their room."

Karen took a deep breath. "My friends from the country club have told me Stan's very angry about us trying to set aside the pre-nup."

Beth said reassuringly, "If he raises his voice, or makes any threats, we'll walk out of mediation and report his behavior to the judge."

Karen nodded.

The divorce had been pending for six months, and each side had taken depositions and reviewed all the financial affidavits. The judge on the case had ordered both sides to attend mediation immediately before the trial was scheduled to begin. There was a knock on the door and Mrs. Barnes walked in first, followed by Mr. Purvey and Stan. Mr. Purvey stepped forward and extended his hand to Beth, "Good morning, Ms. Mancini."

"Good morning, Mr. Purvey," Beth said. She looked at Stan to see if he'd be receptive to a handshake, but he'd already chosen his seat and sat down, looking out the window at the sky to show his disdain for the mediation.

Mr. Purvey extended his hand toward Karen. "Good morning to you, Mrs. Jacoby."

Karen stood up and politely shook his hand. "Good morning."

Mrs. Barnes was an experienced divorce attorney that had retired after thirty years of practice. But she had gotten bored after six months and started doing mediation three days a week. Her silver hair and power red business suit perfectly accented her firm voice. Mrs. Barnes sat at the head of the large oval table with the women to her right and the men to her left. Beth looked to her right momentarily and saw Karen fidgeting nervously. Beth then looked diagonally across the table at Stan, who was glaring at her. Beth stared back at him for a few seconds before glancing across the table at Mr. Purvey, who had leaned back in his chair to listen to Mrs. Barnes's introduction to mediation.

Mrs. Barnes said, "Mr. and Mrs. Jacoby, Judge Sanchez has signed a Mediation Order that requires you to come to mediation this morning."

"Excuse me," Stan interrupted, "it's Dr. Jacoby."

Mrs. Barnes bit her lip momentarily and nodded politely. "I apologize, Dr. Jacoby. Let me start over."

Mrs. Barnes took a deep breath and forced a smile. "Dr. and Mrs. Jacoby, Judge Sanchez has signed a Mediation Order that requires you to come to mediation this morning. If your case settles today, the case is over, and everyone goes home. If it doesn't, you have a trial set for next Monday before Judge Sanchez. The question for both of you is, can we reach an agreement, or do we want a stranger, a judge, to divide up your assets? On one hand, there is a pre-nuptial agreement that limits the amount the wife would get. On the other hand, the wife's attorney has raised legitimate questions about whether there was full financial disclosure by the husband before the pre-nuptial was signed. If the judge finds there was not full financial disclosure, then the pre-nuptial is invalid. If the judge rules the pre-nuptial is invalid, then there are substantial assets to be divided between the parties, as well as the issue of alimony."

Mrs. Barnes hesitated and looked at everyone in the room before she continued. "At this time, we're going to separate. Dr. Jacoby and Mr. Purvey need to go back to their room, and I'll be down there in a while to discuss the case. You have time for a bathroom break, and for Mr. Purvey, a smoke break that I know he needs before I come over. I'll meet with Mrs. Jacoby and her attorney first to discuss the issues in the case."

Mr. Purvey nodded at Mrs. Barnes as he stood up and said,

"You remember my evil habit."

Mrs. Barnes slowly shook her head as she lamented, "I can never settle a case with you when you need a cigarette."

Mr. Purvey was wearing a blue suit and a starched white shirt with a solid green tie and looked the part of the country gentleman that he was. His salt and pepper mustache was sparse and unruly, but his gray hair was slicked back perfectly. As Mr. Purvey gathered his notes and put them in his briefcase, Stan abruptly stood up.

Stan looked at Beth and said loudly, "If Ms. Mancini would just read the goddamn pre-nup, this case would've settled a long time ago. She's just milking this case for her fucking fees!"

Beth felt the heat and flushed from head to toe in anger. She stood up, slamming her rolling chair into the wall behind her.

Before Beth could speak, Mrs. Barnes responded in a stern voice. "Dr. Jacoby, there will be no profanity during this mediation. If you continue, I'll notify the judge of your actions and ask that you be found in contempt of court. If you had read the Mediation Order, you would know Judge Sanchez requires both parties to attend mediation and try to settle the case in an amicable fashion. I assure you Judge Sanchez will consider profanity a violation of his order and could throw you in jail for contempt of court. Do I make myself clear, Dr. Jacoby?"

Stan scowled at Mrs. Barnes before he walked toward the door. "I understand perfectly."

Mr. Purvey watched his client walk down the hall and then looked apologetically at Beth and Mrs. Barnes as he raised his eyebrows. Mr. Purvey walked toward the door and said quietly, "I'm sorry, ladies. I'll try to calm him down and see if we can reach a settlement."

Mr. Purvey stopped at the door's edge and looked directly at Karen. "However, there's a lot of money at stake here, and he feels very angry that Mrs. Jacoby is challenging the pre-nuptial. Maybe we can come up with some more money, but it takes two to reach an agreement."

Mr. Purvey shut the door politely as he left the room, and the three women each took a deep breath.

Mrs. Barnes looked up at Beth and said quietly, "Ms. Mancini, please have a seat and relax. That outburst by Dr. Jacoby was totally uncalled for and everyone, including me, is flustered. I'm going to take a five-minute coffee break and come back. That'll give you and your client time to talk. I'm going to leave my file and notepad here."

Beth sat down and nodded. She looked over at Karen for the first time since the yelling started and saw her pale face.

Karen whispered, "I told you about his temper."

Mrs. Barnes walked toward the door. "I'll see you in five minutes."

After the door shut, Beth leaned back in her chair and tried to relax.

Karen stood up and walked to the window, staring silently at bustling downtown Ft. Myers on a sunny spring day. She let her mind wander away from the stress of the mediation as she gazed down from the fourth floor of the Courthouse Annex Building. She looked across Second Street at the reflective glass walls of City Hall and then across Broadway Avenue at the Veranda, a restaurant in two converted plantation homes. She looked down Broadway about a half mile and saw the spring training home of the Boston Red Sox. The team was in town for spring training, and Karen hoped to go to the afternoon game with two of her single girlfriends if the mediation had ended. They had told her about a party at the beach after the game with some of the ball players. Karen thought that might be a good place to look for her future husband, and she was daydreaming about muscular baseball players with big bank accounts when her thoughts were interrupted by Beth. "I realize that was tough. Are you okay?"

"Yes, I'm fine," Karen said as her thoughts focused back on ending her current marriage.

Beth shook her head as she said, "I've never had an outburst like that before during mediation."

"I told you he yelled when he gets mad," Karen said as she sat back down. "Now you know what I've been dealing with."

Beth nodded as her thoughts drifted to what Mr. Purvey was telling Stan at this moment. Was he reprimanding him, or was he secretly congratulating him? Was he counseling Stan to end mediation and take his chance at trial?

Karen turned to Beth and asked, "What do you think we should do?"

Beth pulled her chair toward the table and put her hands together on top of it, fingers interlocked. "The first thing we do is talk with Mrs. Barnes about our settlement offer.

She'll then go down to their room and talk about it with your husband and Mr. Purvey. If they make a reasonable counter offer, we can continue to negotiate and try to settle today. If not, we have a trial next Monday and Tuesday in front of Judge Sanchez, and he'll decide the case. Of course, if it goes in our favor, your husband can appeal the ruling, and the case could be tied up for another year. The appeals court could rule either way. More time, more uncertainty, and more attorney fees."

Karen shook her head. "I'm so afraid of his outbursts. I'm not sure how much more of this I can take. Maybe we should just take the money from the pre-nup and be done with it."

"You're the boss," Beth said. "However, let's look at the facts. Florida law says that a pre-nup is invalid if a spouse doesn't make full financial disclosure to the other spouse before signing the pre-nup. Your husband disclosed his forty million dollars in Google stock, his five million dollars in bonds, and his real estate. The house on the river here in Ft. Myers and his mountain condo in Aspen totals just under five million. The cash in his money market account was around $100,000, so the total assets disclosed in the pre-nup were about fifty million dollars. However, he failed to disclose the five hundred gold Krugerrands that were in his safety deposit box at the time of the pre-nup. They are worth $1,000 a piece, so he failed to disclose an asset worth $500,000."

"So does that make the pre-nup invalid?" Karen asked. Beth replied, "There has to be full financial disclosure, and the cases have interpreted this to mean 'substantial' full disclosure. The issue is, does the failure to disclose the Krugerrands mean that substantial full disclosure was not made?

"Our argument." Beth continued, "is that $500,000 is a substantial amount, and therefore, the pre-nup is invalid. Their argument is that $500,000 is only one percent of his net worth, so it was an inadvertent mistake, and substantial disclosure was made. It is an interesting situation, and there is no case law on point."

Karen asked, "What do you think we should offer?" "If the pre-nup is set aside by the judge, based on the standard of living during the marriage, I think you're entitled to 3.5 to 4 million in alimony. You own half of the beach cottage, and there is approximately $600,000 in equity after the mortgage is paid off. Of course, you're entitled to half of the beach cottage even if the judge doesn't set aside the pre-nup, because it's jointly owned. And if I remember correctly, you said you wanted the beach cottage outright in the settlement?"

Karen nodded emphatically.

Beth continued, "I think we should offer to settle if he pays you two million in cash, signs over his portion of the beach cottage, and pays my attorney fees. Of course, that's our initial offer. We can always negotiate if he makes a reasonable counter-offer."

Karen contemplated Beth's analysis for a few seconds. "I want the beach cottage and as much cash as I can get, but I think I'm definitely worth more than $250,000."

Beth nodded. "I understand."

Karen looked back out the window toward the Red Sox training field. She started thinking about how much fun it would be to invite her two girlfriends and three eligible bachelors from the Red Sox out to her beach cottage this weekend since it was her weekend to have it. Stan and Karen had agreed, through their attorneys, to alternate weeks at the beach cottage. One spouse would have it from Wednesday at two p.m. until the following Tuesday at six p.m., and they would alternate weeks. Of course, on Wednesday morning a cleaning lady would take a water taxi to the island and clean it before the other spouse showed up in the afternoon.

Beth looked over at Karen staring out the window and wondered about her emotional state. Beth was confident she would get over the divorce and find another husband as soon as she was ready. Karen was a petite blond with curves in all the right places, and stunning turquoise eyes. Her college education, sense of humor, and looks made her quite a package. Beth chuckled to herself and wondered how many future divorces she would handle for Karen.

Chapter 3

Mrs. Barnes walked back in the room with a smile on her face and said in a cheerful tone, "I hope we're ready to make some progress after that unfortunate beginning."

Beth followed the skilled mediator's lead. "We're ready to make a reasonable offer. I hope Mr. Jacoby has calmed down."

"Don't you mean *Dr.* Jacoby?" Mrs. Barnes asked sarcastically.

Beth rolled her eyes and Karen snickered.

Mrs. Barnes sat down at her seat at the head of the table and pulled her file and pad close. She looked at Karen and began, "You have a standard pre-nuptial that contains a clause that requires the wife to pay the attorney fees of the husband if she challenges the pre-nuptial in court and loses. Mrs. Jacoby, that means if the judge rules against you, your husband's attorney fees are deducted from your pre-nuptial pay-out. Let's assume your husband's attorney fees after trial are $75,000. If you lose, that means his attorney fees of $75,000 are deducted from your $250,000, for a lump sum payment of $175,000 to you.

"As far as the beach cottage goes, you're entitled to half of the equity, which is $300,000. Your husband could buy you out, or the beach cottage would be sold and the cash distributed. Therefore, if you lose at trial, you would get approximately $475,000 cash, less after attorney fees."

Mrs. Barnes looked at Beth. "What are your fees at this point, and if the case doesn't settle, how much more for trial?"

Beth opened her file and did a quick calculation. "At this point, the total fees are just over $50,000, and I've been paid $25,000 so far. I would estimate another $15,000 for trial of the case."

Mrs. Barnes wrote down the figures and said, "That means the current amount owed of $25,000 combined with the projected $15,000 for trial is an additional out-of-pocket $40,000 for Mrs. Jacoby. This amount is deducted from the $475,000 for a net payout to Mrs. Jacoby of $435,000, if she goes to trial and loses."

Mrs. Barnes let the figure sink in and looked at Karen until she nodded that she understood. Mrs. Barnes then looked at Beth and asked, "What have you calculated as the best-case scenario if Judge Sanchez throws out the pre-nup and gives you alimony?"

Beth looked down at her own notes and then at Mrs. Barnes. "Based on the standard of living during the marriage, I think she is entitled to 3.5 to 4 million in alimony plus the $300,000 of equity in the beach cottage. If the judge throws out the pre-nup, Mr. Jacoby will have to pay my attorney fees of $65,000. Therefore, a best-case scenario is $4,365,000."

Mrs. Barnes wrote down this figure and pulled her cell phone from her pocket. She used the calculator mode in her phone before she looked up. "I think this case could go either way. Therefore, I added up the best-case scenario and worst-case scenario and divided by two. The average is $2,400,000."

Beth nodded. "I've discussed the issues with Mrs. Jacoby and we've got an offer we would like to make: he pays two million in cash, signs over his portion of the beach cottage, which is worth $300,000, and pays my outstanding attorney fees of $25,000. The value of this offer is $2,325,000."

Mrs. Barnes wrote down the offer and looked up at Beth. "It seems we're on the same wavelength."

"What about his affairs?" Karen asked. "They're what started the downfall the marriage. Does he have to pay for them?"

Mrs. Barnes leaned back in her chair and said, "Florida is a no-fault state. It doesn't matter the reason for the divorce, and there was no clause in the pre-nuptial that penalized either side for affairs. So, it really doesn't make a difference, Mrs. Jacoby."

Beth looked sideways at Karen and said quietly, "We really don't want to open up that can of worms, do we?"

Karen grabbed her chair's arms and blew out her breath. "I only had my affair after his second affair," she said as she shook her head. "I couldn't be loyal to him after he slept with my cousin."

Mrs. Barnes and Beth exchanged looks, and the silence was heavy for a moment. Mrs. Barnes took the high road and said, "Well, it doesn't affect the financial analysis, so there really is no logical reason to bring up affairs in the marriage. By either party."

Karen frowned, but didn't say anything. She thought back to when she found out about Stan's first affair. Karen's mother had been diagnosed with breast cancer two summers before, so during summer break she spent six weeks in Chattanooga, Tennessee helping take care of her with her dad. Her mother's lumpectomy was successful, followed by radiation, and she returned home at the end of the summer. She noticed that Stan seemed distant, but she wasn't concerned because he was always moody, and she'd learned to accept it. He claimed he was playing poker with his friends three nights a week, but she didn't care because she was depressed her mother declined to have a mastectomy, and the odds of the cancer returning were greater. She never thought of an affair because no man had ever cheated on her, or broken up with her, during her entire life. She had always ended the relationships when she became bored or decided to trade up for a newer model.

One night, Stan came home late and smelled of Scotch and cigars. Karen was watching an old movie, curled up on their leather couch, underneath a quilt her mom had made for her when she was a child. Stan kissed her sloppily, stripped down, and crawled underneath the quilt with her.

He wanted sex and Karen agreed, but she convinced him to wait until the movie ended in fifteen minutes. Stan stretched out on the couch and relaxed. By the time the movie was over, Stan was passed out and snoring, with his head on her lap. Karen gently put a pillow under his head and got up from the couch. She put her quilt over him and left him to sleep for the night.

She picked up his clothes and took them to the utility room for the housekeeper to wash in the morning. She turned on the light to check for anything in his pants pockets that might get wet and took out his cell phone, wallet, and keys before she threw his pants into the hamper. She grabbed his shirt, socks, and white underwear to throw in the hamper and that was when she noticed the long red hair on his underwear. Stan had short black hair, the housekeeper had gray hair, and she had blond hair, so there was no other explanation for this errant hair. Karen was stunned as her suspicions grew that Stan had cheated on her.

She checked Stan's cell phone and looked at his recent call log. There had been two calls that day to someone named Tami, so she scanned the text messages and found Tami's name. She clicked on Tami and read texts between her and Stan, starting at ten that morning:

10:00 Stan:— can't wait to c u tonite!

10:03 Tami:— woke up this morning & thought of u. had to get out rabbit & play. gonna hurt u tonite!

6:14 Stan:— just finished golf. do u want me to bring food over?

6:15 Tami:— bring what u want, but when u get here, I'll b ur all u can eat buffet!

Karen was enraged and threw the phone against the wall. She felt her blood roaring in her ears and in her forehead. Her first thought was to run into the family room, wake Stan up with a powerful slap, and confront him. But then she remembered what one of her friends had told her about how to get back at cheating husbands: don't get mad, get even.

She picked up Stan's phone and was glad to see it was still working. She texted Tami:

I was in shower & found crabs on my balls. u nasty whore!!! what else hav u given me??? never want to c u again!!! have a good life!!!

Karen walked over and put the stopper in the utility sink and turned on hot water. She grabbed a bottle of bleach and poured half in the sink. She dropped the phone in the sink and grabbed his wallet. After she took out the cash and threw the wallet in the sink, she turned the water off. She grabbed his car keys and the bottle of bleach and walked out of the utility room.

As Karen walked into the family room, she fantasized about dumping the bleach on Stan's face, but remembered the mantra, don't get mad, get even. She walked down the hall, through the kitchen, past Stan's study, and out into the garage. She opened the trunk of Stan's white Bentley, took out his golf clubs, dumped the rest of the bleach into the trunk, and shut it. She opened all the doors and wondered what she could do to the inside of the car to piss him off the most. She walked over to Stan's workbench, got a box cutter, and proceeded to slice up the leather seats. She looked over at the workbench and saw a can of black spray paint. She grabbed the paint and wrote 'Tami' on the hood of the Bentley and sprayed the doors and trunk.

Karen stepped back and admired her work—she was definitely getting even, and she was enjoying it. She felt momentarily guilty about having fun extracting her revenge, but thought of the red hair, and the thrill returned. She grabbed a seven iron from his golf bag and broke every window and dented every part of the Bentley. She picked up his prized golf bag that was signed by Jack Nicklaus that he'd bought at a charity auction for $25,000 and walked out the side door of the garage, into the pool area, and up to Stan's oversized Weber Grill. She lifted the grill lid and put the clubs on the top of the grilling grate, opened up the gas valve to high, and hit the spark switch. She watched the flames leap up to the bottom of the grate and, after a few moments, smelled the leather on his bag starting to burn.

Karen calmly walked back to their bedroom and packed her clothing and toiletries. She loaded up her three suitcases into her Mercedes and walked back into the house and stared at Stan passed out on the couch. After a few minutes of contemplation, she left a note on the kitchen island:

> *Stan,*
> *I saw the texts from Tami and saw her red hair on your underwear. I got mad and did some things. I'm sure you'll notice if you walk around. Do you want to be married or do you want to fuck whores the rest of your life?*
> *Your loving wife, Karen*

Karen stayed an hour away at the Ritz-Carlton in Naples for a week. She finally agreed to meet with Stan and listen to his sob story about being bored and lonely. She wasn't impressed, but she had done many calculations with the money she would get from the pre-nuptial versus staying with him and enjoying the good life. She decided to give him one more chance and returned home.

A year later Karen's mother died when the breast cancer returned. Karen and Stan traveled to Chattanooga for the funeral and to take care of Karen's father. They stayed at the downtown Hilton, and Karen helped her dad with the funeral preparations since she was the only child. On the day of the funeral, Karen was a wreck and needed two Valiums to make it through the burial. Stan drove Karen, her father, and her cousin back to Karen's parents' house in his new Bentley. Karen wanted to stay the night with her father for support, so Stan agreed to drop off her cousin on the way back to the Hilton. Karen's cousin felt the need to accompany Stan back to his hotel room instead. When Karen showed up unexpectedly at midnight, she made the embarrassing discovery that her cousin was double-jointed and welcoming Stan to Chattanooga in her own special way. At that point, she knew the marriage was over but didn't want to lose her luxurious lifestyle. Karen stayed married and had her affairs, but Stan only discovered the one with the muscular fireman.

* * * * * *

Mrs. Barnes said to Beth, "I'll take your offer down to Mr. Purvey and Mr. Jacoby and see if I can get them to offer some more money. You both have time for a bathroom break and some coffee. If you walk outside, just tell the receptionist up front."

Beth nodded. "Sounds good. I need a break."

Mrs. Barnes left the room with her notes and Beth looked over at Karen. "I'm going to the ladies' room. Want to come along?"

"No, I'll just wait here."

Beth walked out the door and down the hall to the ladies' room with her purse. After she finished and washed her hands, she decided to put on some lipstick. As she concentrated on her lips in the mirror, she noticed the lines starting to form on each side of her lips and became flustered. She moved her glance up to her crow's feet at the edge of her eyes and thought they'd grown from the day before. Beth thought about Botox or getting her eyes done, but it was hard to take a week off to let the bruising heal after the surgery. Many of Beth's female divorce clients got plastic surgery during the divorce to help their confidence as they reentered the dating world, so she knew which doctors to call. One of her clients had told her a little nip and tuck was good for the soul and Beth had agreed.

18

Beth's brother was four years younger than her and had developed Multiple Sclerosis at thirty-nine. He was married with four school-age daughters and had struggled physically and financially since he'd gotten sick. Beth's father died of a heart attack at forty-eight and her mother developed Parkinson's at fifty-nine. She'd been in a nursing home since she turned sixty, and the last time Beth had visited, her mother hadn't recognized her. Beth thought about how healthy Mrs. Barnes looked for her age. Mrs. Barnes was about twenty years older than Beth and in remarkable shape for her age. She played tennis three days a week and hiked mountain trails in North Carolina during the summers at her mountain cabin. Her hair was silver, but stylishly coiffed and well-conditioned. She had lines on her face but looked healthy and vibrant. Beth couldn't help but wonder if she'd age as well.

Chapter 4

Mrs. Barnes knocked and slowly opened the door to Stan's mediation room, which was the mirror image of Karen's room. She saw Mr. Purvey and Stan Jacoby sitting at the table, talking. Stan stood up. "Mrs. Barnes, I'm sorry that I yelled in front of you, but I'm angry about this divorce and how much money it's costing me."

Mrs. Barnes nodded, but didn't say anything until she sat down. She motioned for Mr. Jacoby to sit down and said, "I understand divorce is stressful and expensive. However, if you yell and scream, the case won't settle, and it'll be more expensive. My job is to try and settle this case today and help you avoid the time, stress, and expense of a trial. And remember, if you lose, it'll cost you a lot more money."

Mrs. Barnes let everything sink in before she continued. "Let me ask you something. Do you want to be divorced?"

Stan's face turned red before he stammered, "Of course I do. I can't stay married to a woman that screws around on me with a Neanderthal fireman."

Stan Jacoby was forty-nine years old and stayed active by playing golf four days a week. He was six feet tall and skinny with gray hair, and his large roman nose dominated his narrow head. He was always in a hurry wherever he was going, and when he got there he sat and tapped his right foot for hours until he relaxed. He was a retired dentist that listened to classical music, watched FOX news two hours a day, and read at least one book a week. When he found out his wife was having an affair with a fireman, he had to go into therapy for three months.

Mrs. Barnes said, "Dr. Jacoby, you're a retired professional. Let's think about the divorce from a business perspective. Let's look at the best-case scenario and the worst-case scenario. How does that sound?"

Stan looked over at Mr. Purvey, who nodded. Stan let out a long breath. "Okay, tell me what you think."

"The best-case scenario is if the judge upholds the prenuptial," Mrs. Barnes said. "Your attorney fees are deducted from the $250,000 payout. Mr. Purvey, what are your fees now, and what will they be through trial, if required?"

Mr. Purvey had anticipated the question and didn't have to look at his file. "My fees to date are $70,000 and have been paid. If we go to trial, it'll be another $20,000."

Mrs. Barnes nodded and looked back at Stan. "Best case scenario, you go to trial and win. You deduct $90,000 from her $250,000 settlement for a payout of $160,000. Of course, you either have to sell the Cayo Costa beach cottage or buy out her interest for $300,000. In either event, it'll cost a total cash payout of $460,000."

Mrs. Barnes waited and looked at Stan until he nodded. "Now, let's look at the worst-case scenario. If the judge rules that your failure to disclose the Krugerrands in the safety deposit box is substantial, then the pre-nuptial will be set aside. I'm sure Mr. Purvey has discussed this issue with you."

Stan nodded again, and Mrs. Barnes could see the muscles in his jaw flex as he ground his teeth.

"If the pre-nuptial is set aside," Mrs. Barnes continued, "then the judge will look at the standard of living during the marriage to decide on an appropriate amount of alimony.

Mrs. Mancini thinks this amount is between 3.5 to 4 million. In addition, if the pre-nuptial is set aside, you'll have to pay her attorney fees of $75,000, plus buy out your wife's interest in the Cayo Costa beach cottage for $300,000. Therefore, a worst-case scenario is $4,375,000."

Stan put his head in his hands and didn't say anything. Mrs. Barnes looked over at Mr. Purvey for guidance, and he shrugged slightly. A few moments later, Stan looked up and asked in a quiet voice, "What do they want?"

Mrs. Barnes looked at her notes and said, "The settlement offer is that you pay two million in cash, sign over your portion of the beach cottage to her, and pay her outstanding attorney fees of $25,000. The value of this offer is $2,325,000."

Stan didn't say anything, but he stood up and walked to the window. He thought back to when he met his first wife while he was in dentistry school and she was a registered nurse. They married his final year of dentistry school without a pre-nuptial agreement and divorced four years later with no children. He'd paid her a lump sum settlement of $65,000 in cash and thought that was highway robbery.

One year after the divorce, Stan's parents had died in a plane crash, and he inherited $400,000. His stockbroker, Greg Rasmussen, had convinced him to invest his inheritance in a new company called Google. Five years later, he was worth fifty million dollars and retired from dentistry. He'd enjoyed being a rich bachelor for six years, until he had become lonely. He and Karen met. She'd fallen in love with Stan's money, and he'd fallen in love with her looks. Stan knew she was a gold digger, but he loved how she prospected, and they'd married six months after they met. He thought he'd protected himself with the pre-nuptial, but now she wanted more.

Stan walked back to the table and sat down. He looked at Mrs. Barnes and said calmly, "I'll make her one offer, and she can take it or leave it. I'm not going to sit here all day paying attorney fees and mediator fees. If she doesn't like it, we'll let a judge decide. I'll pay her $650,000 cash, and she signs over her interest in the Cayo Costa beach cottage to me."

Mrs. Barnes finished writing down the offer and looked up. "Dr. Jacoby, I'm pleased you've made an offer to settle, but in my experience, a 'take it or leave it' attitude is not conducive to settlement."

Stan's face turned deep red, and he bit his lower lip. He counted to ten silently and said calmly, pronouncing each word, "Tell her to take it or leave it. Please use those exact words."

"If you insist," Mrs. Barnes said and left the room.

Stan remembered how he'd discovered Karen's affair with the fireman, and he became even angrier. After Karen drove him home from the hospital, he told her to sleep in the guest bedroom, and she readily agreed. The next morning Karen went to work like normal, but the first thing Stan did when he woke up was call Mr. Purvey—his lawyer from his first divorce and the lawyer who had prepared the pre-nuptial for his marriage to Karen. Stan went to Mr. Purvey's office in the afternoon and filed for divorce. After he left Mr. Purvey's office, he stopped at his bank and transferred some money to Karen's bank account and went home. Stan had insisted they keep separate accounts when they got married so he could monitor Karen's spending. However, he didn't know about Karen's savings account until she had filed her financial affidavit for the divorce, and he was surprised at her thriftiness.

Karen got home from teaching at four every day, and he
wanted to be out of the house when she got home. He wrote a note
to Karen and left it on the kitchen island before he went to the
country club bar to get drunk. The note said:

> *Karen,*
>
> *I met with Ralph Purvey and filed for divorce. Have your
> divorce attorney contact my attorney to accept service of
> the petition, or I'll serve you at school with the papers in
> front of your kids. You had a nice life with me, but you've
> screwed it up. I'm at the bar getting drunk. I deposited
> $20,000 into your checking account today. I expect you to
> get your own apartment and be moved out within three
> days. As you know, there is a pre-nuptial, and I owe you
> $250,000. Once you sign the divorce papers, I will pay you
> the money. This should be a quick divorce and you can fuck
> whoever you want!*
>
> *Stan*

Stan accomplished his goal and got drunk at the country
club bar. He told anyone that would listen about what Karen had
done to him. One of the waitresses, who hated Stan because he was
rude, overheard his story and saw his injuries. She happened to live
in the same apartment complex as Lee Atkins, a newspaper
columnist who used to be Stan's patient when he was a practicing
dentist. Lee had a root canal performed by Stan, and it was still
painful after three days. Lee went to a different dentist to fix the
problem because he wasn't happy with Stan's bedside manner. Stan
refused to refund his money from the root canal, and Lee became his
enemy. The waitress and Lee were on friendly terms and enjoyed an
occasional beer together. When the waitress got home that night
from work, she went over to Lee's apartment and told him what
she'd heard and seen.

Lee was ready for payback, and it was just too juicy of a
story to pass up. He correctly calculated that Stan would be back at
the country club the next afternoon for happy hour. He arranged for
a photographer to hide in the bushes at the country club and take
pictures of Stan's bandaged nose and black eyes with a telescopic

lens. The waitress had told Lee that Karen was a teacher at her son's school, so Lee downloaded Karen's picture from the school board's website. The following day he went to the courthouse and got a copy of Stan's divorce petition from the clerk's office to verify his story. The next day Lee knocked on Stan's door at nine in the morning with the same photographer and a digital tape recorder turned on.

When Stan opened the door, Lee shoved the recorder in his face and asked forcefully, "Isn't it true you caught your wife having sex with another man and got in a fight with him?"

The photographer had his camera set to automatic mode and the camera started taking pictures every second. Stan's face flushed as his eyes cinched up in anger and he yelled, "None of your fucking business!"

The headline in Sunday's paper read, *TROPHY WIFE DIVORCE STARTS BADLY*. Underneath the headline were three pictures: one of Stan's injuries to his face taken at the country club, one of Karen from the school board's website, and one of Stan's contorted face yelling at Lee after being confronted at his house. The story gave details of Karen's affair, a copy of the divorce petition, and quotes from an unnamed source at Stan's country club giving details about Stan's fight with Karen's lover.

Chapter 5

Beth and Karen were sitting in their room waiting for Mrs. Barnes to return from her meeting with Mr. Purvey and Stan. They had discussed the issues in the case and how the trial would go if the case didn't settle. Beth decided to kill some time with small talk.

"Do you want to have children?"

Karen shifted in her seat and cleared her throat. She tapped her nails for a few seconds on the table before answering. "Well, eventually I do, I think. I'm thirty-one, so I have plenty of time to decide."

Beth couldn't stop herself from looking at her own, short unpainted nails that she filed herself. She was a reformed nail biter and was proud her nails had grown back to an average length and appearance, except for her left pinky.

During her second divorce, she started biting her nails again. Finally, after three months of nail biting, she made a plea bargain with herself: she'd only bite her left pinky nail and let her others grow back. It had been four years and she'd not violated the compromise with herself. She didn't get her nails manicured because she knew the nail tech would stare at her left pinky and give her a knowing look. Beth didn't think about her nails except whenever she was around a woman with a manicure and her insecurities came flooding back.

Beth's curiosity got the best of her. "Did you and Stan ever talk about kids?"

Karen gave a forced smile before she answered. "Stan had a vasectomy three years before we were married. He said he'd worried about women tricking him and getting pregnant because they knew they'd get a lot of child support from him. He told me if I ever wanted a child, he'd have it reversed or we could adopt. I enjoy my children at school, but I'm not sure I want to change my lifestyle at this point in my life. And besides, I always worried about pregnancy ruining my body."

Beth clenched her teeth and squeezed her chair's arms tightly as she faked an understanding nod. Beth had always wanted children when she was younger, but she had cervical cancer when she was twenty, so it wasn't an option. She enjoyed being around kids and everyone called her the perfect aunt, but it still hurt her psyche that she couldn't have children. She used her nurturing instincts on her two cats, a Persian named Bella and a Tabby named Gracie.

Beth married her college sweetheart, Arthur "Artie" Zimba. Artie was a 5'10" baseball pitcher on scholarship and majored in English, along with Beth. He was a skinny left-hander and couldn't overpower hitters with a fastball so he used changeups and curve balls to strike out the other teams' batters. His freshman year, the game announcer dubbed him a "crafty left-hander" and the nickname stuck. Beth and Artie started dating her junior year, right after she recovered from her cervical cancer, and they married the summer after graduation. Before marriage, they had discussed the fact that Beth couldn't conceive, and Artie said he didn't care because he was in love with her and wanted to spend the rest of his life with her. Beth started law school while Artie started teaching high school English and working on his master's degree. The summer before Beth's third year of law school, he came home one night and confessed to an affair with another teacher and that she was pregnant with his child. The next day, Beth decided she wanted to be a divorce lawyer and she became her first client.

Beth didn't marry again until fourteen years later when she was thirty-nine. She had bought an old house in the historical area of Edison Park, near downtown Ft. Myers. The historical designation didn't allow houses to be torn down; they had to be renovated. Therefore, she had the house gutted down to the brick structure before she began renovations. She hired all the sub-contractors to do the required work and that's how she met her second husband, Alex Martinez.

Alex owned his own electrical company and was a very charming, second generation Cuban. His suave manners, good looks and high energy overwhelmed Beth's reservations about dating someone working on her house. Once they started dating, Beth felt like a lovesick teenager. She thought of him all day and dreamed about him at night.

After six months of dating, Beth proposed to Alex and he accepted.

During their sixth year of marriage, Alex had to do some rewiring at Beth's office and met Beth's young secretary. They started having an affair and hid it from Beth for three months. One morning at the breakfast table, Alex started crying and told Beth he was leaving her because her secretary was pregnant with his child. Beth started biting her nails again.

*　*　*　*　*　*

Karen checked her text messages from her girlfriends going to the Red Sox game. The game started at one in the afternoon and would last until around four, depending on the scoring in the game. Karen was more interested in the party after the game and meeting the players. She texted her friends back that she'd let them know when mediation was over.

Karen looked over at Beth, who was lost in her own thoughts, and asked, "Have you ever been to Cayo Costa?"

Beth focused back on Karen. "I haven't. Tell me about it."

Karen smiled as she thought of her favorite island. "It's a nine-mile-long island, narrow at the south end and wide at the north end. It's just south of Boca Grande and about five miles west of Pine Island, and it's only accessible by boat. It's got a very interesting history. The Calusa Indians lived there from the early-1200s until the Spanish arrived in the mid-1600s and took it over. There are three different Indian mounds spread out over the island."

"What's an Indian mound?" Beth asked.

"Stan told me that the Calusas piled all their used shells from oysters, scallops, and fish bones into mounds. He said over the years they built up, and that's where they held rituals and where the chief lived. Our cottage is built on top of one of the mounds, and Stan always said he was the chief and I was his squaw. I used to think that was cute."

Karen hesitated and looked over at the window for few seconds before she continued. "The Spanish named it Cayo Costa, which means 'key by the coast.' The Spanish established a settlement because there's a fresh water spring on the south end of the island, and small deer lived there. They brought in horses to patrol the island and pigs to eat, along with the deer. They also planted orange and lime trees on the island. The Spanish ships going up and down the coast could stop there to resupply with water and citrus to help avoid scurvy. The pigs and deer are still on the island but all the horses died out in the late 1970s."

Beth said, "Come on. You're telling me descendants of the Spanish horses survived on the island until the 1970s?"

Karen nodded. "Yes. I talked to a fishing guide who was born and raised on the island in the sixties. When he was growing up, he saw the horses run wild up and down the island in a small group of five. They had inbred so much the horses were white with pink eyes and they were mean.

He said they'd chase you if they smelled oranges or limes on you. He told me one time he saw a horse come up to their property and eat a key lime pie that was sitting out on a picnic table."

Beth said, "That's interesting they survived that long."
"The pigs have spread like wild fire," Karen continued.

"They're hundreds of them on the island. They root around our cottage occasionally, but some of them have swum to adjoining islands for fresh feeding grounds. There're a few deer still around, but you only see them in early mornings and late afternoon. There are all kinds of birds—bald eagles, osprey, blue herons, and egrets. It's quite the nature preserve."

"So how long were the Spanish on the island?" Beth asked.

"They were there for about fifty years and then abandoned the settlement because they built forts around Tampa that could better protect the ships from the English and the pirates."

Beth smirked. "Pirates? Are you serious?"

Karen nodded. "Oh yeah. You've heard of the pirate, Gasparilla? In the late 1700s, his main compound was up in Boca Grande, on Gasparilla Island, and they raided the ships going up and down the coast. They'd steal the ships, kill the men, and ransom the women. Apparently, it was very profitable to ransom the women, and virgins were worth a lot more. The non-virgins stayed with Gasparilla and his crew on Boca Grande for their pleasure, but the virgins were protected on a different island so their value didn't go down."

Beth rolled her eyes and put her pointer finger to her

mouth, faking vomiting.

Karen snickered and continued, "Gasparilla kept the virgins on an island south of Cayo Costa, named Captiva, which is Spanish for 'captive.' Gasparilla trusted his older men to guard the virgins from his drunken crew, or anyone else, until the ransom was paid. Stan said the US Navy killed Gasparilla in a battle off Cayo Costa's coast in 1821 and that was the end of the pirates in the area. Of course, there haven't been any virgins on Captiva since that time either!"

Beth laughed and said, "Wait a minute, I've stayed on Captiva at South Seas Resort!"

Karen smiled and held her hands out. "I rest my case." When Beth finished laughing, she asked, "What about pirate treasure on Cayo Costa?"

Karen nodded. "If you walk around the island, all the old oak trees have deep holes dug out around the roots. The rumors among all the old timers were that since the pirates didn't have banks, they buried their treasure around some landmark that wouldn't blow away in a storm, and they could find it in the future. The oak trees are on high ground in the middle of the island, so the treasure chests were buried around them. Of course, when Gasparilla and his crew died in the naval battle, no one claimed the chests. There are rumors among some of the old timers that their distant relatives found some of the buried treasure, but everyone gets real tight lipped when you ask specifics."

Beth was skeptical. "You don't really believe that stuff, do you?"

Karen nodded. "I do. I've seen all the holes around the oak trees. Another reason is Stan and I were drinking at the Cabbage Key bar one night, and the bartender there told me a wild story. His granddad was running a bulldozer on Useppa Island, the island next to Cabbage Key, in 1965 when they were building a golf course. He was removing some old oak trees from an Indian mound they were leveling. One afternoon right before five, he pushed over a big oak tree and they found an old wooden box about four feet long with a rusted, old fashioned padlock. It was too heavy to move, and they couldn't get it opened. The supervisor sent everybody home on the company boat for the night to the mainland, and he said he was going to ask the island's owners about what to do with the chest.

The next morning, when they came back to work, the chest was opened and empty, but they found one gold Spanish doubloon in the sand a few feet away. No one ever saw the supervisor again."

Beth was mesmerized and thought of what she would do if she found buried treasure. She wondered to herself if she'd do the same thing—take the money and run.

Karen continued, "Every time I walk by the old trees and see the holes, I think of the buried treasure on all the barrier islands, and I wonder if there is any left."

Beth smiled. "I'm intrigued. Have you ever looked for pirate treasure on Cayo Costa?"

Karen shook her head. "I asked Stan if he wanted to look one day, and he told me that Google stock was his treasure, and that we should be happy with that."

Beth started to ask why he didn't want to share his treasure with his wife, but she didn't want to offend her client. She decided to steer the conversation back to the safer topic of Cayo Costa. "What happened on the island after Gasparilla was killed?"

Karen said, "Remember your history about Florida. It didn't become a state until 1845, so Spain still owned it in the early 1800s. Cuban fisherman came up to Cayo Costa and started 'fishing ranchos.' They caught the fish, dried them, and transported them back to the Cuban markets. This went on until Florida became a state and the Cubans abandoned the fishing ranchos. After Florida became a state, some settlers from the Southern states moved on to the island."

Karen went on, "Boca Grande pass is about two miles wide and separates Cayo Costa and Gasparilla Island. Boca Grande is on the southern tip of Gasparilla Island, and it became a thriving port for cattle and phosphate exports because the railroad brought everything from the center of the state. The United States government set up a quarantine station on the north side of Cayo Costa, across the pass from the port at Boca Grande. All immigrants entering the country through the port had to stay there for a week to make sure they didn't have yellow fever. The government put in limestone rocks on the north beach to help avoid erosion around the dock. The docks have been torn down since, but you can still see all the rocks and walk the old quarantine trail on the island."

Beth said, "I had no idea there used to be a quarantine camp on Cayo Costa."

Karen nodded. "They had a school, post office, and a general store. It was a thriving, small settlement, and a lot of workers on Boca Grande lived there because it was cheaper than living on Gasparilla Island. Some of the workers homesteaded there, and other people on the mainland bought property there for weekend getaways. In 1976, a state park was established on Cayo Costa, and the state bought about ninety-five percent of the land, but a few people didn't want to sell to the State. Stan bought our property about six years ago from a local family that had a weathered shack on it. He tore it down and built us a modern beach cottage."

"Do you have electricity and running water?"

Karen smiled. "We do, but it's not from the mainland. We dug a well that provides our water, and our electricity is from solar panels and propane gas."

Beth was perplexed. "How do you get electricity from propane gas, and where does the gas come from?"

"Once a month," Karen explained, "a barge brings a propane truck to the island and ties up at different docks. The truck runs long hoses to fill up the propane tanks at all the cottages it can reach. The propane runs a generator that stores the electricity in some system that Stan had installed. The system also stores the electricity from the solar panels on the roof. I don't know exactly how it works, but we have electricity."

Beth said, "I've only been concerned about the financial aspects of the beach cottage, so I never thought about the history of your cottage or the island."

Karen nodded. "I love it out there because it's so isolated and beautiful. It's a one-of-a-kind property, and we both enjoy it. I hope to celebrate my divorce settlement out there this weekend."

Beth was amused by Karen's optimism. "It's too bad you've got to teach school on Monday, or you could celebrate longer if we settle today."

Karen said giddily, "I don't have to teach Monday or Tuesday because I took personal days off for the trial in case we don't settle today. If we do settle today, I'm still gonna use my personal days for some retail therapy at the mall and go to the spa for a pedi and a mani."

Beth nodded and leaned back in her chair. "Why did you become a teacher?"

Karen smiled and said fondly, "My eighth-grade teacher, Mrs. Brand, was one of my childhood heroes. She was a very intelligent lady and dressed impeccably. Her husband was a very successful architect, and every summer they traveled to Europe. When we studied world history, she'd bring in a slide show of all the famous places she'd been. We saw her at the famous places as we studied them in our books.

I thought it was the coolest thing to see her in the Roman Coliseum in shorts and sunglasses.

"She also was in charge of our spring dance and was very particular about having all the decorations just right. She told us dances were just as important as academic subjects because everyone needs fun in their life. Her favorite saying was, 'What good is it to be successful if you don't have fun?' I thought she was the coolest lady with a wonderful life, and that's when I decided I wanted to be a teacher."

Beth took a deep breath and lamented, "It's been a long time since I got dressed up and went to a spring dance.

Maybe I'll drag Frank out dancing this weekend."

Karen laughed. "You go, girl! Text me some pictures of you dressed to the nines.

Chapter 6

Mrs. Barnes knocked softly on Karen's door and opened it slowly. She looked at Beth and Karen as she walked to her seat and said, "We've had some progress, but I'm not the least bit happy with Mr. Jacoby's attitude."

Karen looked over at Beth and shook her head. "I told you about his temper. Once he starts, there's no going back."

Before Beth could answer, Mrs. Barnes said, "Actually, his temper has calmed down. He apologized to me, and we had a good discussion about the issues in the case. He was very thoughtful and calculated when he talked to me about a settlement. What concerns me is that he told me his offer is a 'take it or leave it' offer. In fact, he insisted that I use those exact words when I told you his offer."

Beth rocked back in her chair and looked over at Karen, who was focused on Mrs. Barnes.

Karen quickly asked, "What's his offer?"

Mrs. Barnes looked at her notes for a second. "He'll pay you $650,000 cash if you sign over your interest in the Cayo Costa beach cottage."

Beth wrote down the offer and did a quick calculation. "He's basically offering $100,000 more than what he owes with the pre-nup and a buyout of the beach cottage."

Karen looked angry. "That's bullshit. He had seven years with me in the prime of my life, and I put up with all his crap. I'm worth more than that."

Karen walked to the window, crossed her arms, and fumed. Beth and Mrs. Barnes looked at each other but didn't say anything. Beth knew from her experience that she should wait for Karen to lead the conversation. It was at this point in negotiations that a spouse had to decide to settle or risk a trial, and each client required different amounts of time and advice. Beth waited.

After a minute, Karen walked back to the table and sat down. "I'm irritable and hungry. Can we take a lunch break? I can decide what I want to do over lunch."

Mrs. Barnes looked at her watch. "It's eleven twenty-five,

and I think this is a great time to break for lunch. We'll beat the noon rush. I'll let you choose which restaurant you want to eat at, and I'll suggest they go somewhere else."

Karen looked over at Beth and shrugged.

Beth looked at Mrs. Barnes. "We're going to the Veranda. How about we meet back here at one?"

Mrs. Barnes nodded. "Perfect. You two go ahead, and I'll let them know. I'll see you back at one."

* * * * * *

The Veranda restaurant was formed by lifting an old plantation home from its original supports and moving it two hundred feet next to an adjoining old plantation home, between which a kitchen was built. It's a wooden restaurant with an old South décor in the middle of the downtown cement jungle.

You enter by walking up wide brick steps to large wooden doors with artistic wrought iron grills with stained glass at eye level. The doors open to a large parlor area with a high ceiling and a piano bar in the middle of the room. The waiting area and hostess podium are to the left with decorative wrought iron windows looking out over the parking lot. To the right is an L-shaped bar that ends at a swinging door going back to the kitchen area. Past the L-shaped bar is a floor-to-ceiling wine rack on the wall. Behind the piano bar is a large fireplace that separates sections of the restaurant.

A hallway to the dining room is to the right of the fireplace, and the windowed terrace to the left looks out over a lush outdoor garden dining area, bordered by oak trees and bamboo clusters. There are nine tables in the bar area that are used for dining during lunch. All the walls have patterned mahogany paneling covered with old black and white photos of Ft. Myers and the famous people who had visited, and the carpet is hunter green. The high ceilings, wooden construction, wrought iron windows, and old-fashioned light fixtures make you feel like you're in the early 1900s in a New Orleans restaurant. The Veranda is one block from the courthouse, so it's a favorite lunch spot for lawyers and downtown businessmen.

Beth and Karen entered the Veranda, and the cool air refreshed them from their walk from the mediation building. There was a party ahead of them being seated, so Beth looked around and saw a couple of regulars eating lunch at the bar and waved to them. They waved back to Beth but were ogling Karen and undressing her with their eyes.

Karen noticed them and gave a polite nod as she turned back toward Karen and rolled her eyes. Beth was certain Karen had endured similar stares from other men on a daily basis since she was in high school.

The hostess walked up and asked Beth, "Would you like to be seated in the bar, the dining room, or the courtyard?"

Beth looked around the room. "How about the table in front of the wine rack?"

"Sure," the hostess said, and led them over to the table and gave them menus.

"This is one of Stan's favorite restaurants," Karen said as she sat down. "I'm sure it pissed him off when Mrs. Barnes told him we were coming here and that he should go somewhere else."

Beth smiled. "Actually, that's why I asked for this table. Everybody that's seated in the dining room has to walk by this table, and we can see everybody else that goes to the courtyard or sits in the bar. I'll bet you Stan shows up here and tries to intimidate us by his presence. I didn't want a table in the back where he has to look for us. I wanted us front and center so he sees us as soon as he walks in."

Karen leaned forward and asked, "You think he'll show up here even when Mrs. Barnes asked him not to?"

Beth nodded. "I've seen other arrogant men like him—doctors, lawyers, businessmen—and they like to play games during mediation. They try to intimidate their wives during mediation by saying things like 'take it or leave it,' or saying mediation will end in two hours because they have an important business meeting. And I've seen a few husbands show up at the restaurant I choose, even when the mediator asks them to go elsewhere. So, I figured I might as well play games with him."

Karen cocked her head to the left and asked, "Games, as in plural?"

Beth told her about how she was wearing the same outfit as the day of Stan's deposition and thought he'd remember because he always insisted on choosing Karen's outfits. Karen howled with laughter, and the curious guys at the bar turned around to look at the gorgeous woman again. The waitress walked up and took their drink orders—tea for Beth and a very dry martini for Karen.

Beth looked over to the entrance and said, "Told you—game on!

Karen turned and saw her husband and Mr. Purvey walking in the front door. The hostess was seating another party, so they stood at the podium waiting their turn. Stan scanned the room quickly until he spotted them, and Beth gave him a small wave with her right hand.

Karen snickered. "I need to go to the bathroom. I'll see you in a few minutes."

After Karen walked back toward the restroom, Beth looked at Stan, who was glaring at her, and then Mr. Purvey, who quickly looked away. The hostess picked up two menus and motioned for them to follow her to the dining room. Mr. Purvey was behind the hostess and clearly uncomfortable with being at the Veranda.

As he approached Beth's table, he gave a feeble smile and said politely, "Hope you have a nice lunch, Ms. Mancini."

"You too, Mr. Purvey."

Beth looked back at Stan, and said in a saccharine voice, "I'd stay away from the gumbo. It's a little too spicy."

Stan's face turned red. "I like the damn gumbo."

Beth smiled and shrugged her shoulders as he walked by. She watched him walk away, but after a few steps he glanced back and gave her a nasty look. Beth smiled again, and he snapped his head forward and walked faster. She was pleased with herself because his attempted intimidation was shot down in style. Beth decided Stan was a classic bully— he walked all over people until they stood up to him. Beth was sure he wasn't used to many people, especially a woman, standing up to him. However, Beth hoped his anger would calm down before they went back to mediation so that they could reach an agreement.

Beth looked back to the entrance and was pleasantly surprised to see her boyfriend walk in. Frank Powers was a prosecutor with the State Attorney's Office and handled violent crime cases. Frank was fifty-two and had been a prosecutor ever since he had gotten out of law school. He was 5'11" with gray hair that he'd had since he was thirty, but he was in good shape because he rode his bike every morning. He and Beth had been dating for a year, and she was the happiest she'd been since her second divorce.

Frank was there with three prosecutors, and the hostess led them to a table on the other side of the room. As Frank walked around the piano bar, he spotted Beth and smiled. He told his companions he was going to walk over to Beth's table and to order him an iced tea. Beth forgot about the stress of the mediation, and her heart beat faster as

he got closer. She stood up and Frank gave her a peck on the cheek. Frank was never comfortable with public displays of affection, but in private, he was a passionate lover.

Frank asked, "Who are you here with?"

"Karen Jacoby, my divorce client whose husband has all that Google stock. We're in the middle of a nasty mediation."

Frank nodded. "I remember that one. You're trying to get the pre-nup set aside."

The waitress brought the drinks to the table and told Beth she'd be back to take their order in a few minutes. Beth saw Karen walking up to the table and turned toward her. Frank turned around and faced Karen, as Beth gestured toward Karen with her right hand.

"Frank, this is Karen Jacoby. Karen, this is my boyfriend, Frank Powers. He's sitting across the room with three other prosecutors from his office."

Karen shook his hand. "Nice to meet you, Frank. Your girlfriend is earning her money today dealing with my soon-to-be ex-husband."

"You're in good hands," Frank answered. "I hope you can reach a settlement today and avoid the stress of a trial."

Beth stepped toward Frank and rubbed his back gently with her left hand. "I know you're busy with your trial today, so we won't keep you. Call me tonight when you're done."

Frank nodded. "This afternoon I cross-examine the defendant, so we're brainstorming over lunch. I'll tell you about it tonight." He turned and looked at Karen. "It was nice meeting you."

Karen answered, "It was nice meeting you too."

As Frank walked back toward his friends, Beth sneaked a quick peek at his butt. Beth was thoroughly impressed that Frank hadn't given Karen the quick up-and-down gaze like every other man in the Veranda. Beth decided she was in love at that moment.

She'd been holding back because she feared being hurt again, but Frank hadn't even noticed Karen's looks because he'd been focused on her. She'd always trusted Frank, but now, in some primordial way, her heart knew that Frank only wanted her. Endorphins flowed through her body, and she felt like a giddy teenage girl after her first kiss.

Beth and Karen sat down as Karen whispered, "He's cute."

Beth answered proudly, "I know, and he's smart too. He's the senior trial attorney in the major crimes division at the State Attorney's Office and handles murders and rapes. He's on day three of a nasty murder case where a husband allegedly strangled his wife out of jealousy because she was having an affair. There were no eyewitness to the murder, and when the husband was questioned, he blamed the boyfriend. The defense is that her boyfriend actually strangled the wife because she was ending the affair and he was angry. It's purely a circumstantial evidence case."

Karen took a sip of her martini and asked, "What does that mean?"

Beth explained, "The evidence against the husband is that the neighbors heard some yelling at three in the morning, looked out the window, and saw the husband's SUV in the driveway. The next morning the husband called 911 at seven in the morning to say he just came home and found his wife strangled in their bed. The husband claimed the night before he was upset about the affair and had been drinking, so he walked a mile to his favorite bar at 10:00 p.m. and left at closing time. His credit card receipt confirms he paid $47 at 1:58 a.m., but his story is he was so distraught, he walked around town until he got home at seven in the morning and found his wife dead. And here's the kicker—both the husband's and boyfriend's sperm were on the sheets, but it's impossible to tell how long either one had been there."

Karen took another sip of her martini. "I can't believe she brought her boyfriend to the house and didn't wash the sheets."

Beth was irritated by Karen's analysis of the proper way to have an affair, but she bit her tongue. Fortunately, the waitress walked up to take their order and rescued Beth from her thoughts. Beth ordered chicken piccata with linguini, and Karen ordered a garden salad with vinaigrette on the side.

Beth decided it was time to steer the conversation back to

mediation. "What do you think about your husband's offer?"

Karen took a longer sip of her martini and focused for a few seconds. "I think it's good and bad. It's good because I didn't think Stan would ever offer more than the pre-nup, but it's bad because I deserve more. What do you think?"

Beth answered, "You heard my legal analysis earlier. But at this point, you have to ask yourself, 'Is the offer close to what I would settle for?' If the answer is yes, let's make a counter-offer. If the answer is no, let's end mediation and get ready for trial."

Karen drained her martini as she contemplated her dilemma. "Let's offer one million cash and he signs over the beach cottage."

Beth nodded. "That's a reasonable offer. How far would you come down if he made a counter-offer?"

"I've been thinking about that. I'd come down to $850,000 cash and him signing over the beach cottage to me, or 1.3 million cash and I sign over the cottage and he keeps it."

Beth smiled. "That sounds like a good resolution to the case. Hopefully, we can settle after lunch if your husband wants to avoid a very expensive trial that he might well lose."

Chapter 7

Mrs. Barnes walked into Karen's room. "I hope everyone had a good lunch."

Beth nodded. "We had a very nice lunch at the Veranda, even though Mr. Jacoby showed up."

Mrs. Barnes sat down and shook her head. "I can't say I'm surprised. He's such an arrogant and pompous man. He didn't bother you, did he?"

Beth smiled. "No, but I think I might've gotten under his skin a bit."

Mrs. Barnes noticed Karen's smirk and decided not to ask for details, instead steering the conversation back to the mediation. "What have you decided to do with the offer?"

Beth answered, "Mrs. Jacoby wants to counter-offer one million cash, and he signs over the beach cottage to her."

Mrs. Barnes wrote down the offer on her pad and looked up. "That's certainly a reasonable counter-offer. Is there any wiggle room with these figures?"

Beth looked at Karen and said, "I think we could move a little bit, if they make a realistic counter-offer."

Mrs. Barnes stood up as she said, "I'll be back in a few minutes. I hope their lunch has settled well, and we're able to make some progress."

Mrs. Barnes walked down the hall and knocked softly on Stan's door. When she opened it, she saw Mr. Purvey and Stan sitting stiffly at the table, but they didn't appear to be engaged in a conversation or have any notepads or calculators on the table.

Mrs. Barnes walked into the room as she said, "I hope everyone had a good lunch."

Stan said abruptly, "Lunch was fine. Did she accept my offer?"

Mrs. Barnes sat down and took a deep breath. "Your wife has made a counter-offer. She'd be willing to settle if you gave her one million cash and sign over your portion of the beach cottage to her."

"Doesn't she understand English? I told her to take it or leave it, and I meant it." Stan shook his head in anger and said firmly. "I withdraw my offer to settle—we're going to trial, and that little gold digger is going to lose. This mediation is over."

Mrs. Barnes was shocked and looked over at Mr. Purvey. "We've made progress in negotiations. I don't think it's prudent to end mediation so soon."

Mr. Purvey looked at Stan quizzically and Stan adamantly shook his head. Mr. Purvey said evenly, "I'm sorry, Mrs. Barnes. My client has made up his mind."

Mrs. Barnes looked at Stan. "You're serious? You want to take a chance at trial that you might lose four and half million?"

Stan answered, "I told her to take it or leave it. It's her fault, and I don't care if I lose at trial. I'll just appeal and win it there. Meanwhile, she doesn't have any play money to go on all those vacations she loves so much."

Mrs. Barnes said, "If that's the way you feel, I'll declare an impasse and tell them. I suggest that you go ahead and leave the building while I tell them the news."

Mr. Purvey nodded. "We'll leave right away." Mrs. Barnes cleared her throat and stood up.

As she walked to the door, Stan looked over at Mr. Purvey and said irritably, "You know what? It would've been cheaper to hire a different prostitute every month. I would've had variety, and they would've been thrilled with the money. And, most importantly, I wouldn't have had to listen to any bullshit."

Mrs. Barnes was livid. When she reached the doorway, she turned and asked Stan, "Do you know the difference between sex for money and sex for free?"

Stan answered sarcastically, "No, I don't."

"Sex for free is more expensive," Mrs. Barnes said icily.

She gave a fake smile and shut the door. As she walked away, she could hear Stan calling her a fucking bitch and felt some satisfaction knowing she'd gotten under his skin. She walked back down the hall to Karen's room and knocked on the door before she entered.

Karen blurted out, "What did he offer?"

Mrs. Barnes didn't say anything until she sat down. "Mrs. Jacoby, I'm sorry to say your husband didn't respond well to your counter-offer. He said no and withdrew his prior offer to settle. He ended mediation and said he's going to trial."

"What?" Beth asked incredulously.

Karen was quiet and walked over to the window.

Mrs. Barnes looked at Beth. "When I told him the counter-offer, he said, 'I said take it or leave it, and I meant it. The settlement offer is withdrawn, and mediation is over.'"

Beth shook her head. "What a son of a bitch."

"I tried to talk him into continuing mediation," Mrs. Barnes said, "but he'd have no part of it. I've never had mediation end so abruptly by withdrawing the settlement offer after one round of negotiation. He is certainly a bitter man."

Beth leaned back in her chair. "I've never had a mediation end so quickly either. I hope Judge Sanchez throws out the pre-nup and gives us five million in alimony. That'll teach him to keep his ego in check."

Everyone was quiet for about ten seconds before Mrs. Barnes said, "I told them to go ahead and leave the building, so give them about five minutes. It probably wouldn't be good to run into them in the lobby."

Beth nodded. "I agree. We'll stay here and talk for a few minutes."

Mrs. Barnes stood up and extended her hand to Beth. "I'm sorry we weren't able to settle. Good luck at trial."

Beth shook her hand and thanked her. Mrs. Barnes said to Karen, "It was nice meeting you, Mrs. Jacoby. Good luck next week."

Karen didn't say anything or turn around, but she lifted her right hand and gave a weak wave. Mrs. Barnes took the clue and left the room without saying anything else.

After the door shut, Beth pulled her cell phone from her briefcase and called her secretary. "Hi Audrey, we just reached an impasse at mediation, so I'll be in trial starting Monday. I need you to clear my calendar for tomorrow, Monday, and Tuesday. I'll be back to the office in a little while."

Chapter 8

Beth and Karen walked out of the mediation office and to the elevator in silence. Beth had never seen Karen so absorbed in her thoughts before. She wasn't sure if she should try to engage her in conversation. She decided to let Karen instigate any conversation, so when the elevator door opened, she quietly stepped in first, and Karen followed. Karen didn't look at Beth or say anything on the ride down. When the elevator door opened on the first floor, Beth looked over at Karen and gave her a sympathetic smile.

Karen said quietly, "It's all about control with that son of a bitch," and stepped off the elevator before she continued. "He doesn't like his Barbie doll standing up for herself, and he knew I wanted this to settle today."

Beth followed Karen out the exit to the parking lot. "I agree. But at this point, we have no choice but to be ready for trial on Monday. I feel good about your case, and I hope Judge Sanchez will agree with us."

"Is there anything I can do to help you prepare?" Karen asked as they walked toward her red SL550 Mercedes in the parking lot.

Beth shook her head. "No, I need to organize all the financial information in a cataloged trial notebook for the judge to review. After that, I'll prepare my questions for Stan to make him look bad to Judge Sanchez. He's such a hothead, that it should be easy to push his buttons. You enjoy your time on Cayo Costa this weekend. Come to court looking tanned and fabulous. That'll drive Stan crazy."

Karen opened the door to her car and finally smiled. "That sounds like a great plan. You have my mobile number if you need me."

"Let's plan on meeting at my office at eight on Monday morning to go over some trial questions for you," Beth said. "Why don't you bring Starbucks coffee for both of us, and after that we can walk over to Judge Sanchez's courtroom together?"

"Sounds good. See you then," Karen said and waved goodbye.

Beth turned to walk toward her office and her other clients' problems. Her office was on the third floor of a building that was one block from the courthouse. She had a receptionist and a secretary to help her manage her eighty pending divorce cases. Beth had developed a reputation for handling tough cases, and her phone was ringing constantly with prospective clients. She was able to pick and choose which cases she wanted because of this demand for her services. She'd been practicing long enough to spot problem clients and referred them to other firms to help keep her sanity. She enjoyed helping clients get through this depressing and stressful part of lives.

It was only a three-minute walk back to her office, but she enjoyed the fresh air and sunshine. In Ft. Myers, the springtime was usually sunny and in the low eighties with low humidity. The blazing one hundred-percent-humidity summer was still a few months off. Beth walked into her building and dutifully took the stairs to her office, wondering how many phone messages she had waiting. She opened her door and saw one of her most needy clients, Mrs. Shany, waiting in the reception area.

Mrs. Shany was getting divorced and was in a nasty custody battle for her ten-year-old daughter, Mistee. Mrs. Shany alleged her husband was a chronic alcoholic that was endangering the child. And not to be outdone, her husband had alleged Mrs. Shany was addicted to alcohol *and* marijuana, which was endangering the child. Beth suspected they were both right about their vices, but both parents loved Mistee and thought they should have sole custody because the other parent was unfit. The judge had entered a temporary order that split custody with alternating weeks with each parent.

He had also ordered a parenting evaluation done before he set the case for trial.

Mrs. Shany saw Beth walk in and blurted out, "You won't believe what he did. He bought Mistee a black lab puppy, and now she wants to go over there all the time to see the damn dog. She's always wanted a black lab, and now he has one at his house. I know she's going to tell the parenting evaluator that she wants to live with her father. I want the judge to do something!"

Beth shrugged her shoulders and asked, "What do you want the judge to do?"

Mrs. Shany hesitated and started to tear up. "I want the

judge to order him to get rid of the dog."

"The judge isn't going to do that," Beth said sympathetically.

Mrs. Shany started crying. Beth didn't know what to say. Mrs. Shany continued crying and sat down in her chair with her face in her hands. Beth sat down and tried to think of something to say to console Mrs. Shany as she looked through the window at her receptionist, who was on the phone trying to help one of Beth's other clients while another line was ringing. Beth could faintly hear her secretary, Audrey, talking on the third line to a client in the back office. Beth didn't have time for this type of problem and needed a solution to get Mrs. Shany out of her office.

"I know how you can beat him at his own game," Beth said.

Mrs. Shany looked up with hope. "How?" Beth smiled. "Go buy two black lab puppies."

Mrs. Shany hesitated for a second and dried her tears. She smiled slyly and arched her eyebrows. "I've got a better idea—I'll buy three puppies, a black lab, a yellow lab and a chocolate lab. And I'll let Mistee name them, since he didn't let Mistee name his puppy, and she'll like all the different colored lab puppies."

Beth thought of all the furniture that would be chewed up and all the puppy accidents, but she forced a smile. "Sounds like a great idea."

Mrs. Shany stood up and thanked Beth as she walked out the door on a mission. Beth was certain that she'd outspend her husband in the puppy wars.

Beth walked through the inner door and waved to her receptionist on the phone, who smiled back. She looked over at Audrey in the back office talking on the phone and lifted her head in greeting at her as she walked toward her office. Audrey looked up at Beth and held out her right hand, moving her fingers up and down, signaling a persistent talker.

Beth walked into her office and set down her briefcase as she looked at the red light blinking on her phone. She sat down and listened to her twelve voicemails, writing down messages and organizing them in order of importance. Before she could start returning calls, Audrey walked into her office.

"I've cleared your calendar, but you're gonna have to call

Mr. Baer and Mrs. Wilson because they're not happy about being rescheduled. I explained to them when their case goes to trial, they'd get the same treatment, but they both demanded that you call them today, so I put them through to your voice mail. I'm sorry I couldn't make them happy."

"Yeah, I heard them already." Beth sighed. "Don't worry about it. I'll call them back and let them bitch about their spouses for a while, and they'll feel better. They just need a little hand holding."

"Okay." Audrey shrugged and walked back to her desk. Beth looked at her messages and decided to first call an old client, Ms. Edwards, who wanted to refer one of her tennis team members from the country club that just got served with divorce papers. Beth knew that anyone from Ms. Edwards' country club was loaded and would be a lucrative case for her. Mr. Baer and Mrs. Wilson could wait a few minutes before she listened to them complain about their unreasonable spouses. Beth had a mischievous thought about playing matchmaker and introducing Mr. Baer to

Mrs. Wilson and they could talk to each about their divorce dilemmas. Beth let her amusing thoughts about fixing up her clients fade away as she called Ms. Edwards.

Ms. Edwards answered on the second ring and started talking rapidly. "Beth, thank God you called me back. My best friend, Joyce Sinclair, just got served with divorce papers while we were playing tennis, and she's devastated. She's been married for twenty-six years, and they have three kids in college. She had a little indiscretion a few months back when she was drunk, and her husband just won't let it go. When can we see you?"

"I have a big trial on Monday and Tuesday of next week, and I'm going to be preparing tomorrow. So, how about next Wednesday at ten?"

Ms. Edwards persisted, "Can't we come in today? She's got all kinds of questions that I can't answer. Please?"

Beth looked down at her calendar. "I'll tell you what. We can meet at five for an hour, but I won't be able to file a response until next week."

"We'll be there. I'm going to drive Joyce because she's taken a couple of Valiums. Thanks so much for seeing us today."

Audrey walked into Beth's doorway and held up a finger.

Beth nodded.

Beth finished her call with Ms. Edwards. "If Joyce is your friend, I'm sure we'll get along, and I'll do my best to help her. See you at five."

Ms. Edwards said goodbye and hung up. Beth looked up at Audrey. "What's up?"

Audrey shook her head as she said, "You're not gonna believe this. Judge Sanchez's judicial assistant just called. Judge Sanchez's daughter is up at college in Gainesville and got in a bad car wreck this afternoon. She's in intensive care, and the judge just left his office to drive up there. He's cancelled everything on his docket next week, so the Jacoby case got continued to next month."

Beth leaned back in her chair and said quietly, "I hope his daughter will be all right. I met her once at a judicial appreciation banquet. She was very sharp."

"Your calendar has been cleared through Tuesday. What do you want me to do?"

Beth rolled her neck, cracking the vertebrae before she answered. "I'm not sure. Let me think about it. First, I need to call Karen and let her know her case got continued."

"Let me know what you want me to do with the schedule," Audrey said, and she turned and walked back toward her office.

Beth called Karen and told her what happened.

"That's disappointing. I was hoping to have the trial next week," Karen answered in a monotone voice.

"I agree. My calendar is clear, and I was ready to make Stan's life miserable during trial after he showed his ass today. He really needs to be put in his place."

Karen hesitated for a second before she said cheerfully, "I've got a great idea! Why don't you come with me to the beach cottage this weekend? I'm leaving tomorrow morning and coming back Sunday morning."

"I don't know," Beth said. "I've got so much going on."

Karen chided, "I heard you tell Audrey to clear your calendar. We'll be back in town by noon on Sunday, and you'll be rested for next week. Come on, it'll be fun."

Beth hadn't had a full week away from her practice in three years. A couple of times a year, she'd take a long weekend, but it'd been at least six months since she'd done that. Beth considered her new lucrative case coming in at five that afternoon and told herself she deserved to have a little fun.

Beth answered happily, "You talked me into it. What time do we leave tomorrow morning?"

Chapter 9

Beth called Frank on his cell phone at a quarter till seven that evening. "Hi, honey. I just finished up with my new divorce client. What're you doing?"

"I just got home with a nice bottle of champagne for us to celebrate my guilty verdict," Frank said proudly.

"That's fantastic, honey. I'm going to celebrate too. I just got a big case in, and I'm spending the weekend with Karen Jacoby at her beach cottage because the trial got continued."

"That's wonderful. We can both have a drink and not worry about driving."

"Great. I'll be over in a few minutes. I'm just leaving the office."

Frank lived on the tenth floor of the Downtown Towers condominiums, looking over the mile-wide Caloosahatchee River.

The Caloosahatchee River starts as a narrow river leaving Lake Okeechobee and flows west, emptying into the Gulf of Mexico by Sanibel Island. Frank's condo was about halfway between Beth's office and her home in Edison Park, so it was a five-minute drive for Beth either way. Frank's condo was two bedrooms with two baths and had two dedicated parking spots in the gated parking garage on the first two levels. Frank had given her a gate opener and a resident's sticker for her white Toyota Camry. There was a large swimming pool and club house on the third level that was popular with the residents. Each unit had a ten-foot closet by their parking spaces for storage. Frank kept his bike there and rode it five miles every morning before work.

Beth parked in her spot next to Frank's blue Explorer and got out. She took off her suit jacket and left it in the car. She knew Frank would like her white camisole. Beth loved falling asleep next to Frank after making love and feeling his warmth all night long. As she walked to the elevator, she thought about what had happened to her at lunch. She had stopped fighting her feelings for Frank and allowed herself to fall in love for the first time since her second divorce. She prayed that Frank felt the same about her.

Beth had only been in love four times in her life. Her first love was her high school sweetheart, and that relationship had ended when they went away to different colleges. Her second love was her first husband, but the marriage only lasted two years. She was single from twenty-five to thirty-nine. She had dated some nice men but had never fallen in love. Her third love was her second husband and that marriage lasted six years. Beth didn't date for a year after her second divorce. She dated a few men after that, but experienced no emotional connection until Frank came along. Now, he was the fourth love of her life. She hoped he would be the last.Beth got out of the elevator and used her key to open Frank's condo. She heard Frank's favorite CD playing on the stereo—Sinatra's greatest hits. When she first met Frank, she thought it was a little old fashioned, but it'd grown on her and she'd learned that Sinatra's music meant great sex.

Sinatra's music had an immediate effect on her body, just like Pavlov's dog responding to stimuli.

"Hi, honey. Where are you?" Beth asked.

Frank walked out of the kitchen barefoot, wearing old khaki shorts that showed off his muscular calves and a faded orange t-shirt. "Over here, lover. Come give me a kiss!"

Beth and Frank walked toward each other and met in a full embrace. Beth had on two-inch heels, so she only had to lift her head up slightly to meet Frank's lips. Beth let her tongue explore Frank's mouth, and he pulled her tighter as they kissed like teenagers on their third date. Beth came up for air and looked at Frank's green eyes as she ran her hands through his hair.

"I love you," Beth said quietly.

Frank's nostrils flared slightly as he smiled and looked into Beth's brown eyes. "I love you, too."

They kissed, and Beth felt the heat between them in crease. Beth thought of Frank's dating history and wondered how he felt about her. Frank had never been married and had no children. Since he got out of law school, he'd been in eight long-term relationships that had lasted between one and three years. When Frank's last girlfriend broke up with him because he didn't want to get married, she called him a serial monogamist. Beth wondered if a man who had never married would consider marrying a twice-divorced divorce lawyer. Beth decided she wasn't going to obsess over the marriage issue. Instead, she'd enjoy the moment.

After the long kiss ended, Frank asked, "Are you ready for some champagne?"

"Of course," Beth said sultrily.

Frank turned and walked into the kitchen with Beth following behind him. He opened his refrigerator and pulled out a bottle of Dom Perignon.

"Oh my, you got the good stuff," Beth said as her taste buds tingled.

Frank smiled. "Only the best for the best."

As Frank opened the bottle and poured it into the flutes, Beth slid out of her shoes and walked to the sliders that opened on to the porch. She looked to her left at the stunning sunset. There were no clouds on the horizon, and the top half of the sun was peeking over the Midpoint Bridge to Cape Coral. There was no wind, so the river was flat except for a boat wake behind a yacht heading toward the Gulf of Mexico. Beth opened the slider and stepped out on the screened porch. She sat down at the patio table and faced the setting sun. Frank brought the two flutes of champagne out on the porch and sat down.

Frank picked his up as he said, "I have a toast." Beth lifted her own flute as Frank continued, "May we both celebrate all our good times together." Beth felt her heart melt, and she gently touched her flute to his. "That's the best toast I ever heard." They both looked at each other as they took a healthy drink.

Beth thought about Frank's childhood and wondered how much it had affected his aversion to marriage. When Frank was twelve, his father was convicted of trafficking in cocaine and was sentenced to thirty years in prison because of his two prior drug convictions. One year after Frank's father went to prison, his mother married the defense lawyer that had represented his father. Frank's mother assured him the romance only started after Frank's dad went away, but Frank had lingering doubts and hated his stepfather. When Frank was seventeen, his stepfather died of a heart attack, and his mom collected on the one million-dollar life insurance policy.

Three months later, Frank's mom married a slick yacht salesman in Las Vegas. Within two years, the money was gone and Frank's second stepfather divorced his mother. Frank's mother lost her house in foreclosure and moved to a trailer park, which is where she met her fourth husband. During the marriage, he had been arrested four times for domestic violence, but Frank's mother always dropped the charges and took him back. Frank only saw his mother when her husband wasn't with her because he was concerned that he might beat him senseless.

Frank's father got out of prison and met Frank once for lunch. After that, he moved to Columbia and hadn't been heard from since.

* * * * * *

Frank set down his flute and said, "Isn't Ralph Purvey the lawyer on the other side of the Jacoby case?"

Beth nodded.

"He was always a little too smooth for my taste," Frank said. "And that damn mustache of his is goofy-looking. It looks like a bad eyebrow."

Beth snickered. "His mustache is a distraction, no doubt about it. But he was quite the gentleman at mediation. It was Mr. Jacoby that showed his ass."

Beth told the story of the failed mediation while Frank drained his flute and brought the bottle out to the porch for refills. The temperature was dropping as the sun fell toward the horizon, and thankfully, Beth could feel the exquisite warming effect from the champagne by the end of her story. She told Frank about Judge Sanchez's daughter being in the hospital and the case being continued. Frank seemed genuinely happy about Beth's beach weekend, but she felt slightly guilty about not calling Frank before she committed. Their normal weekend entailed them relaxing at Frank's condo and cooking dinner together Friday night. On Saturday, Frank played golf with the guys and went to a sports bar afterward. Beth would sleep in and work at her office for a half day. On Saturday night, they ordered takeout and stayed at Beth's house and watched movies. Sunday was their day together, and Beth looked forward to it every week. Some days they drove to the beach, and other days they went looking for antiques at garage sales, but it was always a fun day together.

Frank said, "Tell me about your new divorce case." Beth

took a sip of her champagne before she started.

"Joyce Sinclair and her husband live at Sanibel Harbor Golf Club and have been married twenty-six years. They have three kids in college, and I guess the empty nest syndrome started about a year ago. They've been having arguments, and Mr. Sinclair started going out to the dog track and gambling ship at nights with his buddies to get away from her. Mrs. Sinclair was feeling neglected and started taking tennis lessons. Apparently, the tennis pro started giving Mrs. Sinclair private lessons at his apartment, and Mr. Sinclair found out about it and filed for divorce. She wants them to go to counseling, but he doesn't want anything to do with it. They have a chain of tire stores throughout the state, so there are substantial assets to divide up."

Frank asked, "What would you say are the most common reasons for divorce?"

"Sex, money, and kids from prior marriages," Beth said. "When you boil down all the different reasons, it's really those three things ninety percent of the time."

Frank nodded. "Ninety percent of my murder cases are because of sex, money, or drugs."

They took a hearty drink of their champagne, and Beth observed that they both made their living on human frailty. They looked at the setting sun in silence for a few seconds. "Enough about my day," Beth said. "Tell me about the trial."

Frank took a big swig of his champagne and leaned back into his recliner. "The husband took the stand and claimed he and his wife had been drinking all night and talking about the reasons for her affair. She agreed to end it with the boyfriend if her husband would forgive her and make some changes to his lifestyle. He was upset when he found out how long the affair had been going on. He was unsure if he could take her back, so he said he needed time to think. He was too drunk to drive, so he walked to his favorite bar and drank some more and talked with some of his buddies about his situation. He left his cell phone at home because he didn't want his wife calling him.

"At closing time, he left the bar and took the long way home, down by a lake. He gave some bullshit reason that that was their favorite place to go and feed the ducks, so he felt drawn there. He said he just sat there on a bench and thought about their ten-year marriage and whether he could trust her. He finally decided that if she'd go to counseling with him, he'd take her back. He said when the sun started to rise, he started walking home and got there around seven. He walked in, found his wife strangled, and called 911. He put on a pretty good act.

"I started cross-examination by asking how much he had to drink at his house before he left, and he said between seven and nine beers, but he wasn't sure. The bartender testified earlier in the trial that he had three beers and four tequila shots, and the husband said that sounded about right. He agreed with me that he was drunk when he left the bar, but he claimed that's why he walked—he knew he was going to get drunk because his wife had broken his heart. There were two female jurors who actually had tears in their eyes after he said that. So, I decided I needed him to show his temper in front of the jury."

Frank continued, "I asked him if he had read all the police reports and lab results from his case, and he said yes. I asked him if he'd seen the lab report that showed his semen and the boyfriend's semen on the marital bed's sheets. He glared at me and admitted he'd seen the report. I asked him how often his wife washed their sheets, and he told me Saturday was laundry day. His wife was killed on a Thursday night, so I asked him how he felt when he found out his wife had had sex with her boyfriend in their bed, at least once, in the five days before her death. His face turned red, and he squirmed in his chair before he said he hated it. I had him riled up, so I started boxing him in to show he was lying.

"I asked him if his 2006 Chevy Tahoe had OnStar navigation, and he said yes," Frank went on. "I asked him if he was aware that OnStar could tell the location of the vehicle by GPS technology. He fumbled with his answer and admitted he didn't know that. I picked up a file that had OnStar written in big letters on the outside and thumbed through it slowly. I asked him if he knew that OnStar could tell if his vehicle had been at the bar the night of the murder. He turned pale and admitted he didn't know that. I hesitated a few seconds, letting him dangle in the wind."

Frank smiled. "I told him that OnStar could only do that if he'd made a call while he was at the bar. I told him he was lucky he hadn't called with OnStar when he was at the bar, and then I turned the file upside down to show him, and the jury, that it was empty. It was a bluff, and his lawyer jumped up and objected. We had a sidebar and the judge got a little pissy, but I argued my questions were proper. The judge scowled at me and told me to move on. When I got back to the podium and looked at the husband, he had sweat running down his forehead, so I moved in for the kill.

"I asked him if it was true that he left his cell phone at home the night of the murder, and he said yes. I asked him how he checked his e-mail account with Yahoo, and he said either with his cell phone or his home computer. I asked him if his wife knew his account password, and he said no. I asked him if he had any reason to dispute the medical examiner's testimony earlier in the trial that his wife's time of death was between two forty-five a.m. and four a.m., and he answered no. I had the trap set, so I moved my papers around for a few seconds, acting like I was reviewing my notes. I got a drink of water and let everybody wonder what was next.

"I then asked the husband if it was true that he hadn't made any calls on his cell phone between ten p.m. and when he called 911 at seven-oh-one a.m. He got indignant and told me of course he didn't because he'd left his phone at home when he went to the bar. I walked back to my table and picked up another file that had Yahoo written in big letters on the outside. I walked back to the podium and asked the husband if he had checked his e-mail an hour before he called 911.

He hesitated and said it was impossible because he was still at the lake. I took out Yahoo's records from my folder and asked the judge if I could approach the witness. The judge agreed, and I walked up to the stand and showed the husband Yahoo's records showing that he checked his e-mail at six-oh-two a.m. the day of his wife's murder. After he looked at the records for a minute in silence, he blurted out that his wife's boyfriend must have done it when he was still at the house to try and set him up. I asked him how his wife's boyfriend got his e-mail account password, and he shifted in his seat and looked down. After about fifteen seconds of silence, I looked at the judge and said no more questions. It was a ten-minute guilty verdict."

Beth smiled and gave a quiet clap. "That was masterful, honey."

Frank held his hands out with his palms up and said, "I'd rather be lucky than good, but sometimes I'm both."

Beth drained her champagne flute and said, "Let's finish the bottle in the bedroom, and you'll be both."

Chapter 10

Beth and Frank rode the elevator down together early the next morning at eight. After a goodbye kiss in the parking garage, Frank went to work, and Beth drove home to get ready for her beach weekend at Cayo Costa. As Beth was driving home, she got the feeling that she was playing hooky from school, and it felt so refreshing not to be worried about her clients' problems. Three days away from reality at an isolated beach cottage sounded thrilling. After a great night of making love with Frank and a deep restful sleep, she was ready to enjoy the weekend.

Beth's house was an old Spanish style house, built in 1925, with three bedrooms and two baths in Edison Park. It had a rough stucco finish, painted dark tan with a red tile roof. There were old Florida pine wood floors throughout the house, except for the tiled bathrooms. The dining room had cypress paneling on the walls and there was crown molding in every room. There was a gazebo in the back yard that was next to a fire pit that Beth used during the winter months. Her St. Augustine grass was deeply fertilized and perfectly manicured. Beth was very proud of all the work she'd done since she bought the house and fixed it up.

Edison Park has wide curving streets, tall trees, and lush vegetation. It's adjacent to Thomas Edison's winter home and laboratory on the Caloosahatchee River. In Edison's will, he donated his property to the City of Ft. Myers for a museum, and it has been a popular destination since then.

The houses in Edison Park are an eclectic mix of old Spanish, modern ranch and old Florida with tin roofs and brick fireplaces. There are a mixture of young families, retirees, and childless middle-aged professionals like Beth, but everyone is friendly and participates in the neighborhood watch program to keep out crime.

Beth parked in her covered carport on the right side of her house. It was open on three sides, but it protected her car from the sun and rain. There were three cement steps to the kitchen door on the left side of the carport. There was a fifty-foot Poinciana tree in front of her house that provided shade and blossomed stunning red buds in the early summer. As she got out of her Camry, she could smell the gardenias in bloom and hear a cardinal chirping for her mate. One of her old divorce clients owned a lawn service and kept her yard in perfect condition.

Beth walked in her kitchen door and her two cats, Bella and Gracie, greeted her with loud meows as they rubbed against her legs. They were typical cats—if Beth was home they'd hide under the bed or in other rooms, but if she spent the night at Frank's, they complained when she returned. She had water and food canisters that automatically filled up the bowls, so they never suffered when she wasn't home. She needed to give them some love before she left, so she picked them up and held them to her chest as she kissed them. They both purred loudly and rubbed their chins on Beth's neck. After a minute of love, she set them down and they walked away, seemingly disinterested.

Beth spent the next two hours washing clothes, stocking the cats' food and water canisters, cleaning the two litter boxes, packing, showering, and worrying about how she'd look in a bathing suit. She packed light because Karen said to bring only bathing suits, shorts, casual blouses, flip flops, and sneakers. She stuffed an oversized hat, a beach towel, SPF 50 suntan lotion, lip gloss, and aloe lotion on top of her clothes. She rolled her suitcase out to the front door and set her sunglasses and purse on top. She sat down on her couch at nine fifty-five and called her cats over. They had seen Beth packing and knew she was leaving, so they jumped up on the couch for some more attention.

Beth loved going to the beach. Every summer when she was a child, the family spent two weeks at St. Pete Beach at the Don Caesar resort. She learned to body surf and boogie board when she was ten. When she was twelve, she learned to sail on a Hobie Cat through the gentle surf of the Gulf of Mexico. However, when she was fourteen, she learned the teenage girls' favorite beach pastime—kissing older boys. Beth felt giddy to be going away to the beach for the weekend.

Karen pulled into the driveway in her red SL550 Mercedes only ten minutes late. Beth kissed her cats goodbye and walked to the front door. She waved at Karen, who was still in her car talking on her phone. Karen waved back and held up her left pointer finger.

Beth put on her sunglasses and pulled her purse over her shoulder before she wheeled her suitcase outside. She locked the door and turned on her security system with a remote control on her keychain. As she approached the Mercedes, Karen finished her call and got out.

"You have a beautiful house. I love this neighborhood," Karen gushed.

"Thank you," Beth said. "I've been here about seven years. The best part is it's only a short drive to the office."

Karen looked at Beth's suitcase. "It's a little tight in the trunk. I've got a cooler full of food and my duffle bag is back there. Let me put my bag behind the seats, and there'll be room for your suitcase." Karen opened the trunk and made room while Beth admired the sleek sports car and wondered how fast it would go. She doubted if Karen knew that red cars got more speeding tickets and were involved in more wrecks than any other color car. Beth thought about telling her, but she didn't want to be a killjoy at the start of the weekend.

After Karen secured Beth's suitcase she shut the trunk and asked, "Are you ready for some fun?"

"You bet," Beth said as she opened the passenger door and sat down.

Karen got in and started the car, gunning the engine to show off. Beth nodded her head in approval and smiled. Karen pointed forward and asked, "When are you gonna get something a little more exciting than a Toyota?"

Beth was mildly offended but let it slide. "I've had it for five years, and it's paid off. It gets good gas mileage and runs great, so I plan on keeping it for a long time."

Karen asked, "If you hit the lottery and money was no object, what car would you buy?"

"I played the Florida lottery once when it got up to 280 million," Beth answered. "I bought a ticket on Monday, and I obsessed six or seven hours a day over what I would do with that much money if I won. It was a wasted week, and I told myself never again." She shook her head and continued, "I haven't bought a lottery ticket since, so I'll probably drive the Camry until it dies."

Karen smiled and slowly backed out of the driveway.

"You're very practical. My friend, Gayla Stough, said that

about you when you handled her divorce."

Beth fondly remembered Gayla Stough's divorce and the good settlement she helped secure for her. Gayla was a trophy wife who was lucky enough to marry a rich man without a prenuptial. After eight years of marriage, Gayla's husband became impotent, and Gayla promptly hired Beth to file for divorce. At the mediation six months later, they were $100,000 apart after four hours of negotiations, and the parties were separated in different rooms. The mediator told Beth that Gayla's husband said the case could settle if Gayla would talk to him privately. Gayla reluctantly agreed but asked Beth to wait outside the door. Gayla's husband came down the hall to Gayla's room, smiled at Beth, and went inside. After a minute together, Gayla came out and shut the door quietly as she looked at Beth and blushed.

Gayla whispered, "He said he'd give me the $100,000 if he could kiss my boobs for ten minutes." Gayla looked down the hall to make sure no one was listening and asked, "What do you think I should do?"

Beth arched her eyebrows and said wryly, "I'm sure you've done worse for less."

Gayla thought for a second and nodded. "Stand at the door and don't let anybody in."

During the next ten minutes, Beth calculated Gayla was being paid $600,000 dollars an hour for her time. That was certainly better than Beth's hourly rate.

* * * * * *

Beth asked, "How is Gayla doing?"

"We work out at the country club together and push each other on the elliptical machines," said Karen. "All the tight faces at the club are jealous because their husbands stare at us."

"What's a tight face?" Beth asked.

Karen snickered. "That's what Gayla and I call the older women who've had plastic surgery."

Beth unconsciously felt her chin line with her right hand, hoping Karen couldn't see her lift from two years before.

Beth decided her surgeon must've done a great job because

Karen didn't even flinch when she talked about tight faces. Beth decided to change the subject.

"So, what do you have in the cooler?"

"I stopped at Publix," Karen said. "I got some grapes, black pepper and olive oil hummus, pita chips, potato salad, and rice. My fishing guide buddy is meeting us at the cottage tomorrow morning and we always catch fish, so tomorrow night we'll have fish and rice. Tonight, we're going to go to Cabbage Key for dinner. They've got a great menu."

"Sounds great!"

Karen had a devilish grin. "I splurged on Oreo ice cream for a treat. And for drinks, I picked up tea, Coke, bottled water, Gatorade, wine, and tequila for margaritas."

"You sound like a girl after my own heart," Beth said.

Karen laughed like a coed driving to spring break with her girlfriends. As they topped the US 41 Bridge over the Caloosahatchee River and headed into North Ft. Myers, Beth asked, "Just how do we get to the beach cottage?"

"We go straight on forty-one until we hit Pine Island Road and make a left. We stay on it for about fifteen miles and go through Cape Coral and the old fishing village of Matlacha until we come to a four way stop on Pine Island. We make a right and go six miles to the north end of Pine Island, and Four Winds Marina is on the left. We park there and my boat should be tied to the dock, gassed up, and waiting for us. It's about a twenty-minute ride to our dock at Cayo Costa."

Beth asked, "Why is your boat waiting for you at the marina?"

"The marina has two boat barns that store boats three levels up, and our boat is stored there. I call ahead, and a giant fork lift puts our boat in the water and the staff fills the boat up with gas and puts ice and drinks in the cooler.

When we get there, the boat is ready to go, and everything is simply added to the monthly bill."

Beth considered all the conveniences and nodded. "That's the way to do it."

After a few minutes of riding in silence and listening to reggae music on the radio, Karen asked, "How did you end up in Ft. Myers?"

Beth answered, "I grew up in Tampa and graduated from the University of South Florida there. My parents always came down here and vacationed at Ft. Myers Beach. I fell in love with the beaches and fishing here. I went to law school at Mercer, up in Macon, Georgia, and realized how much I missed the beaches and salt water, so I applied for jobs in Ft. Myers after law school. I got a job as an associate at a big firm in Ft. Myers doing divorce work. After four years of making the partners rich, I hung out my own shingle, and I've been on my own since then."

Karen asked, "Do you like working for yourself?"

"Most of the time," Beth answered. "The problem is my boss is one demanding bitch."

Karen laughed. Beth continued, "I like working for myself, but it's hard to relax sometimes. If I don't do it, it doesn't get done. Even when I'm not at work, my mind is racing and wondering when I'm going to have time to do all the work. That's why I'm so excited about this weekend."

Karen thought for second. "What happens to your practice if you get sick or if you're in an accident?"

Beth shrugged. "There are other sole practitioners I'm

friends with, and we cover for each other. But if I were in a serious accident or sick for a long time, it'd be a major problem."

"Have you ever thought about starting a firm?"

"Every lawyer thinks about it," Beth said. "The downside is that you have to deal with everyone else's problems, and invariably, one partner feels like he's doing more work and not getting paid enough, so the firm splits up and costs everybody money. That's why there are so many sole practitioners and small firms out there."

They rode in silence for a few seconds and listened to the reggae music. Beth finally asked, "How did *you* end up in Ft. Myers?"

Karen took a deep breath and answered. "I grew up in Chattanooga, but we spent every July at Panama City Beach, aka the Redneck Riviera, and I loved it there. I was an only child and loved playing with all the vacationing kids. Of course, when I became a teenager, I became boy-crazy, so I loved the beach even more. I got an academic scholarship to Florida State in Tallahassee and went there knowing it was only an hour drive to Panama City Beach. I joined Tri-Delta my freshman year at Florida State, and one of my sorority sisters was from Ft. Myers. We became best friends. Her parents had a condo at Ft. Myers Beach that they always let us use when we visited. So every summer, I stayed with her at the condo, and we worked waitress jobs. I fell in love with the area and decided to come here to teach after I graduated."

Beth said, "So you're a beach bunny at heart?" Karen grinned, "To the core!"

Beth asked, "Who'd you date before Stan?"

Karen reflected for a second before answering. "I met a general contractor who built condos, and we dated for two years. He was a really nice guy, but I wasn't in love with him. I met Stan and he pursued me relentlessly, showering me with gifts and promising me the world if I'd marry him. So, I did."

"How'd he treat you in the beginning of the marriage?"

Karen sighed. "The first four years of our marriage were great, but then everything started going to hell."

Karen drove in silence for a few seconds and then asked Beth, "How long have you and Frank been together?"

"We've been dating a little over a year," Beth said cheerfully, "and I'm the happiest I've been since my second divorce."

Karen looked over and arched her eyebrows. "So, how many guys did you date between your second divorce and Frank?"

Beth was a little taken aback by the question but decided since tequila was making the trip with them, she might as well answer now because tequila was a powerful truth serum. "I didn't date anybody for a year because I was depressed. One day, an old boyfriend from college called me out of the blue because he'd just gotten divorced. He lived in Jacksonville, and we talked and texted for a few weeks. I invited him down for a weekend. We had a great time the first night. We were drinking and telling stories about our college days, and then we kissed."

Beth hesitated and debated about how revealing she should get.

Karen plowed forward. "You know, you're not really over a guy until you sleep with the next one. My best friend from Tri-Delta always said, 'The best way to get over somebody is to get under somebody.'"

"Well, you know there's some truth to that rumor," Beth snickered. "The only cure for lack-a-nookie disease is to get an injection of petercillin."

Karen giggled and Beth snorted, which caused Karen to start laughing contagiously. They amused each other for few minutes. Beth felt more relaxed as they bonded and felt the weekend was shaping up nicely.

After they got their breath back, Beth said, "My mom's sex talk was, 'Don't do anything on a date that you can't do on a bicycle.'"

Karen chuckled and held up her right pointer finger. "Ah, but bad decisions make for really good stories!"

Beth said, "All men are like animals, but some make good pets."

They snickered at their silliness and were then quiet for a few seconds and enjoyed the reggae music.

Karen broke the silence. "How long did you date your old college sweetheart?"

"We'd get together every other weekend for a few months, and then he started to get very serious. I knew there was no future for us, so I broke it off."

Karen looked over at Beth. "Do tell, who was after him?"

Beth sighed. "I didn't date anybody for a few months. I went out with my girlfriends on the weekends, but I didn't meet anybody that interested me. One night, I was bored and drove out to Captiva and had a drink at 'Tween Waters Resort. The Swedish bartender was funny, tanned, and muscular. He was twelve years younger than me, so I guess that was my cougar stage."

Karen looked over at Beth with amusement. "Get out! You?"

"It was a very sweet romance, but I knew again there was no future. It lasted eight months until he moved back to Sweden because he missed his family."

Karen asked, "And who was after that?"

Beth shook her head. "I didn't date anybody for a few months. After that, I went out with a couple of older guys on first dates, and they bored the hell out of me, so no romance. Then I met Frank at a Christmas party at Ft. Myers Court Reporting, and it's been awesome since then."

Karen said, "I saw in the paper this morning that Frank

won his case. I guess he was in a good mood last night?"

Beth nodded. "He was ecstatic and brought home a bottle of Dom Perignon, and we had a fantastic night. He was celebrating his big win, and I was celebrating our beach weekend. And then we celebrated each other."

"Sounds like fun." Karen shifted in the driver's seat and said, "The article also mentioned his other big wins the past couple of years. He's been really busy."

"He's very good at what he does," Beth said proudly, "and he's able to communicate with jurors in language they understand, without talking down to them. My favorite argument he made was in a murder trial eight months ago. His only eyewitness against the murderer was a prostitute, and the defense brought in a thief and a drug dealer as alibi witnesses to refute her testimony. So, the entire closing argument was about credibility and who should the jurors believe. Frank argued, 'You have a thief and a drug dealer that tell one story and a prostitute that tells a different one. Who do you believe? Always believe the prostitute because she works hard for a living.'"

* * * * * *

Karen parked her Mercedes about one hundred feet from the dock at Four Winds Marina in the long-term parking area. Beth opened her door and immediately smelled the salt air and heard mechanical sounds coming from the boat barn. By the time Karen had opened her trunk, a young, tanned muscular worker from the marina, wearing sunglasses and a hat, was walking toward her pushing a gray Rubbermaid wheelbarrow used for transporting supplies to boats. The plastic bin moved on two bicycle wheels and a handle ran horizontally along the back end. The young man was in his early twenties and wore a tight employee work shirt with a name badge that read "Billy."

"Can I help you, Mrs. Jacoby?" he asked eagerly.

Karen vamped it up. "Billy, you know I'm getting divorced. Call me Karen."

Billy blushed and gave a sheepish smile. "Okay…Karen."

Karen pointed toward Beth. "This is my divorce lawyer and

friend, Beth Mancini."

Billy nodded toward Beth. "Hello, ma'am."

Beth was disappointed momentarily he'd addressed her with such a maternal term, but realized he was just being polite.

Billy loaded Beth's suitcase and the duffel bag into the wheelbarrow, set the cooler down on the asphalt, and extended the handle up from the back. Karen stepped forward and pulled the cooler handle toward her, tilting it on its wheels. Billy lifted the wheelbarrow and led the way to the dock.

Beth grabbed her hat and purse from the car and followed them.

As they walked around a line of cars parked by the ship store, Karen pointed to a dark green boat tied up at the dock. "That's our boat by the fuel pump."

Karen's boat was a twenty-two-foot Pathfinder with a two hundred Yamaha outboard engine. It had a green T-top that provided shade over the center console. Behind the center console, there was a three-foot-wide leaning post, with a back support, for the captain and mate to use while driving the boat. You could either stand up and lean back, or step up on the footrest, and sit back while running the boat. On the bow was a trolling motor, locked in the storage position on the port side. There were three fishing rods in rod holders on the port side of the console. Another marina worker was in the boat, putting three bags of ice and a six-pack of bottled water in the cooler at the front of the console. The boat's name, *Cayo Costa Cutie*, was painted in white script lettering with a gold border on each side.

Karen was wearing khaki shorts with a white Columbia buttoned fishing shirt and a pink bikini on underneath. As Billy was loading the luggage and cooler into the boat, Karen took off her fishing shirt and tied it around her waist. All the workers in the boat barn and the mechanics shed stopped what they were doing and stared at her bikini top. A middle-aged stocky guy with a mustache stepped out of the ship store and walked down the wooden steps toward Karen. Beth was amused by Karen's unapologetic flirting and exhibitionism.

"Hey, Karen," the stocky guy said. "Are you spending the weekend at your cottage?"

Karen turned around and smiled. "Hi, Eric. Yeah, we're

staying for the weekend." She held her hand out toward Beth, "This is my divorce lawyer and friend, Beth Mancini."

Eric stepped back and feigned fright as he joked, "I hope you don't know my wife."

Beth decided to flirt a little herself. "I'm sure your wife would never see a divorce attorney."

Eric smiled at Beth and laughed. "I hope not."

When Karen turned to Beth, Eric snuck a discreet look at Karen's extraordinary cleavage.

"Eric is the manager of the Lazy Flamingo restaurant here at the marina, on the other side of the ship store. They have the best oysters on the island."

Eric motioned toward the restaurant. "You ought to come have lunch."

"We'll eat lunch on Sunday when we come back," Karen answered.

"Sounds good to me," Eric said as he walked off toward the restaurant. "I'll look for you two then."

Billy stepped off the boat and said, "Everything is loaded in the boat. Have a nice weekend, Karen."

Karen turned to Billy to give him a perfect view as she pulled a twenty from her pocket and gave it to him. Billy thanked her and backed away without moving his eyes from her chest. He tripped over a cleat on the dock and nearly fell down. The marina workers laughed at Billy and gave Karen one last appreciative look before they went back to work.

Karen looked at Beth and smiled devilishly as she raised her eyebrows.

Beth pointed at the boat. "Who named the boat?" "Stan did when we bought the beach cottage. He used to like it when the guys looked at me on the boat and his ego swelled then," Karen said wryly. "But probably not now."

Chapter 11

Karen drove the boat slowly out of the marina basin and headed west down the narrow channel. She motioned toward the wheel. "Please steer the boat for me while I put on some sun tan lotion."

Beth grabbed the wheel and asked, "Where am I going?"
"Just stay to the left of the markers."

"They're red and green markers. Which ones do you mean?"

"Red, right, return." Karen gently chided. "What are you talking about?" Beth asked.

Karen rubbed some lotion on her left leg as she answered. "When you're returning to port from sea, you keep the *red* markers on your *right*, when you *return*. Since we're leaving port, the red markers are on your left and the green markers on your right. It's easy when you have two markers together, just stay between them. But when there is just one marker, you have to remember red, right, return. So just stay to the left of these green markers while we're in the creek."

"Okay," Beth said uncertainly as she did the nautical algebra in her mind.

"We're in Jug Creek now, and we'll follow it out to Pine Island Sound," Karen said as she finished rubbing lotion on her left leg.

"Why's it named Jug Creek?" Beth asked as she looked at condos to her right and mangroves to her left.

Karen started rubbing lotion on her right leg as she answered, "During prohibition, a lot of bootleggers ran booze up here because it was a winding creek with unmarked channels. The cops that tried to follow them would run aground on sandbars or oyster beds. I guess the name just stuck."

The narrow channel opened to a bay about a half-mile wide, and Beth saw two bald eagles gliding above her, searching for an unsuspecting meal swimming below. They were riding with the wind, so they kept their wings straight until they saw a potential meal. They vectored left simultaneously and dove down toward the water, gaining speed with each second. At the last possible second, they brought their talons out as they splashed into the water. A few seconds later, they flapped their majestic wings and lifted out of the water, a wriggling mullet in each of their talons. Beth watched in awe as they flew off to land in their favorite tree and have lunch.

Karen held the lotion out and asked, "Could you put some on my back?"

"Sure," Beth said.

After Beth finished rubbing lotion on her back, she handed it back. Karen rubbed her stomach and chest with lotion as Beth watched the eagles flying off in the distance with the mullet clutched in their talons, still moving their tails back and forth.

Karen asked, "Do you need to put some lotion on?"

Beth shook her head. "I put some on before I left my house this morning."

Karen smiled. "Of course, you did. That's the practical thing to do."

Beth was wearing navy blue shorts with a long-sleeved white blouse. She had on flip flops and her oversized straw hat with polarized sunglasses. The wind was blowing comfortably from the west, and the temperature was in the mid-eighties with low humidity. There were no clouds in the sky and the sun was warming them nicely. It was low tide, so the smell of exposed mangrove roots and seaweed blended with the salt air for a coastal marsh aroma. It was a beautiful spring day in Southwest Florida, and Beth was feeling thoroughly relaxed.

Karen took over her captain duties at the wheel and sat back on the leaning post. Beth followed her lead and leaned back on the support as she gazed out at the bluish-green water.

"Here we go, hold on," Karen said as she pushed the throttle forward with confidence.

As the engine accelerated, the front of the boat rose up and skimmed on top of the small waves. Beth could feel the wind rushing through her hair and pushing her cheeks back. She hoped the minor scars from her face lift weren't more noticeable with her skin being pulled tight by the wind. After a few seconds of worrying about this vanity, Beth chastised herself over wasted mental energy. She was an attractive middle-aged woman, but she felt she could

74

never compete with Karen's looks, so it was ridiculous to even try. She reminded herself that Karen could never compete with her in the courtroom, and she felt slightly better.

Karen guided the boat through the winding channel in Jug Creek at 45 mph and out into Pine Island Sound. The Sound was wide open water and the waves were bigger, so she reduced the speed to 35 mph for a smoother ride. She followed the channel to the left as it led to the east side of Patricio Island, which was undeveloped and overgrown with mangroves. As they passed the eastern end of Patricio Island, Beth could see the next island fully developed with modern houses.

Beth pointed ahead and raised her voice to be heard over the engine and wind. "Which island is that?"

Karen answered in a raised voice, "That's Useppa Island, and it has an interesting history. It was bought by a Chicago streetcar magnate, John M. Roach, in 1894 and he built his winter residence there. Many of his friends started to visit and loved the island, so he built a hotel for them. One of the guests was his rich industrialist friend, Barron Collier. He liked the island so much, he bought it and turned it into a fishing resort for the rich and famous. After he died, the resort went out of business in the mid-fifties, and only a few people lived there. The owners allowed the US government to train Cuban refugees for the Bay of Pigs invasion there.

In 1976, new owners bought the island and invested a lot of money in the resort. A lot of private residences have been built there, and only members of the Useppa Island club can stay on the island."

As the boat followed the channel around Patricio Island, a small island on the right became visible. Beth noticed it had a few small houses and a white-water tank above the tree line. The channel went between Useppa on the left and the small island on the right, with about a half-mile of water between them.

Beth pointed to the small island and asked, "What's that island called?"

"That's Mondongo Island," Karen said. "It's owned by a big ranching family from the middle part of the state, and that's their private fishing camp."

Karen slowed the boat down and it came off plane, gently

settling back into the water. She pointed to the right of the bow, and Beth looked over to see what she was pointing at. A few seconds later, two large dolphins jumped in the air, followed by three baby dolphins. Beth squealed with delight and reached for her camera in her pocket. The dolphins were swimming in the direction of the boat, so Karen turned off the engine, and they quietly drifted. Beth walked to the front of the boat with her camera ready and looked in the direction of where the dolphins last jumped. About thirty seconds later, the two large dolphins jumped again, and Beth pointed her camera, clicking as the three babies jumped.

She looked down at her digital screen and saw her picture had caught them in the air. She walked back and proudly showed Karen her lucky photo that would become her computer's newest screen saver.

Karen started the engine and idled toward another boat a few hundred yards away. As they got closer, Beth could see a man standing on the front of the boat with a taunt fishing pole, fighting a fish.

Beth asked, "What kind of fish does he have on?"

"I'm not sure," Karen answered, "but he has on a fighting belt and has a big rod, so I think it's a tarpon. This is the time of the year they start migrating up the gulf coast from the keys. They gather in Boca Grande pass, and people come from all over the world to fish for them."

At that moment, a six-foot tarpon leaped completely out of the water and shook its head, trying to throw off the hook in its mouth. Beth and Karen could hear its gill plates rattle as it violently shook its head. It landed in the water with a splash, and they heard the man on the front of the boat swearing. His pole was straight up in the air and was no longer bent.

Karen said, "The line broke when the tarpon landed. He's pissed."

"Goodness, that was a big fish," Beth said in amazement.

"It takes an hour or so to boat a fish that big," Karen said. "That is, if the sharks don't get to him first."

"Sharks?" Beth asked.

Karen nodded. "Tarpon are the favorite food for hammerheads. With all the thrashing during the fight, the sharks are attracted to the struggling tarpon if they're nearby."

"Uh, how big are the hammerheads?" Beth asked seriously.

"I've heard people have seen a twenty-footer in Boca Grande pass. I watched Stan catch one in the pass that was fourteen feet long and weighed over 2,400 pounds. The guide put a shotgun to its head and killed it before we tied it to the side of the boat. We brought it to the marina and took pictures of it hanging from the scale. The guide cut the jaws from the head and gave them to Stan. He put them outside the cottage for a few weeks, and let the raccoons and ants eat the flesh off it. After it was picked clean, he bleached it and let it dry out. He mounted the jaws above the bed in the guest bedroom, so you'll see them later."

Scrunching her face, Beth asked, "You're serious?"

Karen smiled and wiggled her eyebrows. "It's actually pretty cool. On the left side of the jaws, we have a picture of Stan fighting the fish and on the right side, a picture of it hanging from the scales with Stan and me standing on each side."

Beth shook her head. "You're telling me I'll be sleeping below a shark's jaws that killed fish bigger than me?"

Karen nodded.

"I'm glad you brought the tequila."

Karen laughed and started the engine. They idled back toward the channel, and Beth noticed a smaller island behind Useppa, across the Intracoastal channel. It had some wooden cottages and a large wooden building with a lot of dockage. There were boats idling into and out of the island's channel, and a white-water tank rose above the trees.

Beth pointed to the island and asked, "Which island is that?"

"That's Cabbage Key. It's open to the public. The restaurant is built on top of an Indian mound, and at thirty-eight feet, it's the highest point in all Lee County. It was developed in 1938 by the son of playwright and novelist Mary Roberts Rinehart as a winter home. In 1944, it was sold and turned into a resort. The main building is a restaurant and bar with six rental rooms, and there are seven rental cottages and a marina with overnight dockage. In 1976, the current owners, Rob and Phyllis Wells, bought it and upgraded it. In 2004, the eye of Hurricane Charlie passed over it with one hundred forty-seven mile an hour winds, but it survived. We're gonna go there for dinner tonight."

Beth said, "I'm looking forward to it. Where's Cayo Costa?"

Karen pointed west, beyond Cabbage Key. "It's the next island behind it. We've got about a five-minute ride."

"How'd you learn to handle a boat so well?" Beth asked. Karen remembered her childhood fondly. "My grandfather had a pontoon boat on the lake near our house, and he always let me drive it when I was a kid. I started waterskiing when I was eight, and by fifteen, I was driving the boat and pulling my friends skiing. Every summer during college when I came to Ft. Myers with my best friend, we'd be in boats every weekend with our boyfriends. Actually, we had an agreement that at least one of us had to be dating a guy with a boat, so we'd be able to get out on the water. I always insisted they let me drive the boats at some point during the day."

Beth laughed heartily. "Let's go to your cottage, Captain."

Karen laughed, gave Beth a friendly hug, and then pushed the throttle forward and the boat jumped back on plane, cutting through the waves. They headed toward the Intracoastal channel and had to slow down for the big waves from two yachts that were heading south. After they crossed the waves, Karen powered the boat back to 45 mph as they crossed a shallow grass flat and headed to Cayo Costa.

There were a couple of small oyster bars in front of Cayo Costa that Karen drove around in wide arcs. A minute later, they came off plane near a dock that extended about fifty feet into the small bay. Beth could see the sun reflecting off the tin roof of a gray cottage behind some mangroves.

Karen pointed proudly at the cottage. "There she is."

Chapter 12

The five feet wide, sun-bleached dock led to a crushed shell path, and the two-story cottage was about one hundred feet away, built on top of an Indian mound, which was about ten feet tall. The top of the mound had been cut off and leveled for the cottage foundation. The deep green mangroves were cleared ten feet on both sides of the dock but lined the shoreline as far as you could see in either direction. The property was a three-acre parcel between the bay and the beach, with sea oats and sandspur clumps covering it. It had been cleared of the Australian pine, sea grape, and gumbo limbo trees that grew on the high spots of the island for unobstructed views. There was a clear view of the beach about five hundred feet west of the beach cottage, and a crushed shell path led to the beach.

The cottage was built on thirty-five-foot cement pilings, twenty feet deep into the Indian mound and sand and fifteen feet above to protect it from hurricane storm surges. There were square one-foot wooden footers bolted to the top of the pilings that supported the cottage. The outside walls were painted gray with a royal blue trim, and all the windows and sliders were impact resistant glass. There were wide wooden steps leading straight up to a covered entry way to the front door. The entry way was ten feet square with screened sides and a screened door. Underneath the fifteen wooden steps to the entryway, there was a large clump of fragrant southern jasmine in bloom.

Beth smelled the jasmine as she walked up the steps, pulling her suitcase behind her. Karen opened the screened door and walked inside the shaded entryway and set her duffel bag down on the deck. Beth followed her inside the entryway with her suitcase and immediately felt a ten-degree difference in temperature. The screened door was anchored by a spring and shut slowly as Karen pulled the keys from her pocket.

Karen motioned with her head toward the screened door and said, "Keeps the bugs out at night, and the cover is great when it's raining. We can leave our sandy shoes out here so it doesn't get so dirty inside."

From the elevated entryway, Beth looked back out at the bay, surrounded by the mangrove forest, and said, "This is breathtaking."

Karen smiled as she unlocked the door. "This side is great but wait until you see the beach view."

Karen picked up her duffel bag and walked inside, leaving it on the white tile floor. Beth followed her in with her suitcase and shut the door behind her. The stairs to the second floor were directly ahead of her. She walked to the right of the stairs a few feet and gazed through the sliders at the light green Gulf of Mexico glistening in the distance.

She saw a thirty-foot sailboat just offshore, with its main sail and jib filled with the onshore wind, heading north toward Boca Grande Pass.

Karen stared at the sailboat. "Now you know why I love this place."

"Yes," Beth said as she looked around the room. "Now I understand."

Karen said, "Let me give you the tour. This is the room where we spend most of the time. The big screen TV is over in the corner, and the dining table looks out over the gulf.

The kitchen is to the left, looking out over the deck."

Beth admired the open room and the wraparound porch that went around three sides of the house.

"Why don't you have the porch go all around to the front of the cottage?" Beth asked.

Karen said, "Our architect suggested it'd give us more security and privacy if you could only access the porch through the front door that has a deadlock."

Beth nodded slowly, "Ah, I understand."

Karen beckoned her with her right hand. "Let me show you the bathroom."

Karen walked back toward the front door and past the stairs to the second level. She walked into the bathroom and said, "We've got a full bathroom inside, but the coolest part is just outside."

Beth followed her and looked at the tub on the right side and the commode and sink on the left. Beth observed the marble countertop on the sink and the tile work was nicer than at her house. Karen opened the door to the outside deck and stepped out to the right. The wooden deck went to the right toward the gulf and wrapped around the cottage. Beth followed her out on to the deck and Karen pointed up, toward the outside wall. Beth looked up and saw an outside shower head coming out of the wall. Beth looked lower and saw water controls and two pegs on the wall for robes and towels. There was a small, white plastic table next to the wall with shampoo, conditioner, and soap. The water drained between the slits in the deck and landed in the sand below.

"There's nothing better than showering outside," Karen said enthusiastically.

Beth looked around to see who could enjoy the spectacle of Karen showering outside. There was nothing but mangrove forests to the bayside, and the house was angled so passing boaters couldn't see from the bayside. She looked to the gulf side, and there was nothing but sand and water in the distance. The deck above her, on the second level, provided shade so private parts didn't get sunburned.

Karen smiled. "The nearest house is a half mile on the other side. You have total privacy out here, unless someone is walking the beach, which is five hundred feet away, so they can't see much."

"I can truthfully say I've never showered outside before," Beth said. "I'm looking forward to it."

Karen walked back into the bathroom and motioned for Beth to follow her. "Let me show you the bedrooms upstairs."

They walked out of the bathroom and up the stairs. At the top of the stairs, the master bedroom was on the left and the guest bedroom on the right. Both bedrooms had sliders that opened to a wraparound wooden deck on the upper level. At the top of the stairs, there was a wide hallway leading to the deck. The bathroom was on the left side of the hallway and the utility room on the right. There were wood floors in all the rooms on the second level.

The tin roof angled to the front and back of the house with vertical sides. On the gulf side, there was a widow's walk above the roof, supported by four twelve-by-twelve-inch posts through the roof. The widow's walk was ten square feet and accessed by a wooden stairway from the second level deck, next to the master bedroom slider.

                        *   *   *   *   *   *

As they topped the stairs to the second floor, Beth pointed
to the wood floors and asked, "What kind of wood is this?"

"Bamboo," Karen said proudly. "It's environmentally
friendly because it's easy to regrow, and it helps the third world
countries that export it."

Karen walked to the right and said, "This is the guest
bedroom."

Beth walked into the room and her eyes immediately went
to the shark's jaws mounted on the wall. She pointed to the jaws and
said, "Tell me the story about how Stan caught this."

"You have to understand Stan a little bit to appreciate the
story," Karen said.

Beth said sarcastically, "I think I understand him." Karen
chuckled and continued. "He's very competitive, and he loves tarpon
fishing. He enters the tournaments every year at Boca Grande, and
he's won three of them. Well, a few years ago, Stan was fishing with
our guide during a tournament and hooked this huge tarpon. The
guide estimated the fish to be around two hundred twenty-five
pounds, and Stan had fought it for over two hours. He finally had
the fish tired out and was bringing it to the boat to gaff it and tow it
to the weigh station on the beach. The tournament director's boat
had come close to watch the action, and one guy was filming the
fight.

Karen continued, "The tarpon was about twenty feet from
the boat when this giant hammerhead showed up. He bit the tarpon
in half and ate the back section. Stan was cussing like a sailor for a
while but decided to get a scale off the tarpon for a souvenir and a
picture of the carcass. He pulled what was left of the tarpon next to
the boat and was getting ready to grab a scale while the captain took
a picture. Well, the hammerhead came back to finish his bloody
meal and swam up next to the boat. Stan reached down with the rod
and tried to jab the shark in the eye. The shark grabbed the rod in its
mouth and shook its head, pulling the rod from Stan's hands. The
shark twisted its head back and forth, and slammed the rod butt into
Stan's face, before it swam off with the rod, the tarpon remains
dragging by hook and line.

"Stan was humiliated because he ended up with a black eye and had to explain to everybody at the dock what happened. Of course, the guy with the video played it on a big screen TV at the awards banquet that night. I've never seen Stan so angry. He spent the rest of that tarpon season catching and killing hammerheads for revenge. Once he'd fought them to the boat, he'd kill them with a shotgun blast to the head and haul them to the marina for pictures. He'd keep the jaws as trophies and give the carcass to crabbers for bait. He caught eight that summer, but this fourteen-footer was the biggest, so he mounted it here. At first, I thought it was a little gruesome, but it's grown on me."

Beth asked, "What did he do with all the other jaws?" Karen pointed out toward the gulf. "He hauled them out off the beach in about ten feet of water, next to a limestone ledge that runs parallel to the beach. He set them side by side on the bottom as a warning to other hammerheads, he always claimed."

Karen pointed to a spear gun in the corner and continued, "We use that when we swim out to the ledge and shoot snapper for dinner. The jaws look very creepy on the bottom when you have a struggling, bleeding snapper on the spear. We always just got two and raced back to the beach, before some of the shark's relatives got revenge."

Beth said, "My young Swedish bartender liked to go down to the keys and spearfish. I would snorkel with him and watch, but I never shot a fish."

Karen pointed to fishing rods in another corner of the room. "I love fishing, but sometimes they don't bite. With a spear gun, you always have dinner."

Beth looked around the room at all the fishing pictures in blue frames on the white walls. There was a bright yellow comforter on the queen size bed, and the nightstands were painted lime green. There were orange lamps on each nightstand and the drapes were red.

"This room has very bright, vibrant colors," Beth commented.

"I call this the Key West bedroom," Karen said proudly. "When I decorated the room, I wanted it to be a fun, exciting room for our guests." Beth looked out the slider and saw the sailboat continuing its northward track. She wondered how far they'd sailed and where the boat was from.

Karen motioned to the other bedroom and said, "Stan, however, decorated the master bedroom. There's mahogany furniture all around, and it matches the master bedroom furniture at the river house and the Aspen condo. Stan says it makes him feel comfortable sleeping in the same environment. I always thought it was a little rigid, but he's the chief and I'm his squaw, as he always told me."

Beth shook her head in disgust and Karen laughed. "Follow me," Karen motioned with her right hand, "and

I'll show you the best view from the cottage."

Beth was incredulous. "There's a better view?" Karen nodded. "The next level is the widow's walk."

Beth followed Karen into the master bedroom and the wood floor creaked as they entered. Beth was amused that everything in the bedroom was mahogany—even the picture frames. Beth concluded that Stan must make his therapist a lot of money with his obsessive-compulsive disorder. Karen opened the slider and stepped out on the deck, motioning for Beth to follow.

As Karen walked up the wooden stairs, Beth was two steps behind. When they reached the widow's walk, the clean salt air from the strong onshore wind was invigorating. Beth instinctively looked north toward the sailboat, and the sun was glistening off the mast. She turned and looked south, toward Captiva Pass and saw dozens of boats drifting with the outgoing tide, fishing for dinner.

Karen pointed at the beach, and said, "Look at the momma pig and her piglets."

Beth looked down toward the surf and saw a large black hog with her four piglets walking behind her. They were rooting through the seaweed at the high tide mark. The mother hog was moving her tusks through the seaweed and sand, looking for dead crabs or fish to feed her family.

Beth looked around the deck and asked, "Why do they call this a widow's walk?"

Karen leaned against the railing. "In the old days, before radios and cell phones, the highest point at fishing villages along the coast allowed families the first view of returning ships. From the highest windows, at the tallest houses, people would look on the horizon for returning ships. When they saw a ship through a

84

spyglass, they'd shout down to people walking on the street which one was returning, and the news spread quickly. Of course, when a ship was lost at sea, the families of the lost crew didn't know for sure they were dead. They kept looking on the horizon, hoping the ship was just late in returning. When the doomed ship didn't return after a few weeks, most families accepted the fact their relatives drowned at sea."

Beth stepped forward and rested her elbows on the rail. She looked out into the gulf and wondered how that loss must've felt for the relatives.

Karen continued, "However, as the legend goes, one pregnant newlywed couldn't accept the fact her husband's ship had sunk at sea. She convinced sympathetic neighbors to build her a higher tower on her roof, so she could see her husband's returning ship on the horizon sooner. She'd climb the tower every morning at sunrise and spend an hour looking for her husband's returning ship. She'd do the same thing at noon and the hour before sunset. All the people in town named her tower the widow's walk. However, after a while people realized it provided a beautiful view of the sea and started building them on their own houses. Of course, the term 'widow's walk' was forever linked with the towers."

Karen noticed Beth wiping a tear from her right eye. "It's sad, isn't it?" Karen said quietly.

Beth nodded and took a deep breath. They looked out toward the horizon for a minute of silent reflection and enjoyed the view.

Karen walked to the far side of the widow's walk and pointed north. "See that large pond of dark water in the sand, with mangroves on the bay side and sand on the gulf side? It's about 400 hundred yards from here and one hundred feet in from the beach."

Beth walked over and looked. "Yes, I see it. What is it?"

Karen said playfully, "That's where the Tunnel of Love ends."

"What's the Tunnel of Love?" Beth asked, puzzled.

Karen answered, "It used to be a narrow creek that went from the bay to the gulf, but it filled in with sand during the winter of 1982 when a nasty storm blew in from the gulf.

Historically, it was a passage of water that smugglers used because the big police boats couldn't follow. It's about a quarter of a mile long and opens at that pond area, but it's shallow and overgrown with mangroves back toward the bay. It bends to the left and right and some branches have fallen across it. At the entrance in the shallow bay, it's only about four feet high and six feet wide because of the overgrowth.

It's real popular with kayakers and small skiffs because it's shaded and looks like you're going through a tunnel. Over the years, it's sort of become a lover's lane for boaters, so that's how it got its name."

Beth was intrigued. "Have you seen any couples doing it?"

Karen laughed. "Most people stay in the shade for privacy and avoid sunburns. A lot of day-trippers from Cabbage Key and Useppa will come through the Tunnel of Love and pull their boats up on the sand at the end of the pond.

They'll walk the last 100 feet to the beach and sunbathe. Sometimes, they skinny-dip, so I'll pull out the binoculars and get a free show."

They both chuckled over Karen's voyeurism confession. Beth slowly turned around 360 degrees and took in all the sights. To the north, she could see Boca Grande Pass and the condos lining the shoreline of Gasparilla Island. To the east, she could see Cabbage Key, Useppa, and Pine Island. To the south, Captiva Pass, North Captiva, Captiva, and Sanibel Island. To the west, was the Gulf of Mexico, sparkling green and no clouds in sight.

She looked at Karen and gushed, "This is really a special place." Karen stared out at the gulf for a few seconds. "The first three years we had this cottage was wonderful. It was like I'd found my own prince charming, and I was blissfully happy. Stan was respectful to me and showered me with compliments and gifts. We'd come up here at night with an air mattress and make love for hours."

Karen was quiet while Beth fantasized about bringing Frank out to the cottage for a weekend. They could experience the widow walk at midnight and the Tunnel of Love in the afternoon. Beth's naughty thoughts turned into an erotic daydream as she stared at the gulf.

After a minute of silence, Karen said, "Let's go get the cooler from the boat and turn on the gas and water."

* * * * * *

Karen lifted the cooler up and rested it on the edge of the boat. Beth was up on the dock and reached down and grabbed the left handle. Beth pulled, as Karen lifted the cooler, on to the dock. Beth pulled the extension up from the back of the cooler, tilted the cooler on its rubber wheels, and pulled it up the dock. She pulled the cooler along the shell path to the wooden stairs as Karen walked behind.

"Leave the cooler here for now," Karen said as she pointed to the left, "and walk with me over here. I need to turn on the generator and the well."

About one hundred feet south of the cottage was a wooden shed built on top of a cement base. It was painted the same gray with blue trim as the cottage and had a matching tin roof. There were two doors on opposite sides of the shed, which were opened when the generator was running to allow ventilation. On the east side of the shed, there was a six-foot-long propane gas tank, secured to a cement base. On the west side of the shed, there was a heavy-duty pump that ran the two hundred-foot deep well that provided fresh well water to the cottage. There was a shell path through the sand and sandspur clumps to the shed from the cottage.

Karen opened both doors of the shed one hundred eighty degrees and latched them to an eye bolt on the outside wall the shed. She walked over to the propane tank and opened the valve that controlled the PVC gas line. The gas line ran down to the ground, across the sand, up the outside wall the shed, and through a hole in the wall to the generator. She walked back inside and flipped the start switch on the wall, next to the generator, and it fired up.

"We've got electricity and water now," Karen said matter-of-factly.

Beth was studying the connections and the switch on the wall. "What powers the switch on the wall that turned on the generator?"

"That's a very practical question," Karen said tongue-in-cheek.

Beth raised her left eyebrow and smirked.

"Actually," Karen said, "that's a very observant question. The solar panels on the roof of the cottage are connected to the electrical system that powers the house, the shed, and the outlets on the dock. However, the panels only produce a small amount of electricity. It's enough to run the water pump for a short time, the generator switch in the shed, and the dock lights and power outlet on the dock. That way, if the generator is broken or we run out of propane, we can still have basics at the cottage until the generator is running again."

Beth asked, "How do you fill up the propane tank?" "There are about fifteen private houses on the island,"

Karen answered, "and the state park has employee housing next to the main dock. Everybody uses propane, so we chip in and charter a barge once a month to bring a propane truck to the island. The barge docks here and the truck runs a long hose to our tank and fills it up. That works with cottages that are close to the bayside docks, but some of the cottages are right on the beach, and some in the interior of the island. These cottages are too far away to run a hose from the propane truck on the barge. Those people have to use golf carts and bring their small propane tanks, like the ones for grills, to the main dock at the state park, and have them filled up when the employee housing tank is refilled."

Beth nodded toward the shed. "It's a very ingenious set-up."

Karen motioned back toward the cottage. "Let me show you our toys underneath the cottage." As they walked back on the shell path, Beth asked, "What kind of toys?"

Karen pointed underneath the cottage. "We have two four-wheelers we use on the paths around the island. The park staff maintains the paths all up and down the island. Only the park rangers and the residents can use 4-wheelers, so there's not much traffic. A lot of the day trippers walk on the paths going to the beach, on the north end of the island. Down south, where we are, it's pretty deserted going back and forth. We'll see a lot more deer, raccoons, and tortoises than people.

"We also have two kayaks for the backwaters. It's nice this time of year because it's not as hot and the rainy season hasn't started. During the summer, the mosquitoes will carry you away if heatstroke doesn't get you first."

Beth walked underneath the cottage and looked up at the underside of the first level. She could see all the PVC plumbing pipes and the stainless steel electrical pipes, running up the cement pilings and spread out everywhere. She noticed a few wasp nests in the corners and hoped they stayed away from her. The kayaks and 4-

wheelers were chained to cement pilings in the middle of the cottage to keep them out of the rain and midday sun. There were two red five-gallon gas canisters next to the four wheelers. There was also a weathered picnic table, covered with tools and odd parts.

Karen said, "Help me up the stairs with the cooler, please."

Beth nodded and followed her over to the cooler. Karen tilted the cooler on its wheels and started walking up the stairs, pulling the cooler, and Beth lifted the cooler from behind at each step. When they reached the top of the stairs, Karen opened the screen door and pulled the cooler into the entryway. They had started to sweat and were winded, so it felt good to be in the shade.

Karen pulled her hair from her sweaty forehead and said, "It's time for a swim."

Beth smiled. "Sounds good to me."

"I'll unload the groceries, while you go change into your swimsuit," Karen said cheerfully.

* * * * * *

As they walked toward the beach, Karen asked, "What do you like best about being a lawyer?"

Beth considered her answer for a few seconds. "I'm a student of human nature, so I learn a lot about people in my job. Lawyers, clients, judges, bailiffs, court reporters, and witnesses all have different views on things. I enjoy waking up every morning and knowing that I'm going to hear divergent views on things. There's not much monotony in my job."

Karen asked, "Tell me the quirkiest thing that one of your clients did."

Beth laughed. "Give me a second to go through the list." "I hope I'm not on your list," Karen said in a fake indignant tone.

"Not at all," Beth said. A few seconds later, she snapped her fingers. "I've got one for you."

"Do tell."

Beth continued, "I represented this guy in his early sixties, on his fifth divorce. He was a successful contractor that always married women with bleach blond hair and fake boobs. Between his divorces and his business disputes, he'd paid a ton of attorney fees over the years, so he always complained about his bill. When I was representing him, he had eight residential rentals, so he always had problems collecting rent. During a break at mediation, I asked him which attorney in town handled his eviction cases. He chuckled and said he didn't use evictions because he'd found a better way to get rid of delinquent tenants.

"He'd wait until his tenants were at work," Beth said, "and then he'd go to the outside of the rental house and open up the sewer cleanout. He'd stuff newspaper in the four-inch PVC pipe on both sides of the cleanout intersection, and then pour a gallon of cement. He'd screw the lid back on the sewer cleanout and leave. The cement would dry and clog the outflow of water and sewage from the house. After a couple of days, the sewage would back up and the house would stink, so the delinquent renters would call and complain. He'd tell them the plumbing lines were broke and he couldn't afford to fix them. They'd be gone in two days. He said it was cheaper and quicker to replace the sewer cleanout than pay attorney fees for the eviction."

Karen snickered. "Who was the wisest judge you ever met?"

"That's an easy one," Beth said quickly. "Judge Samuels is retired now, but when I was a young lawyer, I was in his chambers one day with opposing counsel. We were talking about scheduling on a case, and after we finished, I asked him if he ever lost sleep over a decision. He pointed at two banker boxes in the corner of his office. One had SOB in black letters and the other had POB in black letters. He'd kept all the letters sent to him over the years that congratulated him, or criticized him, on his decisions. The congratulatory letters were called the 'pat on the back' letters, or POB letters, and he kept them in the POB box. He looked at me over his reading glasses, and said mischievously, 'Not all the letters I received over the years praised my decisions. The critical letters I keep in the SOB file.'

"He told me that whenever he had a hard decision, he'd look at the two boxes. He said he realized that no matter how he ruled, he'd make someone mad. He told me he applied the law to the facts of the case as best he could, and when he went home, he didn't think about it anymore. He told me he never had to take any sleeping pills at night."

Karen said, "I hope that's what Judge Sanchez does on my

case."

Beth nodded. Karen asked, "Who's the funniest lawyer you ever met?"

Beth laughed. "That's got to be a lawyer I've known since law school, Barbara Eastly. She's a public defender in Miami, and she's the most liberal non-conformist I've ever met. Her family is very wealthy, and her trust gives her plenty of money to live on. She only works because it's a hobby, and she loves fighting for the underdog. She also loves her pot and proudly calls herself a 'trustafarian'. Whenever she loses a hearing, she always argues with the judges, and they yell at her. She'll call me afterward and say, 'The judge performed legal liposuction on me again.'"

Karen looked confused and asked, "What's that?" "That's code for she got her ass chewed out."

Chapter 13

Beth was nude and ready for the first outside shower of her life. She timidly peaked out the outside door of the bathroom and looked down the beach to make sure no one was there. She stepped out on the wooden deck and felt very exposed as she hung her towel and wash cloth on the pegs.

She turned the valves until a warm flow of water came out of the showerhead. She looked down and watched the water drain between the boards of the deck and heard it splattering on the sand below. She closed her eyes and stepped under the warm stream.

Beth felt more relaxed with her eyes closed and slowly turned around to wash all the salt and sand off her body from the beach swim. The gulf water had been slightly cool, but very refreshing after her body had adjusted to the temperature. Karen had swum out to the deeper water, but Beth thought of all the shark's jaws just offshore and stayed in waist deep water where she could see the bottom. Karen had made a crack that the sharks wouldn't eat her out of professional courtesy.

Beth washed and conditioned her hair as she looked at the waves breaking on the beach. A flock of seagulls had landed on the beach, faced the onshore wind, and settled down into the sand to rest. Karen had turned on a jazz album inside, and the speakers on the deck were providing relaxing music. The deck from the second level was providing shade, and the afternoon breeze was better than air conditioning.

After an invigorating twenty-minute shower, she turned off the water and grabbed her towel. Beth walked toward the gulf and stood at the railing, looking seaward as she dried off in the afternoon sun.

* * * * * *

Karen turned the blender on and made margaritas while Beth sat in a rocking chair on the deck. Beth watched a pod of tarpon crashing into a school of shiners just off the beach. Some of the shiners were leaping out of the water to avoid being eaten, but the tarpon followed them into the air. The feeding frenzy lasted about thirty seconds before the school of bait scattered away. Karen brought two Tervis tumblers out to the deck, filled with tasty green goodness, and handed one to Beth.

"It's officially happy hour," Karen said as she sat down in a rocker.

Beth took a healthy sip of her margarita. "Oh goodness, that's very tasty. What kind of tequila?"

"Patron silver, of course," Karen said playfully.

They rocked slowly and drank their margaritas as they watched the sun getting lower on the horizon. Beth was feeling slightly sunburned, even though she'd reapplied sun tan lotion once she'd gotten to Cayo Costa. She was thinking how quiet the island was and realized her mobile phone hadn't rung all day. Her secretary must have taken her seriously when she told her no calls.

Karen asked, "How about we get one to go for the ride to Cabbage Key?"

"Sounds good to me," Beth said heartily.

Karen was dressed in blue jeans with a yellow Columbia fishing shirt and Sperry topsiders. Beth had on khaki pants and a green cotton sweater with white tennis shoes. They filled their cups, grabbed their purses, and walked down to the boat. After they untied the lines and idled away from the dock, Beth looked back toward the cottage. The sun was setting, and the cottage's cement pilings made long shadows toward the dock.

Karen pushed the throttle forward and the boat eased up on plane, cruising comfortably at 30 mph over the calm water. She steered the boat in a wide arc around the sandbar and oyster bars toward the marked channel. The noise from the prop scared all the mullet, and they scurried away, up into the shallows, and created hundreds of V-shaped wakes. Karen drove the boat toward Mondongo Island and then turned due south when she reached the Intracoastal channel, the deepest channel in Pine Island Sound.

Beth watched a flock of fifteen pelicans flying north in a V-formation and marveled at their perfect spacing. Karen pointed to the right of the boat, and Beth saw a family of dolphins surfacing for air two hundred feet away. Karen smiled at her and held out her Tervis tumblers for a silent toast to the day. Beth lightly touched her Tervis tumbler and took a drink of her margarita. Beth looked to her left and saw dozens of yachts, trawlers, and sailboats anchored between the channel and Useppa Island. Most boats were anchored at least fifty yards apart, but a few were tied up together. People from every boat were on their decks enjoying the sunset.

"Why are all the boats anchored there?" Beth asked.

Karen pointed to her left. "It's deep between the channel and Useppa, so it's safe to anchor for the night when the tide falls. The wind is mostly blocked by Useppa and Cabbage Key, so it's calmer than other deep water spots. And more importantly, it's a short ride to take their dingy to Cabbage Key for dinner and drinks."

Beth looked at all the different styles of boats anchored next to the channel. Some trawlers were sparkly clean, and others looked like they just arrived from an around the world cruise. Some sailboats were sixty feet long with radar domes and television satellite antennas, and others were twenty feet long with tattered sails and no evidence of electronic gear. Some yachts were sleek, modern vessels that cost millions, and other yachts were so old and patched they looked like they'd sink in the next storm. Beth imagined all these different people drinking together at the Cabbage Key bar and laughed to herself.

Karen came off plane at channel marker sixty and pointed to her right. "There's Cabbage Key."

Beth looked over to her right and saw a small marked channel heading west toward the main docks. Karen turned the boat and idled up the channel. There were rental cabins on the left of the channel, with their own small docks, and a long sandbar on the right protected the boats in the basin from waves from passing boats in the Intracoastal channel.

They docked the boat at the marina's dock and walked by the gift shop at the base of the dock.

After they passed the gift shop, Karen stepped to her left and pointed toward a wide sidewalk that led up the Indian mound. "The restaurant and bar is at the top of the mound."

As they walked up the sidewalk, Beth could see a dozen people sitting at round cement tables on the outside patio, underneath a Poinciana tree with white rope lights winding around the trunk and branches. Some people were smoking, but all seemed to be enjoying their drinks. To the right of the restaurant was a wooden water tower that was about forty feet high. As they got closer, they could hear beach music from the outside speakers and laughter inside the screened windows.

They walked into the restaurant and bar and saw about forty people spread out between the front dining room and bar. Karen asked to be seated in the rear dining room, and the hostess led them through the bar. As they walked through the bar, Beth noticed that all the walls were covered with dollar bills that had been signed and taped to the walls. Predictably, all the men at the bar gave Karen the once over, but Beth was pleasantly surprised a few men even looked at her. Of course, they were older and had been drinking, she observed.

The hostess sat them at a table on the back wall, where the windows were screened and allowed a comfortable breeze to flow through the building. Beth looked through the screen at large Banyan, Poinciana, and Gumbo Limbo trees outside. She could hear an osprey in a treetop, chirping for its mate to return. The other walls of the back dining room were also covered with signed dollar bills and waterfront paintings.

"What's with all the dollar bills?" Beth asked.

Karen said, "It's an old tradition that started over sixty years ago when the resort opened. There were more commercial fishermen than tourists back then. Of course, when the fishermen had good days, they had plenty of cash for beer. On bad fishing days, they were broke and thirsty. One smart fisherman taped a dollar bill to the wall with his name on it, so he'd always have cash for a drink. The tourists saw it and started doing it for fun. Pretty soon, the walls were covered in dollar bills."

Beth looked around the restaurant and bar for a few seconds. "There's no way that the bills have stayed on the walls this long."

Karen said, "There's some old bills around, but you're right, a lot do fall off the walls. The owners collect them in trash bags and deposit them in a charity account. Once a year, a check is sent to a local charity for all the deposits that year. The owners tell me it's usually around $15,000 a year."

The waitress walked up and asked, "Can I bring you two ladies some drinks?"

"Margaritas for both of us!" Karen said. "With or without salt?" The waitress asked. "I like it salty, don't you?" Karen asked Beth.

Beth said playfully, "That's the way real women drink It. "Women after my own heart," the waitress said. After the waitress walked away, Beth looked at the menu. "Everything looks so good. What do you recommend?"

"If you like seafood, the catch of the day is always good. If you like steak, the New York strip with peppercorn sauce is superb."

Beth smiled. "I need some meat to soak up all this tequila."

The waitress brought them their margaritas with salt and took their order. Karen ordered grilled shrimp over linguine with marinara sauce, and Beth got the New York strip, medium rare, with peppercorn sauce and a baked potato. Beth sipped on her margarita and glanced around the dining room. There was a skin mount of a large snook, tarpon and permits proudly displayed on the walls, surrounded by taped dollar bills. Hanging from the ceiling were antique fans slowly twirling around and more dollar bills taped to the wood ceiling.

Karen said, "I can't believe you've lived in Ft. Myers this long, and this is your first time to Cabbage Key."

Beth shrugged. "I always enjoyed the beach and fishing from the piers, but I've never been much of a boater. However, I'm sure I'll be back here because it's so unique. It would be a perfect romantic getaway for Frank and me."

"There are no TVs in the rooms, so you have to make your own entertainment." Karen said provocatively.

"That won't be a problem with Frank," Beth said as she smiled mischievously.

Karen smiled and held up her margarita for a toast. "Here's to entertainment without a TV."

Beth touched her glass and said, "The world survived quite nicely before TVs." They both sat back in their chairs and took a healthy drink of their margaritas. Beth and Karen heard the noise level from the bar increase, and they glanced over and saw a group of about ten people walk into the bar and say hello to old friends already sitting there. The two bartenders were working furiously to keep up with all the drink orders coming from everyone enjoying happy hour.

"That scene reminds me of my favorite bar from college," Karen said wistfully.

Beth nodded. "I worked as a waitress at Chili's during college and law school, and it was a fun place to work because of all the regulars. I worked hard and made good money, but when my shift was over, I had a drink at the bar with the regulars. It was a perfect college job."

"Amen to that," Karen said as she raised her glass up and took a drink. "Every summer, my sorority girlfriend and I worked waitress jobs at Ft. Myers beach, and we always got invited to the best parties."

Beth pointed into the bar and asked, "What kind of game is that couple playing in the bar with a ring hanging from a string attached to the ceiling?"

Karen looked over and chuckled. "That's a seemingly very simple game, but it's hard to do. There's a two-inch stainless steel ring tied to a string that's hanging from the ceiling and you have to step back from the wall and push the ring toward a hook on the wall. If you make it, your date has to drink. If you miss it, you have to drink. It's the Cabbage Key version of quarters."

Beth watched the man try three times and miss it each time, followed by a drink from his cup. His date made it the first time she tried and raised her hands in victory, followed by the man taking another drink and holding his hands up in surrender.

The waitress brought their meals and they devoured their sumptuous choices in short order. At Karen's suggestion, they shared a delicious piece of key lime pie made with limes from Pine Island. After Beth paid the check, they walked outside onto the patio and gazed out over the marina harbor. A three-quarter moon was rising over Useppa, and the stars were bright in the cloudless sky. To the casual observer they appeared to be best friends enjoying a girl's night out.

"This is beautiful," Beth said.

Karen pointed up toward the water tower. "You can see the widow's walk at our cottage from the top. You want to walk up there?"

"Of course."

Karen and Beth walked down the shell path to the cement base on the water tower. The tower was made of twelve-inch square wooden beams painted white. The wooden stairs zig zagged back and forth to a viewing area just underneath the forty-five-foot high water cistern. After Beth and Karen climbed the stairs they were out of breath and sat down on a bench.

Karen pointed to the west and said, "Just over that Gumbo Limbo tree you can see the light on our dock, and if you look above the tree line, you can see the outline of our widow's walk."

Beth followed Karen's finger and saw the widow's walk. "Well, I think we should climb your widow's walk and have another margarita."

Karen laughed. "I knew I liked you!"

Chapter 14

Karen idled the boat out of the Cabbage Key channel as Beth looked at the lights on all the boats anchored in front of Useppa. The large sailboats had lights at the top of the masts and all along the sides. Some of the large yachts were lit up like bars on New Year's Eve. One of the large trawlers was apparently hosting a party, because the music was blaring and dozens of dinghies were tied up to the stern. A few of the small boats only had one tiny light at the stern of the boat.

Beth pointed at the water next to the boat's wake. "What's all that green stuff glowing in the water?"

Karen looked over the side. "That's phosphorous.

They're microscopic animals in the water and they light up when something moves them."

Karen put the engine in neutral and turned off the running lights on the front of the boat and the stern light. "With less light you can see them better."

Karen grabbed a fishing rod from the rod holder on the port side of the console. She put the tip of the rod in the water two feet down and swirled it around. The phosphorous glowed when it was disturbed by the rod. "I get it," Beth said.

Karen put the rod back in the holder and turned off the engine. "Listen to how far sound travels over the water."

Beth could hear conversations from the party at the trawler and it was a half mile away. After a few seconds of listening to the party, Beth heard a loud blast of air coming from the water. She looked overboard and saw about ten feet of disturbed phosphorus glowing in the water.

"What's that?" Beth asked as she stepped back. Karen looked to the side. "It's a manatee." "That scared the hell out of me!" Beth said.

"They're harmless. They eat sea grass from the bottom, and they're very docile. In the old days, sailors who'd been at sea a long time called them mermaids. They must've drunk a lot of rum to think they were women with tails."

Beth and Karen watched the phosphorus glow as the manatee slowly swam away. Karen waited until it was a hundred feet away, started up the engine and turned the running lights back on. The moon and stars provided enough light that she didn't need a spotlight. Karen powered the boat up on plane, and they headed back to Cayo Costa at 30 mph.

As they were heading north on the Intracoastal channel, Beth pointed to lights on the northeast horizon. "Which town is that over there?"

"That's Punta Gorda. That used to be as far south as the railroad went back in the 1920s. Everything south of Punta Gorda had to be accessed by boat. That's how all these old fish shacks in Pine Island Sound got built. The Punta Gorda Fish Company got ninety-nine-year leases from the State for the land and built them on pilings. Once a week, a big boat from Punta Gorda would bring ice and supplies to the fishermen who lived in the shacks. The boat would pick up the week's catch of fish and haul them back to Punta Gorda, where they were put on refrigerated train cars and shipped to the big cities up north. After roads were built to Pine Island, the company didn't need the fishing shacks, so they sold them to locals who used them as weekend getaways."

Beth nodded. "That's so interesting. Any other fascinating local history stories?"

Karen thoughtfully answered, "Fort Myers was a union fort during the civil war. Ft. Myers was originally part of Monroe County, but a dispute over funding for rebuilding a burned down school caused city leaders to lobby the legislature for their own county. The legislature agreed, and the city leaders, most of which were from strong southern families, choose to name the county after Robert E. Lee to atone for the Union fort built there during the civil war."

Beth said, "A psychologist could write her thesis on that split personality."

Karen nodded and said, "Another interesting bit of history is how Captiva and North Captiva formed. Originally, Captiva was one long island, but the 1900 hurricane split the island in two and formed Redfish Pass. They've been separate since then, and the northernmost island is called Upper Captiva or North Captiva, depending on who you're talking to."

Beth said, "I never knew that."

They rode in silence for a minute before Karen asked, "What was your first husband like?"

Beth took a deep breath before answering. "We met in college at Mercer. He was there on a baseball scholarship, but he took his studies very seriously. He was a very smart guy and was on the dean's list every semester. For pleasure reading, he'd always read three or four books at once. That's something I could never do. He was good looking, funny and smart, and I was in love. I thought I'd spend the rest of my life with him," Beth's voice quivered, "but I was wrong."

Karen waited for a few seconds. "What was your second husband like?"

Beth wiped a tear away from her left eye. "He was tall, dark and handsome. Imagine Antonio Banderas with a

deeper voice and three inches taller. I met him when he was doing work on my house and I fell head over heels for him. I actually proposed to him."

Karen laughed. "Did you make him sign a pre-nup since you had more money?"

Beth shook her head. "I thought about it, but I worried it might jinx the marriage. Even though I knew there are studies showing marriages with pre-nups have a lower divorce rate."

"What?" Karen asked incredulously.

Beth continued, "When people talk about finances up front, and what each side expects out of the marriage, it helps both sides understand each other. Of course, many engagements are called off during negotiations of pre-nups, but the ones that get married are more likely to last than marriages without pre-nups."

Karen was quiet for a few seconds before she responded. "When I get married again, I will never, ever sign a prenup."

They rode in silence for a minute before Beth asked, "What traits are you going to look for in your next husband?"

Karen considered her answer for a few seconds. "I want him to be closer to my age. He doesn't need to be as rich as Stan, but I still want financial security. And most importantly, he can't be an asshole, like Stan."

Beth laughed.

They rode in silence for the next few minutes until they

were close to the dock. Karen pulled the throttle back and the boat came down off plane, settling into the water. Beth saw three falling stars and pointed at them. Karen put the boat in neutral, and they drifted as more falling stars appeared.

Karen said wistfully, "Sailors consider falling stars a sign of good luck."

Chapter 15

Karen eased the throttle into forward gear and the boat moved slowly toward the dock, which was lit by a mercury vapor light on a ten-foot pole at the base of the dock. Two feet from the dock she pulled the throttle in reverse, spinning the wheel to her left, and pulling the stern sideways toward the dock as she stopped the forward momentum. As the boat's port side gently stopped against the pilings, Karen put the throttle in neutral, turned the engine off, and walked forward to the bow. She picked up the docking line tied

to the front cleat, and nimbly jumped out of the boat, like a gymnast finishing her routine. She turned and smiled at

Beth. "Isn't this better than looking through files and thinking about a divorce trial?"

"You got that right."

Karen tied the bow line to the piling and pointed to the stern. "Can you grab the rear line and throw it to me?"

Beth walked to the back of the boat and grabbed the rear line with the end tied to the port cleat. She picked it up and threw it to Karen, who had walked down the dock. Karen tied the line to the nearest piling and said, "The boat is secure for the night. Are we ready for a night cap on the widow's walk?"

"Definitely," Beth said and looked at the stars for a second.

Beth stepped out of the boat and walked with Karen down the dock. A mother raccoon and her four babies walked across the shell pathway at the end of the dock, glancing cautiously toward the women before continuing their nightly forage. As Beth stepped on the shell pathway, she heard a mosquito buzz her ear, and she swatted it away.

"Once we get up on the widow's walk, the breeze will keep the mosquitoes away. There are always a few down by the mangroves," Karen said as she walked faster toward the cottage.

Beth followed Karen's pace as she slapped one on her left forearm and heard another buzz her ear. The smell of the night blooming jasmine eased Beth's irritation at the pesky bugs as they approached the stairs illuminated by yellow bug lights on the covered entryway. They scampered up the steps two at a time and quickly went in the screen door.

"Now I understand all the screens," Beth said as she swatted one remaining pest on her right hand.

"A pain at night, but they'll be gone tomorrow when we go fishing with the guide," Karen said as she pulled her keys from her pocket.

As Karen unlocked the front door, Beth took a deep breath and relaxed. She was tipsy from the margaritas and was certain one more on the widow's walk would be just right. Karen went inside first and hit the two light switches on the right wall, turning on the overhead light by the door and a lamp on the far side of the room. Karen stopped in her tracks, stiffened, and gasped.

Beth heard a strange male voice say, "I've been waitin' for both of ya."

Beth looked toward the deep voice and saw a man dressed in black with a clown mask sitting on the couch and pointing a gun at them. Beth felt the hair on her neck raise up and a chill run down her spine. She felt the blood pumping in her ears but didn't move. Karen stepped backward and grabbed Beth's right forearm with her left hand.

The stranger stood up, and Beth felt worse when she saw he was tall and muscular. The white clown mask had a large round red nose, with oversized red eyebrows and lips. Beth focused on the gun, and saw it was a small snub nose revolver. Karen pulled closer and Beth felt the heat from her body.

The stranger had a southern accent. "Your husband sent me to deliver a message to you and your lawyer—ya'll shoulda settled at mediation."

Beth looked intensely at the clown mask, trying to stare at the eyes of the stranger to gauge his intentions. The light was low, and all Beth could see was black in the eye holes of the mask.

The stranger walked toward them and motioned to the stairs with the gun. "Walk up the stairs, both of ya."

Beth led the way, and Karen touched her lower back as they reached the steps. Karen turned the light switch on at the base of the stairs and a single light at the top of the stairs came on. The stranger followed about five feet behind with the gun pointed at Karen's back.

When they reached the top step, the stranger said, "Go to the bedroom on the right and both of ya sit on the bed."

Beth glanced at Karen and saw her eyes were wide open, darting back and forth. Beth hesitated and looked at the stranger.

"Keep goin'," the stranger bellowed.

Beth and Karen went into the guest bedroom and sat on the bright yellow comforter, looking back at the stranger silhouetted by the single light over the stairway. Beth felt

helpless and instinctively slid closer to Karen. The stranger stood in the doorway and stared at Karen.

He pointed to the back corner of the room, next to the glass slider leading to the deck. "Blondie, go sit in the corner on top of your hands."

Karen didn't move, so the stranger stepped closer and pointed the gun at her head.

"Move, Blondie," he said sternly.

Karen stood up and walked slowly to the corner while looking back at the gun. She sat down cross-legged and put her hands under her thighs. Beth could see tears running down Karen's face.

The stranger looked back at Beth. "Lawyer, lay face down with your hands stretched forward, and put your feet together."

Beth looked at the gun as she processed her options and realized none were good. She quickly considered lunging at the stranger, but realized it was suicide.

"Do it, lawyer, or you're gonna have another hole in your body."

Beth slid up onto the bed and lay down as instructed. She turned her head to the left so she could see Karen and the stranger behind her. He put the gun behind him and slid it between his back and his pants. He reached to the dresser top to his left and grabbed a small circular plastic container of fishing leader, pulling out five feet. He pulled a pocket knife from his right pants pocket and cut it. Beth could feel the sweat running into her eyes, so she faced the comforter and wiped her face clean. The stranger wrapped the leader around Beth's ankles and tied a knot, cinching it down tight and pulling Beth's ankles closer together. He wrapped Beth's ankles five more times with the leader and cinched down another knot.

"Lawyer, put your hands behind ya, together-like." Beth

complied and the stranger tied her hands the same as her ankles. After he cut the leader, he closed the knife and stood up, leaving the leader container on the edge of the bed. He put the knife back in his pocket and grabbed the gun behind him with his right hand. He picked up the leader container with his left hand, and said, "Blondie, come with me to the other bedroom. It's your turn."

Karen looked at the stranger and slid backward toward the corner.

"Blondie, if ya don't come with me, I'm gonna shoot your lawyer buddy."

Karen stood up slowly and walked unsteadily toward the door, glancing down at Beth. As she walked past Beth's feet, Beth turned her head to her right. She saw Karen walk out the door with the stranger as he backed up. A few seconds later, they both disappeared out of Beth's line of vision, but she could hear the wood floor creak as they walked into the master bedroom.

The stranger said, "Blondie, get rid of those clothes and lay down. I'm gonna tie ya up, and then we'll have some fun."

Beth imagined Karen undressing in front of the stranger, and him tying her arms and legs to the four corners of the bed. But she heard nothing. Beth's anger was exploding, but she tried to focus on a way to save them and remembered her cell phone. It was in her left front pocket, and she tried to maneuver her hands to get it, but the knot was too tight.

She looked to her left and saw the slider leading to the porch with the moon in the background. She turned her head to the right and saw the nightstand with a ceramic vase and fake yellow roses.

"No," Karen moaned from the other bedroom. Beth heard a slap, followed by the stranger yelling,

"Blondie, we can do this the easy way or the hard way. How do ya want it?"

There was silence for a few seconds before Beth heard the bed springs creaking slowly. Beth felt adrenaline surging through her veins and flipped onto her back to see how she could move with the restraints. She saw no shadows or movement in the hallway, but she heard the bed springs creaking faster. She threw her head back in frustration and saw the shark's jaws mounted on the wall behind her.

Beth quickly processed how she could maneuver to cut herself free with the shark's teeth. If she tried to stand up with her ankles together and fell, she would alert the stranger, so she decided to cut the line around her ankles first. She pushed down with her feet on the mattress and lifted her hip up and over about six inches. She continued this sideways crab crawl until her soles were against the headboard. She took a deep breath and lifted her tied ankles on top of the headboard. She pulled with her heels, as she lifted her butt, and maneuvered herself beneath the shark's jaw. Beth felt the sweat running down her forehead and into her eyes, but she felt energized.

Adrenaline drowning her fears, Beth concentrated on sliding her ankles up and down on the shark's teeth until the leader was cut. When she finally cut the line from her ankles, she maneuvered around on the bed until she was on her knees in the middle of the mattress. She stood up with her back to the shark's jaws and slowly stepped back on the mattress toward the shark's jaws. As she stepped on the edge of the mattress, next to the headboard, she felt her feet sinking as the mattress lifted up from the foot of the bed, like a teeter-totter. She quickly sat down on the headboard, hoping it would hold her weight. It shifted and rested against the wall as the mattress settled back onto the base.

Beth could feel the shark's jaws on her elbows. She leaned forward and lifted her tied wrists up to the shark's teeth. Her shoulders screamed in pain as she moved her wrists back and forth. She felt the teeth cutting the leader and the skin on the top of her hands, but the adrenaline numbed the pain. It took her longer to cut her wrists loose because of the balancing act on the headboard and the uncomfortable angle. Once she was free, she pushed off the wall and lunged to the center of the bed so the mattress wouldn't tip with her weight. The springs of the mattress strained as she landed, and she listened to see if the noise had given away her escape. But she heard the same loud rhythm of the mattress springs in the other bedroom.

Beth frantically looked around the room for some type of weapon and saw the spear gun leaning in the corner. She had seen her old boyfriend use a spear gun while snorkeling, but she'd never shot it herself. She jumped out of the bed and grabbed the spear gun and spear. She hesitated as she looked at the rubber sling and the spear, trying to remember how to load it. She took them and walked to the doorway so the hallway light would be brighter, and she tried to picture her old boyfriend loading his spear gun.

After a few seconds of thought, Beth wedged the front of the spear gun into the mattress, while pushing with her hip, and pulled the sling back to the loading notch. She picked up the spear, loaded it on the sling, and turned the safety off, so it was ready to fire. She walked out of the room holding the cocked spear gun and tip-toed about ten feet to the edge of Karen's bedroom. She heard the stranger making low guttural sounds and smelled his Old Spice cologne. There was no light coming from the bedroom, and Beth knew as soon as she stood in the doorway the stranger would see her shadow.

Beth took a deep breath and stepped into the doorway. She saw Karen tied up spread eagle to the four corners of the bed as the stranger raped her. The stranger stopped his thrusts, turning his head to the door when he saw light from the hallway partially blocked. Beth pointed the spear gun at the stranger's clown mask and yelled, "Don't move or I'll shoot!"

There was a moment of silence, and the stranger slid back on his knees while turning slightly to his left, toward the night stand. Beth looked at the night stand and saw the gun laying there as the stranger lunged toward it. Beth fired. She heard the sling hurl the spear toward the stranger and recoil back into the gun. The stranger fell off the bed and thrashed violently. He grabbed the nightstand with his left hand and pulled himself up to his knees. His back was to Beth, and she saw the spear tip sticking out of the right side of his neck. Beth dropped the spear gun as she watched the stranger's head quiver.

Karen yelled, "No!"

The stranger reached for the gun with his right hand and Beth sprinted toward him. She lunged at the man's neck from behind and grabbed onto both sides of the spear. She shook it and felt blood trickle on to her left hand, but the man was still moving, and she felt his strength overpowering her as he raised his right arm. Beth saw the man had the gun in his right hand and was trying to point it at her head. She held onto the spear with both hands but moved to her left to avoid the gun barrel. She heard a deafening explosion and felt the bullet burn through her hair. She instinctively fell to her left but held tight with her left hand to the shaft of the spear. The spear tip pulled back into the stranger's neck, and she lost her grip as she tumbled to the ground. Beth looked up at the stranger on his knees and saw blood spurt from his neck onto the nightstand. He fell back against the edge of the bed, dropping the gun as more blood gushed out with each heartbeat.

Karen yelled, "Beth, oh God, Beth, are you shot?"

Beth felt the right side of her head for blood and was surprised she didn't find any. "I'm okay. Are you?"

Karen screamed, "Just cut this leader off me!"

Beth looked at the stranger and saw more blood gushing from his neck. She ran to the kitchen, got a steak knife, and ran back to the bedroom. She cut Karen's legs loose first and then her hands. Karen lurched toward Beth and hugged her as she started to cry. Beth looked over at the dead stranger, slumped against the bed in a pool of blood, and pulled a sheet up over Karen, who had begun to violently shake with spasms.

"I'm calling 911," Beth said and pulled her cell phone from her pocket.

Chapter 16

Beth shakily called 911 and then Frank, who answered on the second ring. "Hi, honey. Are you having fun?"

Beth told him what happened.

"Baby, I'll be there as fast as I can," Frank said in a quivering voice. "I'm calling the Captain of Fish and Wildlife to have one of their boats meet me at the marina. I'll call you when I'm leaving the dock."

Beth simply said goodbye and ended the call.

Karen had the sheet pulled tight around her and was staring at the dead stranger. She said flatly, "Pull the mask off."

Beth looked at the dead stranger with the spear through his neck and blood all over his body. He was slumped against the bed, and his head had fallen back on the mattress. Beth didn't want to step in the blood, so she climbed over the mattress on all fours, and pulled the mask off. She left the mask on the mattress and climbed back to the foot of the bed.

"Please, turn on the overhead light, so I can see," Karen said.

Beth was unsteady when she stood up, so she held on to the side of the bed for a second. After she got her equilibrium, she walked to the door and turned the light switch on. Karen clutched the sheet close and stood up at the foot of the bed as she looked at the stranger.

"It's Stan's handyman," Karen said furiously. Beth started chewing her left pinky nail.

* * * * * *

Beth's cell phone rang, and she picked up. "Hello?" "This is the 911 operator. I'm going to patch you through to Detective Dagle. His boat is leaving the marina and needs directions to which part of the island you're on."

"Okay."

There was a second of static and a new voice was on the line. "This is Detective Robert Dagle, ma'am. How do we get to your dock on Cayo Costa?"

Beth said, "Just a second. I'm a guest here. The owner's in the bathroom."

Beth knocked on the door, told Karen who it was, and handed her the phone when she opened the door. Beth saw she still had the sheet wrapped around her and her eyes were puffy from crying. She gave directions to Detective Dagle, said goodbye, and handed the phone back to Beth.

"I'll be out in a few minutes, after I change," Karen said as she closed the door.

It had been fifteen minutes since the initial 911 call, and Karen had been in the downstairs bathroom since then with the door shut. Beth walked with her downstairs to get her away from the body. After Karen was in the bathroom, Beth had walked back upstairs to get some clean clothes for her. When Beth walked back in the master bedroom, she stared at the man she'd killed. The air seemed to be still energized from the struggle, and she instinctively felt her hair where the bullet had burned through, narrowly missing her scalp. She could still smell the Old Spice, but there were other odors from the body that she'd never smelled before. She had a headache from the adrenaline overload, but she didn't feel any regret. It was a kill-or-be-killed scenario, and she felt no remorse.

The bathroom door opened, and Karen walked out in clean clothes.

Beth pointed up and asked quietly, "Who is he?"

Karen breathed in loudly through her nose and exhaled slowly. She said solemnly, "Butch was his first name, but I don't know his last. He was Stan's handyman, and they liked to shoot guns together. Stan used to tell me he was going to the shooting range to meet Butch, the handyman. He'd fix stuff at the house in town and come out here to fix things."

"How many times have you talked to him?" Beth asked. Karen shrugged. "A couple of times. I saw him occasionally when I was leaving for school and would say hello. Stan always took care of all the maintenance of the house and the cottage."

Beth pointed to the deck. "Let's go sit in the rockers until the police get here."

After they sat down, Beth asked gently, "Do you want to talk about it?"

Karen shook her head and said feebly, "No."

They both rocked in silence and relished the fresh breeze coming in from the gulf, absorbed in their own thoughts. After about fifteen minutes, Beth could hear an outboard engine speeding through the water, getting louder as it got closer.

Once the engine slowed down, Beth knew they were close to the dock.

She stood up and looked at Karen. "Stay here. I'll go down to the dock and get them."

Karen nodded.

Beth walked out the front door and could see the flashing blue lights from the Sheriff's boat as it approached the dock. She walked down the shell path to the dock, and by the time she got there, the sheriff's boat was tied up. A short man with a crew cut dressed in khaki pants and a white polo style shirt with the sheriff's logo, stepped out first, and three uniformed deputies followed.

"Hello, ma'am. I'm Detective Robert Dagle, and these deputies are here to help me. Are you okay?"

"Yes, I'm fine, but my friend was raped. She's up on the deck." Beth hesitated, and her voice cracked, "And the dead rapist is upstairs in the bedroom. I escaped and killed him when he tried to grab his gun."

"What exactly happened, ma'am?" Detective Dagle asked in a soothing voice.

Beth told him in detail everything that happened since they arrived back from dinner at Cabbage Key.

Detective Dagle looked up and down the shoreline. "Do you know how he got here, and have you heard any boats leave since you called 911?"

Beth shook her head. "No, I don't know how he got here, and I haven't heard any boats."

Detective Dagle said, "Hernandez and Franklin, follow us to the cottage and look for the bad guy's shoe prints in the sand. Follow the prints, and you'll find out where he hid his boat. Be careful—there might be a getaway driver waiting in the boat, so I want you guys to stay together. Be cautious and be ready!"

Hernandez and Franklin pulled their Glocks and flashlights

from their belts, and looked up and down the shoreline, like bloodhounds waiting to be turned loose. Detective Dagle led the group up the path toward the cottage and Beth wondered if there was an armed accomplice still hiding.

When they got to the stairs, Hernandez and Franklin found the intruder's shoe prints and followed them toward the brush north of the cottage.

Detective Dagle looked at Beth. "Take me to your friend, ma'am."

Karen nodded and started up the steps.

Detective Dagle motioned to the remaining deputy with a duffle bag. "Massey, come with me."

Beth led Detective Dagle and Deputy Massey up the stairs and in the front door. Beth pointed upstairs and said, "The dead man is upstairs to the left, and Karen is outside on the deck."

Detective Dagle looked at Deputy Massey. "Go check out the scene upstairs and gather evidence while I talk to the victim."

Detective Dagle walked into the living room and saw Karen through the sliders, facing the gulf in her chair. He looked at Beth and said quietly, "Ma'am, if you could walk out with me on the deck for introductions, maybe it'll be easier for her. But after that, if you don't mind, I'd prefer if you came back inside while I take her recorded statement. After I finish with her, I'll take your statement."

Beth nodded. "Sure, no problem."

Detective Dagle's cell phone rang, and he picked up. He gave directions to the cottage and said to look for flashing blue lights on his boat.

"That was FWC at the marina, ma'am. They picked up your boyfriend, and they're on the way here."

Beth nodded.

"Frank and I go back twenty years. He's a helluva good prosecutor."

Beth bit her bottom lip and nodded. She led Detective Dagle out to the porch and made introductions to Karen. Her eyes were still swollen, but she'd quit crying and was able to have a conversation. Beth let herself back in and shut the sliders for privacy. She turned the TV on to the Weather channel and sat down to wait for Frank.

* * * * * *

Beth heard Frank running up the stairs and met him as he opened the front door. They embraced and held each other. Frank whispered in her ear, "How are you?"

"I'm fine," Beth said quietly and kissed him.

Beth heard someone walking up the steps and looked up. A uniformed FWC officer stood in the entryway and Frank said, "Officer Loundes, this is my girlfriend, Beth Mancini."

"Hello, Officer Loundes," Beth said. "Thank you for bringing Frank out here."

"Just glad to help, ma'am."

Beth motioned for them to follow her, and they sat down at the dinner table. Beth pointed to Detective Dagle and Karen through the sliders and explained what was going on with them and the other deputies. Detective Dagle saw Frank and Officer Loundes sitting at the dinner table and gave them a nod. Beth told them everything that had happened as they waited for Detective Dagle to finish his interview.

Deputy Massey came down the stairs from the bedroom, and Beth introduced everyone to him. He sat down at the dining room table and caught Detective Dagle's eye through the sliders. A few seconds later, Detective Dagle walked inside and shut the slider. Karen stayed in her rocker, staring out at the gulf, so Beth decided to stay inside.

Detective Dagle sat down at the head of the table and looked at Deputy Massey. "What have you found out?"

Deputy Massey pulled his pocket pad from his left shirt pocket and looked at it for a second. "I got his driver's license from his wallet, and his name is Butch Redding. I called headquarters, and they ran a check on him. He lives in Ft. Myers, has a Ford truck and sixteen-foot boat registered in his name. He has two prior DUIs and a domestic violence conviction against his ex-wife from three years ago. I went through his pockets and found his wallet with nine one hundred-dollar bills in it, his cell phone, truck and house keys, and a pocket knife. I checked his keys, and one of them was for the front door of the cottage."

Frank said, "We need to get a search warrant for his house, boat, truck, and phone records. I need evidence linking him and Stan Jacoby, so I can send that son-of-a-bitch to prison for a long time."

Detective Dagle nodded. "I agree. I also need to call an EMS helicopter to land out here and take Mrs. Jacoby to the hospital to be checked out. They'll also want to collect evidence from the rape."

Beth was perturbed. "I *saw* her being raped. What else do you need?"

"Don't be mad, honey," Frank said in a soothing voice.

"It has to be done in every case to preserve evidence for trial. If you don't do it, the defense will have a field day."

Beth was not happy. "I'm going out to see how Karen is doing."

Beth walked out the slider and shut it quietly. She pulled a rocker close to Karen and sat down. Karen looked over and tried to smile.

"How did he treat you?" Beth asked quietly.

Karen pulled her hair back off her forehead and took a deep breath. "He was fine. He just asked a lot of details about everything, and it was kinda embarrassing. And, of course, I know it's being recorded, so everyone is going to know every detail about how I was raped."

Beth didn't say anything but reached over and held Karen's hand. They sat there for a few minutes in silence until they heard the front door open and close. They turned around and saw Deputies Hernandez and Franklin walking toward the kitchen table. After a few seconds of conversation, Detective Dagle walked over to the slider and opened it. He walked over to them and said, "They found his john-boat in the mouth of some hidden creek, a few hundred yards north of here. Nobody else was in it."

Karen shook her head and said scornfully, "He hid it in the Tunnel of Love."

Chapter 17

The State Attorney's Office is located on the top four floors of the SunTrust building in downtown Ft. Myers, adjacent to the courthouse. It's close to the Caloosahatchee River and offers stunning views of the waterfront. The prosecutors for the State Attorney's Office often meet with law enforcement officers on serious cases to assess the evidence before making arrests. After an arrest is made, most defendants will lawyer up and refuse to make statements. In addition, many potential witnesses are reluctant to talk with law enforcement after an arrest is made.

It was Monday afternoon and Frank was on the phone in his office, talking to a defense lawyer about scheduling depositions on a case, when his secretary walked into his office with a note and set it down on his desk. He read it, nodded, and covered the bottom of the phone as he whispered, "Bring him back."

A minute later, his secretary led Detective Dagle back to his office. He sat down in a chair across the desk from Frank, who nodded at him. While Detective Dagle waited for Frank to finish his conversation, he looked out the eighth floor window at a trawler traveling down the Caloosahatchee River, toward the Gulf of Mexico. It was about forty feet long, and he wondered if the captain had a destination in mind, or if he was just out for a day cruise. Detective Dagle had always hoped to own a trawler in his retirement, but he had two daughters in college, and they were draining his bank account on a steady basis. He chuckled to himself—a canoe was probably in his future.

Detective Dagle was hungry, so he looked at his watch and saw it was three o'clock. He hadn't eaten since he'd choked down a hot dog from 7-11 when he'd filled his cruiser up with gas at eight that morning. He'd worked all day preparing the case and was anxious to arrest Stan Jacoby. But he wanted to go over the evidence with Frank to see if anything else was needed.

Frank hung up the phone and shook his head. "Some

lawyers really like to hear themselves talk."

Detective Dagle shrugged his shoulders. "Mouth pieces talk, cops take action."

"Speaking of which," Frank asked as he leaned back in his chair and put his hands behind his head. "What do you got on Stan Jacoby?"

Detective Dagle sat up in his chair. "We got the duty judge to sign search warrants on Saturday for Butch Redding's truck, boat, house, and phone records. We found his truck at the marina on Pine Island with the boat trailer attached, and we had the key from the key ring in his pocket, so we didn't have to break the glass. All we found in his truck were empty beer cans and a can of snuff. Same thing for his boat, except there were two unopened beers in his cooler. I guess he was gonna drink two on the way back to the marina after he finished his job at the cottage."

Frank leaned forward and put his elbows on his desk. "Beth gave him just what he deserved."

Detective Dagle nodded and continued. "At his house, he had a gun safe, and we got a locksmith to come out and open it. It had the titles to his truck and boat, a Bowie knife, a 20-gauge shotgun, a 9mm Glock, an empty .38 caliber holster—which matches the gun he had with him at the cottage—ammo, and most interestingly, $1,500 in hundred-dollar bills."

"If you add that money," Frank said, "with the money in his wallet, you get $2,400. I can't wait until we get Stan Jacoby's bank records, and it shows a cash withdrawal for that kind of money."

Detective Dagle smiled. "I saved the best for last. Remember, Redding's key ring had a key to the beach cottage. Redding's phone records show he received two phone calls from Stan Jacoby's cell phone on the day of the rape. One call lasted fifteen minutes, and the other call was four minutes. It proves Stan Jacoby called his trusted handyman to do a little dirty work. He gives him money up front, a key to the cottage, and promises him more money once the deed is done."

Frank nodded. "Makes sense to me."

"I've been thinking about the charges and wanted to run it by you," Detective Dagle said.

"Okay."

"We've got an agreement between Redding and Jacoby to tie up Jacoby's wife and her lawyer for revenge, and to try to intimidate them into settling the divorce. When he pointed the gun at them, he used threat of force before he tied the women up, so we've got him on kidnapping both women.

He obviously raped Mrs. Jacoby, but we don't know if he was gonna do anything to your girlfriend. So, I think we charge Stan Jacoby with two counts of conspiracy to commit kidnapping, and one count of conspiracy to commit rape. If the judge maxes him out, he'll get ninety years."

Frank nodded. "It's a circumstantial case, but it's enough. I checked with my boss, and he's gonna let me prosecute the case personally."

Detective Dagle smiled. "I hoped you'd get the case."

Frank moved his head around in a small circle and cracked the vertebrae in his neck. "Go arrest that son of a bitch."

Chapter 18

The criminal courthouse in downtown Ft. Myers is nine stories tall and the judges' offices are on the ninth and tenth floors. The felony trials are in the sixth, seventh and eighth floor courtrooms, which have side windows that look out over downtown and the expansive Caloosahatchee River.

For security reasons, the judges have private elevators that take them from their offices to hidden hallways behind the courtrooms. A bailiff waits for them in the hallway and escorts them to a door behind their bench in the courtroom.

"All rise. Judge Tom McDaniel is presiding over this court," the head bailiff announced.

Judge McDaniel was a tall, portly man with a full head of silver hair and a matching beard that contrasted with his tan face. His bright green eyes, confident gait, and black robe made him an imposing figure as he walked in the doorway behind his bench in courtroom 6B. Everyone in the courtroom was instantly quiet and focused on him as he sat down. Judge McDaniel enjoyed being a judge, and he was happiest when everyone was looking at him and waiting for him to speak.

Judge McDaniel looked up and said in his strong baritone voice, "Please be seated."

As everyone in the courtroom sat down, Judge McDaniel glanced over his bench at the court reporter for the trial, Debby Wilson, and smiled. Judge McDaniel had dated Debby between his second and third divorce and had fond memories of their three months together. Whenever she was assigned to his courtroom, he felt the old fires, and the bottom of his tongue tingled. Judge McDaniel and his live-in girlfriend had fought that morning over taking out the trash, so he was glad to see Debby and was ready to flirt.

Debby had been dating an E.R. doctor for two years and wasn't remotely interested in Judge McDaniel, but she politely returned his smile and looked down. Judge Mc-

Daniel had put on thirty pounds since they'd dated, and she

estimated his ego had increased by the same percentage. She chastised herself for ever dating him, but it seemed like a good idea at the time. Every time she worked in his courtroom, she could feel him undressing her with his eyes.

As you walk into Courtroom 6B, the jury box and jury room is on the left side. The prosecutor's table was closest to the jury box on the left and the defense table was on the right side of the courtroom. The witness stand was to the left of the judge's bench and the clerk sat to the right of the judge. The podium for the lawyers to stand at when questioning the witness was located between the two tables. There were small wheels on the bottom of the podium that were used when the bailiffs moved the podium to face the jury box during opening and closing statements.

Stan Jacoby nervously shifted in his chair at the defense table and looked over at his lawyer, Charley Kline, hoping that he'd chosen wisely. Charley was a short, stocky man in his early fifties with salt and pepper hair that he kept in a closely trimmed military style. Born and raised in Dothan, Alabama, he'd moved to Ft. Myers after law school because his wife's family lived there. Charley was a linebacker in high school, but he was too short for college ball, so he'd used his competitive juices to excel in school. Charley still lifted weights three days a week, but over the years, the combination of fried chicken and Jack Daniels had put a layer of fat over his muscles. After law school, he'd started working as a prosecutor with Frank at the State Attorney's

Office. After four years of prosecuting crimes, Charley went into private practice and started defending clients. Charley's hair had grayed, and he needed reading glasses now, but his steel-trap mind had gotten stronger with experience.

Judge McDaniel looked over at the jury of three men and three women that the lawyers had picked that morning before lunch. The courtroom was filled with curious citizens, courthouse workers and the press, including Lee Atkins, the columnist who wrote the headline: *TROPHY WIFE DIVORCE STARTS BADLY*. Lee had begged his editor to let him cover the trial, and he'd agreed. After a lunch break in the summer heat, everyone was anxious to be back in the air-conditioned courtroom to hear opening statements.

Judge McDaniel took a deep breath and began. "Ladies and gentlemen of the jury, we're going to start with opening statements.

The State will go first and the defense, if they choose, will go second. The burden of proof is on the State, so the defense is not required to give an opening statement or produce any evidence at all. However, if they choose, they can give an opening statement and produce witnesses after the State has closed their case."

Judge McDaniel looked over at Frank. "Mr. Powers, are you ready?"

"Yes, I am, Your Honor," Frank said as he stood up. He walked to the podium in front of the jury box and looked toward the judge. "May it please the court?"

The judge nodded, and Frank faced the jury. "Ladies and gentlemen, this case is about greed and revenge. You'll hear that the defendant, Stan Jacoby, is a very rich man who forced his wife to sign a pre-nup before he'd marry her."

Charley stood up. "Objection, Your Honor. That's argumentative and improper characterization using the work 'forced'."

"Gentlemen," Judge McDaniel said sternly, "approach the bench."

As Frank and Charley approached the bench, Judge McDaniel looked over at the jury. "Ladies and gentlemen, this courtroom has an acoustic device installed that's called 'white noise'. I have a button here at my bench that turns it on, and you'll hear a static noise that's meant to drown out the conversation we have here at sidebar so you can't hear it. I'm going to turn it on now so you can't hear our discussions about the legal issues. Thank you for your patience."

Judge McDaniel hit the button, and a loud humming came from the speakers above the jury box. Debby stood up and put her stenography machine on the small counter on the front of Judge McDaniel's bench. Charley stood to her right and Frank to her left. Debby gave Frank a knowing smile and raised her eyebrows slightly, which caught Judge McDaniel's attention. Debby had dated Frank immediately before she dated Judge McDaniel, and she'd say Frank's name in her sleep on most nights. It drove Judge McDaniel crazy.

"First of all, Mr. Kline," Judge McDaniel said to Charley, "I'll have no speaking objections. State your grounds succinctly and no grand standing."

124

Charley nodded. "Yes, Your Honor."

Judge McDaniel glared at Frank. "Second of all, Mr. Powers, the word 'forced' is argumentative, and you know better. The objection is sustained."

Frank ground his teeth. "Yes, Your Honor."

Charley walked back to his table and patted Stan on his back as he smiled at the jurors. Frank returned to the podium and waited for Debby to sit back down with her stenography machine and secure it to the stand. Once Debby was ready, she nodded, and Frank turned to the jury.

"The defendant is worth fifty million dollars, and before he married his wife, she signed a pre-nuptial agreement that gave her $250,000 in the event of a divorce. After seven years of marriage, the defendant filed for divorce and the wife hired lawyer Beth Mancini to represent her in the divorce. Ms. Mancini found that the defendant didn't disclose

$500,000 in his financial affidavit before the pre-nuptial was signed, so she filed a motion to invalidate the pre-nuptial."

Frank noticed that four of his jurors looked confused and two were slowly nodding their heads. He decided he needed to make the rest of his opening statement easier to understand.

"Ladies and gentlemen, you'll hear all the details of the divorce and the legal issues about the pre-nup from

Beth Mancini, the divorce attorney for the defendant's wife. However, for right now, I want to focus on why we're all here. And the reason we're all here is because of the defendant's actions."

Frank turned and stared at Stan, who didn't look away. "This man," Frank said as he pointed at Stan, "paid his handyman, Butch Redding, to attack his wife, Karen Jacoby, and her attorney, Beth Mancini, while they were out at the Jacoby's secluded beach cottage on Cayo Costa Island. The defendant was mad the divorce case hadn't settled, and he wanted to intimidate them. Mr. Redding wore a clown mask to conceal his identity when he went to the beach cottage with a gun. He'd been given a key by the defendant and waited inside for them to return from dinner at Cabbage Key.

"When they walked in the front door," Frank continued, "he pointed the gun at them and said, 'Your husband sent me to deliver a message to you and your lawyer—you should've settled at mediation.' He forced them upstairs into the guest bedroom and tied

Ms. Mancini up with monofilament fishing leader. He had other plans for Karen Jacoby and took her to the master bedroom. Mrs. Jacoby was forced at gun point to strip, and he tied her up spread eagle to the four corners of the bed and raped her."

Frank hesitated momentarily and let the jury digest what they'd just heard before he continued.

"Ms. Mancini was able to break free and grabbed a spear gun, used for spear fishing, which was in a corner of the guest bedroom. She loaded it and confronted Mr. Redding while he was on top of Mrs. Jacoby in the master bedroom. When he lunged for his gun, Ms. Mancini fired the spear gun and killed him. She called 911, and the sheriff's department responded. The lead investigator is Detective Dagle, and he'll testify about the evidence he found. He subpoenaed the defendant's phone records, and they showed the defendant had two conversations with Mr. Redding on the day of the attack. You'll also hear that the defendant withdrew $5,000 dollars cash from his bank on the day of the attack, and Mr. Redding had $2,400 in hundred-dollar bills in his possession when he was killed. I'm asking you to listen closely to the evidence and return a guilty verdict on all counts. Thank you for your time."

Frank walked back to his table and sat down. Judge McDaniel looked over at Charley and asked, "Mr. Kline, is the defense going to make an opening statement?"

Charley stood up. "Yes, we are."

Charley walked to the podium and looked at the judge. "May it please the court?"

Judge McDaniel nodded and Charley faced the jury. He looked all six jurors one at a time in the face before he began.

"Ladies and gentlemen," Charley said in his southern drawl, "the one thing the prosecutor and I agree on is that this case is about greed and revenge. However, it's the wife's greed and revenge that has caused her husband, Dr. Jacoby, to be accused of these horrendous crimes, and caused you to be brought to this courtroom to smell out her lies."

"Objection, Your Honor," Frank blurted out and stood up.

Judge McDaniel said forcefully, "Gentlemen, approach. Now."

While Debby moved her stenographer machine, Judge McDaniel turned on the white noise and glared at Charley as he approached. The jurors looked at Stan and each other as they weighed Charley's statements. Everyone in the courtroom tried to hear Judge McDaniel over the humming, but it was useless.

"Mr. Kline," Judge McDaniel said, "explain to me how you think the words 'smell out her lies' is proper."

Charley nodded. "Your Honor, in every case, a witness's motives to lie are relevant. I think those words are a proper statement about the wife's bias."

Judge McDaniel shook his head. "Mr. Kline, you may use those words in closing argument, but not in opening statement, so stick to the facts. The State's objection is sustained."

"Yes, Your Honor," Charley said. Frank returned to his table and Charley to the podium while Debby sat back down. Charley looked over at Debby and waited for her to nod before he continued.

"Ladies and gentlemen, you heard the prosecutor mention a pre-nup earlier. However, the prosecutor didn't tell you everything that was in the pre-nup. There's a clause, at the end of the pre-nup, which states if Dr. Jacoby is convicted of a violent crime against his wife, the pre-nup is invalid."

Charley turned and stared at Frank for a few seconds in silence. Charley looked back to the jury and held his hands out to his side in a questioning manner. "Why do you think the prosecutor hid that from you?"

Frank exploded to his feet. "Objection, Your Honor!" Judge McDaniel said, "Sustained."

Charley turned back to the jury and lowered his voice. "If the pre-nup is invalid, Mrs. Jacoby stands to make four million dollars." Charley turned and looked at Frank. He was enjoying turning the tables on Frank, and Frank's face was turning red. Charley turned back to the jury and smiled.

"And that's just the beginning. If Dr. Jacoby is convicted of these crimes, Mrs. Jacoby could file a civil lawsuit for battery. We'll have a lawyer as an expert witness to talk about the value of a civil suit and how punitive damages could be awarded. In other words, Mrs. Jacoby could get all Dr. Jacoby's fifty million dollars with a civil lawsuit, if she found a jury gullible enough to believe her story."

"Objection!" Frank shrieked.

Judge McDaniel scratched his beard for a moment. "Overruled. If a witness is going to testify about this, it's proper to discuss in opening statement."

"Thank you, Your Honor," Charley said in his most polite southern voice.

Frank was seething, but he sat down. Charley continued, "Ladies and gentlemen, we'll prove to you that Mrs. Jacoby staged this attack to help her divorce case. We'll prove to you that she had her lawyer there as a witness to help her credibility. Dr. Jacoby will be testifying in his own defense, and we'll have two other witnesses. I'd ask you to keep an open mind and listen to all the evidence in this case. Thank you for being attentive."

Chapter 19

Beth and Mrs. Barnes, the divorce mediator, were waiting to testify in the witness room, which was adjacent to the courtroom. Beth was fidgety and looked across the small table at Mrs. Barnes. "Tell me why we can't watch opening statements?"

"The defense lawyer has invoked the rule of sequestration," Mrs. Barnes said, "and we can't be present because our testimony might be influenced by opening statements. However, after we testify, we can watch the rest of the trial in the courtroom."

Beth shook her head. "I understand that a witness shouldn't listen to other witnesses testify before it's their turn, but I don't agree with the judge's ruling that we can't listen to opening statements. In divorce cases, we don't have juries, so I guess I never had to deal with this before."

Mrs. Barnes smiled and chided Beth. "Remember, it's all about fairness to the defendant. It's better that one hundred guilty men walk free than one innocent man is sent to prison."

Beth shifted in her seat and took a deep breath. "That concept sounds good in law school, but when you're the victim of a crime, it sucks. I saw that asshole raping Karen and heard him say, 'your husband sent me,' and we both saw Mr. Jacoby's temper at mediation. How much evidence do they need?"

Mrs. Barnes lowered her voice and said, "I have my personal opinion about his guilt, but it's the jurors that have to be convinced."

Mrs. Barnes and Beth were silent for a few seconds before Mrs. Barnes spoke.

"Beth, I want you to think back to your trials, and how some of your clients tried so hard to make their spouse look bad, but it backfired on them, and the judge ruled for the other side. You have to put your anger aside and just answer the questions without giving unsolicited comments. If you do give gratuitous comments, it might alienate the jurors. Mr. Kline is a very talented criminal defense attorney, and he'll ask questions a certain way to help his client. I've watched him win trials over the years he shouldn't have because he made witnesses unlikeable to the juries. Just answer the questions truthfully, and don't be a smartass."

Beth exhaled loudly and nodded. "You're right."

Mrs. Barnes looked down at the newspaper on the table and read the headline: *TROPHY WIFE RAPE TRIAL BEGINS.*

* * * * * *

Frank was wearing a blue suit with a white shirt and red tie to look patriotic. Psychologists had done studies that showed blue being the most believable color for trial lawyers to wear in front of jurors. Consequently, every prosecutor was coached to wear "believable blue" on the first day of trial to get the jurors to trust them.

Charley was wearing a light blue seersucker suit with a white shirt and a yellow bow tie with small white polka dots inside black circles. His rattlesnake skin boots didn't exactly match his outfit, but they conveyed that he was a maverick who wasn't afraid to fight the system. His outfit and his trim hair, combined with his southern accent and politeness, was designed to make the jury receptive to his arguments.

The court reporter, Debby, was wearing a green cotton dress and golden yellow pumps that perfectly accented her sun-kissed golden brown hair and brown eyes. She was tall and thin with a toned body from playing beach volleyball for two decades. She was a picture of health and had an outgoing personality that made her even more attractive. She had thought Frank would make a good father and was surprised that he ended the relationship when she brought up the subject of marriage and children.

Stan was wearing a dark gray Brooks Brothers suit, a white starched shirt, and a burgundy tie that would make a banker proud. He was sitting at the defense table and uncomfortably shifting in his chair as he looked at Judge McDaniel. His gray hair had gotten lighter since his arrest, and dark circles had formed underneath his eyes. He'd also developed a slight case of rosacea on his forehead and cheeks.

"Call your first witness, Mr. Powers," Judge McDaniel said.

Frank said, "The State calls Michelle Barnes."

The assistant bailiff walked to the witness room in the back of the courtroom and opened the door. Mrs. Barnes walked to the front of the courtroom, the clerk swore her in, and she sat down in the witness stand. She was wearing a gray business suit with a white blouse and black pumps.

Frank looked at her and smiled. "Please give us your full name."

"My name is Michelle Elizabeth Barnes." "What do you do for a living?"

"I'm a lawyer, but I'm semi-retired, and I specialize in mediation in family law cases."

Frank looked over at Stan and pointed at him. "Have you ever met the defendant?"

Mrs. Barnes nodded. "Yes, I was the mediator in his divorce case a few months ago."

"Objection. May I approach, Your Honor?" Charley asked.

Judge McDaniel nodded and looked at the jury. "More white noise while we discuss the legal issues." Judge McDaniel turned the button on as the lawyers approached, and Debby again moved her stenographer machine to the counter at the front of the bench. After everyone was in place, Judge McDaniel looked inquisitively at Charley. "What's the basis for your objection?"

"Your Honor," Charley said, "my objection is that everything that is said at mediation is privileged, according to state statute. Therefore, I don't think Mrs. Barnes should be able to testify about anything that happened at mediation."

Judge McDaniel nodded and looked at Frank. "What's your response?"

Frank said, "Your Honor, Mr. Kline is partially correct. The specific words of a litigant at mediation can't be used against him in a later court proceeding on that case. However, I don't intend to have Mrs. Barnes testify about specifically what was said. What I do intend to ask her is, 'Did Mr. Jacoby get upset at mediation and yell profanity at his wife's attorney?' I submit that I'm entitled to ask about acts that happened at mediation, but not exact words that were said."

Judge McDaniel sat back in his chair and scratched his beard.

Charley said, "Your Honor, the reason we have a privilege

at mediation is that we want litigants to be honest about the strengths and weaknesses of their cases, without it being used against them later. That's exactly what's happening here."

Judge McDaniel looked at Frank, "Why do you think this is relevant?"

Frank answered, "Your Honor, it's relevant because the dead rapist that tied up Beth Mancini and Karen Jacoby said, 'Your husband sent me to deliver a message to you and your lawyer – you should've settled at mediation.' I think the fact that Mr. Jacoby was angry at his wife and her attorney at mediation is relevant to this case."

Judge McDaniel sat back and contemplated the issue for a few seconds. "Here's my ruling. Mr. Powers, you may ask about outbursts and anger, but don't ask about exact quotes regarding settlement offers from the Jacobys at mediation.

Mr. Kline, your objection is noted for the record."
Everyone returned to his and her places, and Frank looked back at Mrs. Barnes.

"Mrs. Barnes, during mediation, did the defendant ever get angry at his wife's attorney, Beth Mancini, and raise his voice at her?"

"Yes, he did," Mrs. Barnes said firmly.

"Did he use profanity toward Ms. Mancini?" Mrs. Barnes nodded. "Yes, he did."

"What did you do when this happened?"

Mrs. Barnes looked at Stan momentarily before she answered. "I told him this was unacceptable and if it continued, I'd notify the judge."

Frank looked at Judge McDaniel. "No further questions."

Judge McDaniel looked at Charley and asked, "Any questions for cross-examination, Mr. Kline?"

"Yes, Your Honor," Charley said as he approached the podium.

Charley looked at Mrs. Barnes and smiled. "Good morning, ma'am."

"Good morning, Mr. Kline."

"Isn't it a fact that after Dr. Jacoby yelled at Ms. Mancini, he calmed down later?"

Mrs. Barnes nodded. "Yes, that's true."

"Isn't it a fact that Dr. Jacoby offered to settle the case for more than the pre-nup required?"

Frank stood up. "Objection, Your Honor."

Judge McDaniel looked at the jury. "More white noise while we discuss the legal issues."

Judge McDaniel turned the button on as the lawyers approached, and Debby moved her stenographer machine to the counter at the front of the bench. After everyone was in place, Judge McDaniel looked at Charley. "Mr. Kline, I thought I made myself clear—no quotes."

Charley answered, "Your Honor, I didn't ask her if he offered $100,000 more than the pre-nup required, which is what happened—I only asked if he offered *more*. The State has opened the door because they're trying to show my client was an out-of-control maniac that paid his handyman to kidnap and rape his wife. I'm trying to rebut that by showing that after my client's outburst, he calmed down, and made a rational, logical offer to settle the case."

Judge McDaniel nodded. "I agree the state has opened the door. Objection overruled."

Frank was seething. "Your Honor, that's not proper." Judge McDaniel looked at Frank with flared nostrils.

"I've made my ruling. If you continue to argue with me, I'll hold you in contempt of court. Do I make myself clear?"

Frank took a deep breath before answering. "Yes, Your Honor."

As everyone turned to get back to their places, Judge McDaniel discreetly looked at Debby's rear as she bent over to secure her machine in the stand.

After everyone returned to their places, Charley looked at Mrs. Barnes. "Ma'am, isn't it true that Dr. Jacoby offered to settle the case for more than the pre-nup required?"

"Yes, that's true."

"Isn't it true that Dr. Jacoby made a logical and rational offer to settle the case?"

Mrs. Barnes thought about her answer for a second. She didn't want to help Stan, but she knew that she couldn't win the argument with Charley, and she'd end up looking bad.

Mrs. Barnes said flatly, "He offered more than the prenup, so I suppose that's logical and rational."

Charley's reading glasses were hanging from a strap around his neck, so he put them on and looked at his notes for a few seconds. He wanted to make sure everyone was focused on him for the next question.

"Mrs. Barnes, isn't it true that if Dr. Jacoby is convicted of the crimes he's been charged with, his wife will get more money than the pre-nup allows?"

Mrs. Barnes considered her answer for a second and nodded. "Yes."

Charley looked at Judge McDaniel. "No other questions, Your Honor."

Judge McDaniel looked at Mrs. Barnes. "You're excused, ma'am."

Mrs. Barnes smiled and walked out of the courtroom. Judge McDaniel looked at Frank. "Call your next witness."

Frank turned to the assistant bailiff. "The State calls Beth Mancini."

The assistant bailiff walked to the witness room in the back of the courtroom and opened the door. Beth walked to the front of the courtroom, the clerk swore her in, and she sat down in the witness stand. Beth was wearing the same outfit from mediation and Stan's deposition—her dark purple business suit with a white camisole and black pumps. She glared at Stan for a second before she looked at Frank and smiled. Stan cracked his knuckles and sat back in his chair angrily.

Frank smiled at Beth. "Please give us your full name."

Beth looked at the jurors. "My name is Beth Frances Mancini."

"What do you do for a living?" "I'm a divorce attorney."

Frank pointed at Stan. "Do you know the defendant?" "I do," Beth said and looked momentarily at Stan. "How do you know the defendant?"

"I represent his wife in her pending divorce from him." "Before today, when was the last time you saw the defendant."

"The last time I saw him was the day of mediation."

Frank hesitated to make sure the jury would be focused on his next question. "Was this the day before you were hogtied by a masked intruder at your client's beach cottage?"

Beth glared at Stan. "Yes."

"Did the defendant yell profanities at you during mediation?"

Beth was still glaring at Stan. "Yes." "What did he yell at you?"

Beth sat up in her chair and looked at the jury. "While we were in the mediation room, he said, 'If Ms. Mancini would just read the goddamn pre-nup, this case would've settled a long time ago. She's just milking this case for her fucking fees.'"

Frank turned and stared at Stan momentarily and looked back at Beth. "What happened next?"

"His lawyer sent him down to another room to cool off." "During your investigation of the pre-nuptial, did you find a problem with the financial affidavit?" Beth nodded. "I did."

Frank held his hands out to his side in a questioning manner. "Can you tell the jury why that matters?"

Beth nodded and looked at the jury. "Florida law requires both parties to make full financial disclosure in their financial affidavit before signing a pre-nuptial. If that isn't done, the pre-nuptial is void."

"When you found this out, what did you do?"

"I immediately filed a motion to set aside the pre-nuptial agreement."

"Can you tell us the difference between the pre-nuptial amount and what Mrs. Jacoby would've been entitled to without a pre-nuptial?"

"Yes. The pre-nuptial amount was for $250,000. If the judge found the pre-nuptial invalid, then Mrs. Jacoby would've been entitled to alimony. I estimate the amount to be between three and four million dollars, based on the standard of living during the marriage."

There were murmurs in the courtroom and Judge McDaniel leaned back in his chair and stroked his beard. All the jurors looked at Stan suspiciously. Stan sat back in his chair and shook his head slowly. Charley was looking over his notes and didn't seem to be too concerned with Beth's testimony.

Frank asked, "Was the trial scheduled for the following week?"

"Yes," Beth said wearily. "The judge does that on most

cases because it puts pressure on both sides to settle."

"Did you reach a settlement?" Beth shook her head. "No."

"Did you go back to your office after the mediation failed?"

"I did."

"Did you get an unusual call to your office an hour later from the judge's office?"

Beth cleared her throat and spoke compassionately. "I did. Unfortunately, the judge's daughter was in a bad car wreck up at college, and the judge rushed to the hospital to be with her. His judicial assistant called my office to let

me know the judge had cancelled all trials for the following week. I found out a few weeks later that his daughter made a full recovery."

"Did you call Mrs. Jacoby to tell her the news?"

"I did. She took the news in stride, and we had some small talk."

"Did she invite you to her beach cottage for the weekend since you weren't going to preparing for her divorce trial?"

Beth nodded and said happily, "She did. During breaks in the mediation we had talked about Cayo Costa and her beach cottage. She knew I'd canceled all my Friday appointments to prepare for trial on Monday, so she told me I should enjoy a beach weekend since I was free, and I agreed."

"How did you get to Mrs. Jacoby's beach cottage on Friday?"

Beth leaned back in her chair and smiled. "She picked me up at my house around ten and we drove to a marina on Bokeelia, where they keep their boat. We loaded our supplies on the boat and drove through Pine Island Sound to get to her dock on Cayo Costa."

"What did you do that afternoon at the beach cottage?"

"We unloaded our luggage and supplies. After that we

turned on the water and power and walked to the widow's walk and looked at the gulf. It was so beautiful, that we went for an afternoon swim and then showered."

"Where did you go to dinner?" asked Frank.

"We took the boat to Cabbage Key for dinner at the restaurant there."

"How long were you at Cabbage Key for dinner?" Beth

shrugged. "I would estimate around two hours."

"Did you see any boats around the dock when you came back to the beach cottage?"

Beth shook her head and said firmly, "No."

"What happened when you went inside the front door of the beach cottage?"

Beth took a deep breath and said shakily, "I heard a strange male voice say, 'I've been waiting for both of you,' and I looked up and saw a man dressed in black with a clown mask. He was pointing a gun at us and said, 'Your husband sent me to deliver a message to you and your lawyer—you all should've settled at mediation.' I stood there in shock."

Frank lowered his voice. "How did you feel?"

"I felt . . ." Beth's voice cracked. "I felt helpless and scared."

Frank hesitated a second to let Beth get her composure. "What happened next?"

"He told us to go upstairs and sit on the bed in the guest bedroom, or he'd shoot us. So we did what he told us to do."

Frank turned and stared at Stan for a second. He looked back at Beth and asked, "What happened next?"

Beth sat up in her chair. "He made Karen sit in the corner. And then he made me lie on my stomach, and he hog-tied me with fishing leader."

"How did you feel?"

Beth shifted in her chair and said in a shaky voice, "I felt like I was going to be tortured or killed, or both."

"What happened next?"

Beth took a deep breath and gathered herself together before answering. "He pointed the gun at Karen and ordered her into the other bedroom. She got up slowly and walked into the master bedroom. I was tied up and face down on the bed, so I couldn't see anything in the other bedroom."

"What did you hear in the other bedroom?"

Beth raised her voice. "I heard the man say, 'Blondie, get rid of those clothes and lay down. I'm going to tie you up, and then we'll have some fun.'"

Frank waited a few seconds to let the jury appreciate Karen's predicament. "And then what did you do?"

"I moved around and tried to get to my cell phone in my pocket, but the knots were too tight."

"What did you hear from the other room?"

Beth hesitated before she answered. "I heard Karen say no, and then he slapped her. Afterward, he said, 'Blondie, we can do this the easy way or the hard way. How do you want it?'"

Frank paused momentarily to let the jury consider Butch's words before he continued. "What did you do?"

Beth raised her voice. "I arched my back and flipped over on the bed. That's when I saw the shark's jaws above the bed."

Frank asked, "What do you mean by shark's jaws above the bed?"

Beth looked at the jury before she answered. "Karen told me her husband had caught a fourteen-foot hammerhead shark and killed it for pictures. After the pictures, he cut out the jaws for a souvenir and let the animals and bugs eat the flesh off it outside the cottage. He cleaned it up and mounted it on the wall above the bed in the guest bedroom."

Beth saw two female jurors on the front row look at each other and raise their eyebrows in a disapproving manner.

Frank asked, "What did you do next?"

"I turned around and maneuvered myself on the bed so I could cut the lines off my ankles. After my ankles were free, I stood up and cut my wrists free."

"What were you thinking at that point?"

"I was determined to stop the man from raping Karen anymore," Beth said forcefully.

"What did you do?"

Beth shifted in her chair. "I saw a spear gun in the corner, so I loaded it and walked into Karen's bedroom. I saw the man raping Karen and told him to stop, and he did. But he reached for his gun on the nightstand, and . . . I shot him in the neck."

Beth was breathing heavily, and her face was turning red.

Frank waited and let her get her composure.

Judge McDaniel asked, "Ms. Mancini, would you like some water?"

Beth shook her head. "Thank you, but no. I'm fine."

Frank asked quietly, "What happened after you shot him in the neck?"

138

Beth answered stoically, "He was thrashing on the ground, but he pulled himself up and grabbed his gun. I jumped on him and pulled on the spear in his neck to try and keep him from shooting me. But he fired and the bullet burned through my hair. Luckily, it missed my scalp. After I pulled on the spear, a lot more blood started coming out of his neck . . . and he dropped his gun and slumped against the bed."

Frank asked somberly, "What happened next?"

"I cut Karen loose and called 911," Beth said quietly and looked down.

Frank nodded and looked at Judge McDaniel. "No further questions, Your Honor."

Judge McDaniel looked at Charley. "Cross-examination, Mr. Kline?"

"Yes, Your Honor," Charley said energetically. He walked confidently to the podium with his notes and set them down. He looked up at Beth and smiled. "Good afternoon, ma'am."

Beth felt her face flush and fought the urge to scowl at Charley. She nodded slightly and said, "Hello."

"Isn't it true, the masked man said, 'I've been waiting for both of you' when you walked in the front door?"

Beth nodded. "Yes."

"How did he know you were going to be there?"

"I assume your client told him," Beth said dismissively.

Charley put his reading glasses on and thumbed through his notes until he found the page he was looking for. "I'm looking at Mrs. Jacoby's statement to the police, and she told them she didn't tell her husband you were coming to the cottage. Do you agree with her statement to the police?"

Beth shifted in her seat as she contemplated her answer. "If that's what she told the police, then I assume it's true."

Charley held his right pointer finger up. "So, someone must've told Butch Redding you were going to be at the beach cottage, because he used the words, 'both of you'.

Wouldn't you agree?"

Beth considered the question before answering matter-of-factly, "Someone told him because he knew who I was and that I'd be there."

Charley nodded emphatically. "I agree with you, ma'am,

someone told him," Charley said and looked at the jury for a second before he continued. "In her statement, Mrs. Jacoby said the only people she told you were going to the cottage with her were workers at the marina. So, my question to you is, who told the masked man you'd be at the cottage?"

Beth was flustered and after a few uneasy seconds she answered, "I don't know."

Charley smiled and pointed at Beth. "Who did you tell you were going to the beach cottage that weekend?"

Beth thought for a second. "I only told my secretary and my boyfriend."

Charley looked at the jury momentarily and cocked his head. "Who's your boyfriend?"

Frank exploded from his seat. "Objection, may we approach?"

Judge McDaniel nodded and looked at the jury. "More white noise."

Judge McDaniel turned the white noise button on as the lawyers approached, and Debby moved her stenographer machine to the counter at the front of the bench. Charley chuckled to himself as he approached. He'd talked to his contacts at the courthouse, and found out about the Debby, Frank, and Judge McDaniel love triangle. He'd planned to use this knowledge to his client's advantage and was giddy the time had finally arrived.

When everyone got to the bench Judge McDaniel asked, "What's the basis for your objection, Mr. Powers?"

Frank's face was crimson, and he said angrily, "Your Honor, the question has no relevance. I'm dating Beth Mancini, and Mr. Kline is trying to throw mud on this proceeding by bringing up my relationship with her. There's no relevance to the question."

Judge McDaniel leaned back in his chair and stroked his beard. "Mr. Kline, how's this inquiry relevant?"

Charley spoke in his most polite southern voice. "Your Honor, this question is relevant in two ways. Number one, the State has claimed in opening statement that my client hired his handyman to kidnap and rape his wife. We proved earlier that Mrs. Jacoby didn't tell her husband that Ms. Mancini was going to be at the beach cottage. I'm trying to establish who knew she was going to be there before the attack, and she stated she told her boyfriend.

Therefore, I'm trying to find out who her boyfriend is. This is relevant because someone told the attacker that Ms. Mancini was going to be at the beach cottage, and we need to find out who had that knowledge.

"And number two, and I submit the most important reason, is that bias is always an appropriate subject for cross-examination. Ms. Mancini, the witness, is currently dating the prosecutor, Mr. Powers, and has been the entire time between the arrest and today's testimony. I submit it's a natural human emotion to try and please someone's current lover, and even an old lover under certain circumstances." Charley hesitated for a second and looked at Debby. "I think this shows bias of the witness toward the State, and the jury is entitled to hear about it. The jury can decide how much weight to give it."

Debby looked over at Beth in the witness chair, who heard the exchange, and then at Frank. Judge McDaniel looked at Frank, and then over at Charley for a few seconds, before he glanced at Debby. He started to say something flippant, but he knew the transcript would be reviewed by appellate courts and the press, so he bit his tongue. Frank glanced at Beth and shut his eyes as he tried to think of something intellectual to say, but his mind was a blank.

After a few seconds of uncomfortable silence, Judge McDaniel said flatly, "I'm going to allow the question." They returned to their places slowly, except for Charley, who walked briskly back to the podium and smiled at the jurors.

Charley glanced back at Debby to make sure she was ready. He smiled at Beth and asked politely, "Ms. Mancini, who's your boyfriend?"

Beth looked at Frank. "My boyfriend is Frank Powers, the prosecutor."

There was a collective gasp in the courtroom, and the jurors stared at Beth and then at Frank. Charley was seasoned enough to not ask any questions for a few moments as everyone in the courtroom formed their opinion. Charley looked up at Judge McDaniel, who looked flustered and was glaring at him.

Charley asked Judge McDaniel. "Your Honor, is it possible to take a few minutes for a comfort break?"

Judge McDaniel banged his gavel and said gratefully. "We're in recess for fifteen minutes."

Judge McDaniel walked off the bench and walked out the door behind his bench. He walked down the hallway to the secure elevator and rode it up his office on the ninth floor while he thought of his own marriages and divorces. He entered his office and walked over to his window looking out over the Caloosahatchee River and thought of his first wife.

Maria had been his college sweetheart, and they married while he was in law school. She had their first son on the day he graduated from law school, and he was the happiest he'd ever been in his life. He had always wanted to be married and raise a family in his hometown of Ft. Myers. Three years later, when Maria was seven months pregnant with their second son, she was admitted to the hospital because of high blood pressure. The doctors ran a myriad of tests and ordered her to stay in the hospital until she gave birth. A month later she went into labor and died giving birth to a healthy baby boy.

Judge McDaniel's life changed at that point. When Maria was alive, he was a happy family man who was an associate in a big firm and worked forty billable hours a week. After Maria died, he was heartbroken and hired a full-time nanny to help raise his boys. He threw himself into his career and billed seventy hours a week while he volunteered his time at charity events to help build his resume. He went on a few sporadic dates, but he spent most of his free time with his boys' school and sports activities. However, it wasn't the same without Maria next to him. Eventually, he made partner at his firm and was appointed to the bench two years after that.

Once he became judge, he was the most eligible bachelor in Ft. Myers, and he enjoyed the attention. He only had to work thirty to thirty-five hours a week as a judge, so he had time to start dating again. He met his second wife, Daphne, at a little league game for both of their sons. She had recently divorced a doctor and was ready for a new husband. Daphne was a beautiful woman, and Judge McDaniel soon fell under her spell. It was the first time Judge McDaniel had been in love since his wife died, and he married Daphne three months after meeting her.

Unfortunately, Daphne became bored with Judge McDaniel after three years and started dating another doctor. She had Judge McDaniel served with divorce papers after he finished hearings in his courtroom on a Monday. It was the talk of the town because no one ever remembered a judge being served with divorce papers while he was wearing his robe in his courtroom. It was a quick divorce—Daphne's new boyfriend had plenty of money, and she didn't want any of Judge McDaniel's property. Judge McDaniel's heart was broken again. He became a bitter man after his very public divorce from Daphne.

After six months of random dating, Judge McDaniel met Rachel, a paralegal from Judge McDaniel's old law firm. She was twenty years younger than Judge McDaniel and thrilled his libido long enough for him to marry her. It only lasted for two years, but she wanted every dime she was entitled to in the divorce. After Judge McDaniel paid his attorney fees, her attorney fees, and her go-away-money, he was $75,000 in the hole.

That was his mindset when he started dating Debby, the beautiful court reporter. She was fresh from being dumped by Frank and was entranced by Judge McDaniel's charms. However, after a few months of his braggadocio and snoring, she knew there was no future, so she moved on.

Judge McDaniel had developed a very skeptical view of marriage at this point, but he was still lonely at night and wanted a wife. He was introduced to Janice, a tax attorney from the biggest law firm in town, who he met at a bar luncheon. After six months of exclusively dating each other, he was convinced she was the woman he should spend the rest of his life with, so he married her. However, he lost interest after a year and had an affair with a waitress from his favorite restaurant. The divorce only cost him $15,000, but he decided marriage was a luxury he couldn't afford anymore. He vowed to only have girlfriends for the rest of his life, and that's how Stella became his live-in girlfriend.

* * * * * *

Judge McDaniel looked at Charley. "Mr. Kline, please continue your cross-examination."

"Yes, Your Honor." Charley looked at Beth. "Ms. Mancini, when you returned from Cabbage Key, did you see any sign of forced entry into the beach cottage?"

"No," Beth said icily.

"After you killed your attacker and walked around the cottage, did you see any sign of forced entry around any of the sliders or windows?"

"No."

"Ma'am, are you aware the attacker had a key to the beach cottage on his key ring?"

"Yes, I am."

"Do you know how he got a key to the beach cottage?"

Beth was angry and agitated. "Your client must've given it to him."

Charley had set the trap and Beth had walked right into it. Charley looked over at Stan for a second and then looked back at Beth. "Yes, I suppose that's one possibility. But, isn't it just as likely that Mrs. Jacoby gave him the key before she picked you up at your house?"

Beth was livid. "No, it is not. She barely knew him."

Charley nodded. "Isn't it true, your knowledge is based solely on what Mrs. Jacoby told you?"

Beth shifted in her chair and mentally raced through all other possibilities, but she realized there was only one answer. "Yes, that's what Karen told me."

"Isn't it possible that Mrs. Jacoby lied to you?"

Frank started to object, but he knew he'd be overruled, and it would look like he was trying to hide something or protecting his girlfriend from a bully. He just sat and silently cursed Charley.

Beth felt the jurors staring at her and felt uneasy. "Yes, I suppose it's possible."

"Isn't it also possible that since he was a handyman for the Jacobys, he already had a key for the cottage?"

Beth nodded. "Yes, that's possible."

"Ms. Mancini, I'd like to ask you some questions about what happened after you cut yourself free with the shark's teeth. My first question is, how did you feel when you entered Mrs. Jacoby's bedroom and pointed the loaded spear gun at your attacker?"

Beth felt the blood pumping rapidly in her neck and forehead as her resentment toward Charley spiked. "Adrenaline was pumping through my body, and I was angry. I was going to stop him from raping Karen, no matter what it took."

Charley held up his right pointer finger. "Isn't it true, Mrs. Jacoby said 'no' after Butch was shot, but before he reached for his gun?"

Beth looked up as she tried to remember the exact sequence of events. "Karen said 'no' to warn me that he was reaching for his gun."

"How do you know what Karen was thinking?" Beth shifted in her chair and glared at Charley. "I don't know what she was thinking. You'll have to ask her."

"Oh, I will," Charley said condescendingly. "So, isn't it possible Karen was upset her boyfriend was shot in the neck in front of her, and her plan wasn't working?"

Frank jumped to his feet. "Objection, assumes facts not in evidence."

Judge McDaniel shook his head. "Overruled. You can ask the question."

Charley looked at Beth. "Ms. Mancini, isn't it possible?"

"No, it isn't," Beth yelled. "Karen had been violently raped and watched me shoot her attacker. As he was bleeding, he reached for his gun on the nightstand to shoot me, and she warned me. That's what happened, dammit, and I'm tired of you trying to turn things around."

There were murmurs in the courtroom, and Judge McDaniel banged his gavel. "Ms. Mancini, you will not raise your voice or use profanity in my courtroom. Do you understand?"

There was a moment of total silence in the courtroom. Beth felt her face turn red, and she was embarrassed that Charley had gotten to her. She took a deep breath, faced Judge McDaniel and said politely, "I'm sorry, Your Honor. It won't happen again."

Judge McDaniel looked at Charley. "Please ask your question again, Mr. Kline."

Charley had Beth right where he wanted her.

"Ms. Mancini, isn't it possible that while Mrs. Jacoby was alone in the bathroom for fifteen minutes, before she changed into clean clothes, she was planning what to tell you and the police?"

"Yes," Beth said flatly.

"Isn't it true, she told you she didn't want to talk about the details of the rape while you were in the rockers on the porch?"

"Yes," Beth said flatly.

"Isn't it true, there was no conversation between you and Mrs. Jacoby for fifteen minutes in the rockers?"

"Yes," Beth said flatly.

"Ms. Mancini, isn't it possible that while Mrs. Jacoby was sitting in the rockers for fifteen minutes before the police arrived, she was planning what to tell the police?"

"Yes," Beth said flatly.

Charley put on his reading glasses and looked through his notes for a few seconds before he looked up.

"Ms. Mancini, I'd like to go back to the day of mediation on the Jacoby case. Isn't it a fact that you and Mrs. Jacoby went to the Veranda for lunch that day?"

Beth was flustered. "Yes, that's true."

"Isn't it true, during your lunch, your boyfriend," Charley pointed at Frank, "came to the Veranda for lunch with his friends."

"Yes," Beth said irritably.

"Isn't it true, your boyfriend came to your table and met Mrs. Jacoby?"

"Yes."

"Isn't it true, after he left your table, you told Mrs. Jacoby that he was a prosecutor?"

"Yes, but why does any of this matter?"

Charley was pleased she'd taken the bait again and he said, "It matters because Mrs. Jacoby knew your boyfriend would take a personal interest in a case where you were the victim."

"Objection!" Frank roared.

Judge McDaniel was enjoying the show. "Overruled, but is there a question coming Mr. Kline?"

"Yes, Your Honor," Charley answered and turned back to Beth. "Isn't it true, you called your boyfriend after you called 911?"

"Yes."

"Isn't it true, your boyfriend got a ride to the island with FWC officers on their boat?"

"Yes."

Charley looked at the jurors. "Do you think your boyfriend's judgment is clouded because you're a victim in this case?"

Frank jumped to his feet. "Objection, she can't testify about someone else's judgment."

Judge McDaniel leaned back in his chair and smiled mischievously. "Your objection is sustained. She can't testify

if your judgment is clouded because of her involvement. You'd be the only person that would know that."

Charley looked at the jurors and raised his eyebrows. "No further questions."

Judge McDaniel looked at the jurors. "We're done for today. I need to caution you that there has been media coverage of this trial, and I don't want you to be influenced by what you see on TV or read in the paper. I want your verdict to be based solely on the evidence presented. Therefore, I'm ordering you not to watch the local news on TV, read the newspaper, or research the case on the internet until the trial is over. I'll see you tomorrow morning at nine."

Judge McDaniel took pride in banging his gavel and ending court for the day. He banged the gavel, and everyone stood up to go their separate ways, but he sat and watched the courtroom clear out for a few seconds before he left the bench.

Chapter 20

Frank turned his glass up and drained every drop of scotch off the ice cubes before he set it down on his kitchen counter. He filled it up again and walked toward his lanai to watch the sunset with Beth, who was sitting in a rocker and nursing a glass of Merlot. Beth looked up when he walked through the sliders and smiled. Frank walked over and kissed the top of her head before he sat down and looked out over the river.

"I'm sorry you had to listen to that bullshit today," Frank said softly.

Beth lamented, "I can't believe they're trying to blame Karen for all this."

Frank was quiet for a few seconds. "What other defense do they have? We've got that son of a bitch cold, and the only way he can try to avoid prison is claiming his wife is an evil gold digger that set him up."

"I hope the jury can see that and aren't drawn in by Charley's bullshit. I can't believe he played me like he did today."

Frank took a long draw of his scotch. "I've watched Charley for twenty-five years charm jurors into voting for his clients. We were young prosecutors together before he went into private practice after four years of learning how our office worked. He did that dumb country boy act then, and he's been perfecting it ever since. You know, the state normally wins eighty-five percent of the cases that go to trial. I've had twenty-six trials against him since he went to the dark side, and I've only won fifteen, which is fifty-eight percent." Frank sighed. "Not that I'm keeping track."

Beth looked out at the sunset and tried to relax, but her head was still spinning from her time on the witness stand. She'd been flustered by Charley's questions that were designed to make Karen look bad. Now that she'd finished testifying, she could sit in court and watch everything. She'd cleared her calendar for the week because she wanted to watch Stan be convicted by a jury of his peers and sent to prison for a long time.

Frank drained his glass and set it on the stand between

them. Frank thought back to how fast the case had come to trial after Stan's arrest. He'd been released on a $500,000 bond and immediately hired Charley. Two weeks later, Charley had filed a demand for speedy trial without taking any depositions. Judge McDaniel had a status conference and set the case for trial on May fifteenth, which was fifty-five days after Stan's arrest.

Beth asked, "Why are there only six jurors?"

Frank sat back in his chair and said, "In Florida, you only have twelve jurors in 1st degree murder cases and condemnation cases. In all other cases, you only have six jurors."

Frank stood up and twisted his shoulders back and forth, loosening the stiff muscles in his back for a few seconds and then sat back down.

Beth looked over at Frank and cocked her head to the left. "Why does the judge ride you so hard?"

"We're Peters-in-law," Frank blurted out without thinking.

"What?" Beth asked incredulously.

Frank could tell by Beth's tone of voice that he should've used a more tactful description of the situation. "Judge McDaniel and I have both dated the court reporter, Debby, at different times in the past. I guess he has some type of grudge against me and enjoys trying to make me look bad in front of her."

Beth was silent for a few seconds, remembering the beautiful court reporter. "I'm not sure if I'm more upset that you've never told me about her before, or that you have a nickname for that situation because it's so common."

Frank knew this conversation was not going to go well for him, but he tried damage control and said softly, "Honey, that's just a phrase that guys use when they've both dated the same girl in the past. Maybe it's a little bit crude, but it's guy talk."

Beth looked over at Frank and cocked her left eyebrow. "She's pretty. How long ago did you date her?"

Frank sighed. "It was about five years ago, and we dated for a year or so."

"Was your peter in her before or after Judge McDaniel's?" Beth asked sarcastically.

Frank took a deep breath and considered his answer. "Debby started dating Judge McDaniel shortly after we broke up."

Beth drained her glass of Merlot and set it next to Frank's

empty glass. "Why did you break up with her?"

Frank shrugged his shoulders and said matter-of-factly, "She wanted to get married and I didn't, so we broke up. No screaming or yelling, we just went our separate ways."

Beth remembered Debby's statuesque figure and her perfect tan with flawless hair. Beth calculated she was about ten years older than Debby and got a sinking feeling in her stomach. If Frank wouldn't marry Debby, Beth reasoned, he'd never marry her—she was older and heavier.

Beth felt nauseated and stood up. "I'm going to go. I've still got a headache from court, and I just want to take a nice quiet bath and relax. And besides, I know how you are during trials, so I'll leave you to prep for tomorrow."

Frank knew Beth wasn't happy. "How about we order take-out and you can leave after dinner?"

Beth shook her head. "I don't have much of an appetite. I'll probably just have some yogurt later."

Frank stood up and held his hands out toward Beth. "Can I get a kiss before you go?"

Beth gave him a kiss on his cheek and left.

* * * * * *

Beth pulled her Camry into her covered carport and put it in park. She pulled a Kleenex from the box she kept in her console and wiped the tears from her eyes. She got out, locked her car, and walked up the steps to her door. When she unlocked the door, she heard Bella and Gracie give loud meows. She walked inside, set her purse on the counter, and crouched for some love from her cats. She picked them up and held them to her neck as they purred.

Beth stood up and looked around her quiet house. She wondered if she'd ever come home to a husband that was happy to see her or is this what her future held—coming home to an empty house with cats that needed her. She had a quick vision of herself as an old cat lady, with dozens of cats meowing for attention, and her talking to the cats all night out of loneliness. She held her cats close and started to cry.

Beth's aunt had been a cat lady, and she never wanted to have that lifestyle. Beth's aunt had gone to the Bahamas on her honeymoon. On the last day of the honeymoon, she and her husband had ridden out on a dive boat with twelve other couples to dive on a wreck in sixty feet of water. Beth's aunt didn't dive, so she stayed on the boat and read a book while she worked on her tan. Her husband swam away from the group and drowned while diving. Her grief was profound, but she found out a month later that she was pregnant and rejoiced with her second chance at happiness. However, she had a miscarriage a month later and went into a deep depression.

That's when she started her collections of cats. She died at fifty-seven with twenty-one cats and no dates since her husband died years earlier.

Chapter 21

Beth opened the newspaper at her breakfast table and read the headline: *DEFENDANT CLAIMS TROPHY WIFE STAGED RAPE.* Beth took a drink of her coffee and wondered how many of the jurors would read the headline before court. Judge McDaniel had given the jurors instructions not to read any news stories, or listen to any news reports on TV about the case, but she knew human nature and she guessed 80% of the jurors had read the paper, or Googled the trial on their computers to find out as much as they could.

Beth had taken a hot bath the night before and immediately fell asleep when she crawled into bed. She had a nightmare about shooting Butch in the neck with the spear gun.

However, in her dream, she had only wounded Butch with the spear. He had then tied her up in the other bedroom and raped her with the spear still in his neck and blood dripping on her. The last thing she remembered in her dream was that he was walking out of her bedroom with the spear still sticking out of his neck and blood slowly oozing from the wound. Beth had screamed, but no one had come for them.

She'd only slept five hours and felt cranky. She realized she'd overreacted with Frank at his condo about dating Debby and hoped he wasn't mad. She would be positive when she saw him before court and would remind him she'd be watching how the jurors reacted to the evidence. Bella and Gracie rubbed against Beth's legs and purred their satisfaction with breakfast. She reached down and stroked their necks for a few seconds, and they leaned into her legs in appreciation. She took another sip of her coffee and read the rest of the article.

* * * * * *

Beth walked into the courtroom and saw Frank standing next to his table inside the bar that divided the audience area from the lawyers' area. He was talking to an investigator with a crew cut from the State Attorney's Office who was assisting him with the witnesses' appearances. Frank saw her walk in and gave her a smile, while listening to the investigator. Beth sat down on the front row and glanced over at the defense table. Charley and Stan were huddled together. Stan was moving his hands around in animated gestures and whispering loudly. She couldn't hear every word, but she distinctly heard the words "perjury" and "fucking prosecutor." Beth truly hated Stan.

Out of the corner of her eye, Beth noticed Debby arriving in the courtroom, pulling a rolling briefcase that held her stenographer machine. As Debby walked by Beth, she smiled and walked through the gate letting her inside the bar. She walked to the front of Judge McDaniel's bench and began setting up her stenographer machine. Beth felt inadequate as she stared at Debby's flawless body and focused on how tall she was. Beth knew it was juvenile to be upset that Frank hadn't told her about all his previous girlfriends.

She did a quick inventory of how many old boyfriends she'd disclosed to Frank and realized she had neglected to tell Frank about her younger, Swedish boyfriend before him.

She smiled as she chastised herself about her double standards.

She wondered what it must be like for Debby to work in a high-pressure trial with two of her former lovers. She decided it must be a little stressful, but at the same time, a little bit arousing to hear their voices all day long. Beth decided she was going to introduce herself to Debby and get to know her a little bit during one of the breaks.

"All rise, Judge Tom McDaniel is presiding over this court," the head bailiff announced.

Judge McDaniel walked in and sat down. "Everyone may be seated."

Everyone sat down, and Judge McDaniel looked at Frank. "Call your next witness."

Frank stood up and announced, "The State calls Deputy Massey."

The assistant bailiff walked to the witness room and opened the door. Deputy Massey walked to the front of the courtroom and was sworn in by the clerk. He was dressed in his green uniform and black shiny shoes. He sat down in the witness stand and faced Frank.

"Please give us your full name."

"My name is Alfred Samuel Massey." "Where do you work, sir?"

"I'm a deputy with the Lee County Sheriff's Office." "How long have you worked with the Sheriff's Office?" "Six proud years."

Frank took a deep breath. "Do you remember responding to an emergency call at a beach cottage on Cayo Costa about two months ago?"

Deputy Massey nodded. "I do."

"What did your supervisor at the scene tell you to do?"

Deputy Massey looked at the jurors. "One of the victims told us she'd shot the perpetrator in the neck with a spear gun and killed him in the upstairs bedroom. My supervisor directed me to go upstairs and collect any evidence from the body."

Beth was irritated that the most traumatic hour of her life was condensed to one question. She knew that Frank had designed his questions so the jury would focus on important facts, but it still bothered her. She wanted the jurors to know everything that had gone through her mind when she was tied up, and the panic and fear she felt when she'd cut herself free on the shark's teeth. She wanted the jurors to know how terrified she was when Butch's bullet barely missed her scalp. And most importantly, she wanted the jurors to understand that Stan was the puppet master and paid Butch to do these things.

Frank looked at his notes and picked up some eight-by-ten-inch pictures. He looked up at Deputy Massey and asked, "Did we meet yesterday in my office and go over some pictures of the scene, as well as the evidence that was taken from the rapist?"

"Objection, there's been no proof that Mrs. Jacoby was raped," Charley said as he stood up.

Beth was livid and looked at the jurors. Five had no expression on their faces, but one woman in the front row smiled slightly and Beth almost jumped out of her seat in frustration.

Judge McDaniel looked at Frank. "Please use another term."

Frank controlled his simmering anger and looked back to Deputy Massey. "Sir, yesterday in my office, did you have a chance to go over some pictures of the scene and the evidence that was taken from the intruder?"

"Objection, there's been no proof that Mr. Redding wasn't invited to the cottage by Mrs. Jacoby," Charley said as he rose.

"Approach the bench," Judge McDaniel boomed. He looked at the jury and said in a polite voice, "More white noise while we discuss the legal issues."

Judge McDaniel turned the button on as the lawyers approached, and Debby moved her stenographer machine to the counter at the front of the bench. Frank and Charley walked to the bench and looked up at Judge McDaniel.

Judge McDaniel glared at Frank. "The objection is sustained. Since you chose to put Mrs. Jacoby on later in the trial, there's no evidence at this time she was raped, or that Mr. Redding wasn't invited to the cottage. You will refer to the dead man by his name. In closing argument, you can call him any name you want. But until then, you will follow the rules of procedure in my courtroom. Do I make myself clear, Mr. Powers?"

"Yes, Your Honor," Frank said flatly.

Judge McDaniel glared at Charley. "Everyone, return to your places, and let's get through this without any more objections. The jury needs to hear this evidence without all these sidebars. Do I make myself clear?"

Both Charley and Frank nodded and returned to their spots. Charley patted Stan on the back at the defense table and sat down. Stan looked uneasy and leaned back in his chair. Beth noticed Charley smile at the jurors and two of the male jurors smiled back. Beth glanced at Frank, who was looking through his notes and trying to get his composure at the podium.

Frank took a deep breath and looked at Deputy Massey. "Sir, yesterday in my office, did you have a chance to go over some pictures of the scene, and the evidence that was taken from Butch Redding?"

"Yes, I did."

Frank looked up at Judge McDaniel. "May I approach freely, Your Honor?"

"Yes, you may."

Frank picked up seven eight-by-ten-inch pictures and walked toward Deputy Massey. "Sir, I'm showing you State's

156

exhibits one through seven. Do you recognize these pictures?

Deputy Massey looked through all seven pictures. "Yes, I took them."

Frank walked back to the podium. "On the back of each picture is an exhibit number. Can you please refer to these numbers and describe each picture for the jury?"

Deputy Massey nodded and looked at the jurors. "Exhibit one is a picture of the master bedroom from the doorway showing the body slumped against the bed. Exhibit two is a picture of the decedent's face and the clown mask next to it. Exhibit three is a picture of a pocketknife that was found in the decedent's left front pants pocket. Exhibit four is a picture of a wallet that was found in the decedent's right rear pants pocket. Exhibit five is a picture of a cell phone that was found in the decedent's left front pants pocket.

Exhibit six is a picture of a key chain that had nine keys on it. It was found in the decedent's right front pants pocket. And exhibit seven is a picture of the decedent's gun on the ground."

Frank looked at Judge McDaniel. "I request that State's exhibits one through seven be admitted into evidence and published to the jury."

Judge McDaniel looked briefly at the pictures and admitted them into evidence. He looked at his head bailiff and said, "Please show these to the jurors."

The head bailiff took the photos from Judge McDaniel and walked over to the jury box.

Judge McDaniel looked at the jurors. "You'll have time later to examine these in detail during deliberations. Please look at one photo and when you're done, pass it to the next juror. We'll wait while you briefly look at the pictures."

Beth watched as the jurors saw pictures of the bloody bedroom for the first time. One male juror put his hand over his mouth and two female jurors looked away. It took about two minutes for all six of the jurors to look at the photos, and every juror glared at Stan after they were done. Beth felt slightly better and looked at Frank, who gave her a quick smile. After the last juror finished looking at all the photos, the head bailiff retrieved them and gave them to the clerk.

Frank looked at Deputy Massey and asked, "What did you do after you secured the scene and collected all the evidence from

Butch Redding?"

"I put each piece of evidence in a plastic bag and labeled it. I then put all the plastic bags into my duffle bag with my camera and went downstairs."

Frank looked at Judge McDaniel. "No further questions."

Judge McDaniel looked at Charley. "Do you have any cross-examination?"

"Briefly, Your Honor," Charley said as he walked to the podium.

"Isn't it true, when you came downstairs, this prosecutor," Charley pointed at Frank, "was consoling his girlfriend, Beth Mancini?"

"Yes."

"Isn't it true, he was on the scene before you had even talked to Detective Dagle about what you'd done upstairs?"

"Yes."

"Did the prosecutor seem to have a strong interest in the case?"

Deputy Massey was getting irritated. "I hope so. His girlfriend had just been assaulted and tied up, while her friend was being raped in the other room. So yes, I think he had a strong interest in prosecuting the man responsible for the crime."

Charley looked at the jury and raised his hands in a questioning manner. "Isn't it true, your office prohibits an officer investigating a crime if any member of his family is a victim?"

"Objection, relevance," Frank said as he stood up. "Overruled," Judge McDaniel said firmly.

Charley looked at Deputy Massey. "You can answer the question, sir."

Deputy Massey shifted in his chair and said quietly, "Our office prohibits any officer being involved in an investigation of a crime where any family member is a victim or a witness."

"What's the reason for that?"

"In our training, we were told it avoids the appearance of favoritism or lack of objectivity."

Charley stared at Frank for a second and shook his head slowly. He looked at Judge McDaniel and said quietly, "No further questions."

Judge McDaniel looked at Deputy Massey. "You're

excused, sir."

As Deputy Massey stepped off the witness stand, Judge McDaniel looked at Frank and said, "Call your next witness."

Frank looked at the assistant bailiff. "The State calls Detective Dagle."

The assistant bailiff walked to the witness room and opened the door. Detective Dagle walked to the front of the courtroom and was sworn in by the clerk. He was dressed in khaki pants with a white shirt, which was tight at the neck, and an orange tie with a blue blazer. As he walked to the stand, Beth noticed he was wearing faded black loafers with yellow socks. He sat down in the witness stand and faced Frank.

"Please give us your full name." "My name is Robert Erwin Dagle."

"Where do you work, and what's your job?"

"I'm a Detective with the Lee County Sheriff's Office." "How long have you worked with the Sheriff's Office?" "I've been there fifteen years. My first nine years, I was a road deputy. I was promoted to detective after that."

"Do you remember responding to an emergency call at a beach cottage on Cayo Costa about two months ago?"

Detective Dagle nodded. "I do." "Who was with you in the boat?"

"Deputies Massey, Hernandez, and Franklin." "What did you find when you got there?"

Detective Dagle sat back in his chair and looked at the jurors. "When we were docking the boat, a white female named Beth Mancini met us at the dock. She told us a masked gunman tied her up in one bedroom and her friend up in the other bedroom. She broke free and was able to kill the intruder while he was raping her friend."

"Objection to the words 'intruder' and 'raping'," Charley said.

Judge McDaniel shook his head. "Overruled. He can testify to what she said when he arrived on scene. However," Judge McDaniel looked at the jury, "you will have to decide whether there was actually an intruder and rapist, based on all the evidence."

Frank looked at Detective Dagle. "After you talked to Ms. Mancini, what did you and your deputies do?"

Detective Dagle shifted in his chair and leaned forward toward the microphone. "My first concern was finding the boat that brought the masked gunman to the island. I was worried he might have an armed accomplice, and I was concerned for everyone's safety. So, I sent Deputies Hernandez and Franklin to search the area. Deputy Massey and I went inside the cottage. I interviewed Mrs. Jacoby while Deputy Massey secured the scene upstairs, collected evidence, and took photos."

Frank hesitated and looked at his notes for a second. "When you first saw Mrs. Jacoby, how did she look?"

"Her face was pale, and she had a blanket pulled around her. She was on the back porch in a rocking chair."

Frank lowered his voice. "When you spoke with her, what was her demeanor?"

"She was very distraught and talked slowly. She broke down a few times and cried while I was interviewing her, so it took a while."

"After you completed the interview with Mrs. Jacoby, what did you do?"

"I left Mrs. Jacoby on the porch and went inside. Deputy Massey briefed me on the scene upstairs, and Deputies Hernandez and Franklin came in and told me they'd found the boat in a small hidden creek north of the cottage. I was satisfied the scene was secure, so I called an EMS helicopter to take Mrs. Jacoby to the hospital for treatment and for the doctor to administer a standard rape kit exam."

Frank lifted his left hand toward the jury. "Could you tell the jury what a rape kit is?"

Detective Dagle looked at the jury. "In every rape case, there's a kit at the hospital that doctors use to collect evidence for the criminal case. It has DNA swabs for collecting any semen from the woman's body. It also has a detailed chart of a woman's body to mark any trauma areas with numbers and take pictures documenting any trauma that corresponds to these numbers on the chart. Sometimes," Detective Dagle cleared his throat and continued, "the trauma is to the inside of the vagina and it's hard to take pictures, so the doctor makes detailed notes and marks the diagrams. The doctors also search for hair and any trace samples of carpet or clothing. This can be useful if we have to track the rapist down. In this case, it wasn't an issue, but we're still required to perform all the tests in the kit."

Frank waited a second to let the jury digest all the information. "After you called the EMS helicopter, what did you do next?"

"I called the coroner's office and made arrangements for Deputy Hernandez to drive our boat back to the marina and pick up the coroner's assistant. He took custody of the body and transported it back to their office for an autopsy. After that was done, I did a taped interview of Ms. Mancini."

Frank pointed to Stan. "The following Monday, did you arrest the defendant at his home?"

Detective Dagle stared at Stan and nodded. "I did." "Please describe to the jury what happened when you went to the defendant's house?"

Detective Dagle raised his voice. "I went there with two other deputies to arrest him and search his house, pursuant to the search warrant the judge signed. I knocked on his front door and he answered in his blue silk bathrobe. I told him he was under arrest for conspiracy to commit kidnapping and rape. I asked him to turn around so I could handcuff him, and he became disruptive."

Frank turned and stared at Stan. "What do you mean by disruptive?"

"He stepped away from me and said, 'What the fuck are you talking about? If you arrest me, I'll sue you for false arrest and have you fired. I'm calling my lawyer.' So, at that point, I pulled my taser and told him I'd be forced to use it unless he let me handcuff him. He finally let me cuff him, and I took him to the cruiser and put him in the back seat.

He was cussing like a sailor when I left him and went back to his house to search for evidence with the other deputies."

"What did you find when you searched his house?" Frank asked.

"We found $1,500 in his dresser drawer and $642 in his wallet, and it was all hundred-dollar bills, except for the $42. We found his cell phone on his dresser and checked it for evidence. His speed dial was programmed for his divorce attorney, Butch Redding, his stock broker, aChinese take-out restaurant, and his two girlfriends. We searched his computer for any recent e-mails or correspondence to Butch Redding, but we didn't find any."

"Did you subpoena the defendant's bank records to check for any cash withdrawals on the day Butch Redding went to Cayo Costa with a clown mask and a gun?"

"I did."

Frank turned and stared at Stan. "Did you find any cash withdrawals on the day Butch Redding went to Cayo Costa?"

Detective Dagle nodded. "I did. The defendant withdrew $5,000 cash from his checking account at ten a.m. on the day of the attack."

"When you arrested the defendant, did he have a total of $2,100, in hundred-dollar bills, in his possession?" 4

"Yes."

"Butch Redding had how many hundred-dollar bills in his wallet?"

"Nine."

"Did you get a search warrant to search Butch Redding's house?"

"I did. When we searched it, we found $1,500 in his gun safe."

"Did Butch Redding have a total of $2,400 in his wallet and in his house?"

"Yes—in hundred-dollar bills."

Frank held up his right pointer finger. "Isn't it true that if you combine the $2,400 in Butch Redding's possession with the $2,100 in the defendant's possession, you get

$4,500?"

"Yes, that's true."

"Isn't it true, the defendant withdrew $5,000 from the bank the day of the attack?"

Charley stood up. "Objection. Asked and answered."
"Sustained. Move along, Mr. Powers."

"Yes, judge," Frank said irritably.

Frank walked over to his table and picked up some papers and returned to the podium. "Detective Dagle, did you subpoena the defendant's phone records for the day before the attack and the day of the attack?"

Detective Dagle nodded. "Yes."

"Isn't it true, the divorce mediation ended abruptly at two

p.m. the day before the attack?"

"Yes, that's what all the witnesses told me."

"Can you tell the jury about the incoming calls to Butch Redding's phone after two p.m. on the day of mediation?"

"Yes, I can," Detective Dagle said and looked at his notes. "At three fifty-eight p.m., he got a call from a customer, confirming Butch was coming to fix his porch the following week. The call lasted seven minutes. At 5:12 p.m., he got a twelve-minute call from a pay phone at a 7-11. At six p.m., he got a five-minute call from a friend he played pool with on Thursdays. And at 10:12 p.m., he got a four-minute call from his girlfriend who came over to his house and spent the night."

"How do you know what the conversations were about?"

"We interviewed the people who were assigned the numbers that called Butch Redding's phone."

"Were there any outgoing calls that day from Butch Redding's phone?"

"Only one. He called his five-year-old son in Georgia, who is living with his ex-wife, and the call lasted twenty three minutes."

"Were there any incoming calls to Butch Redding's phone on the day of the attack on Cayo Costa?"

"Yes," Detective Dagle said and looked at his notes. "At 8:55 a.m., there was a call from the defendant's cell phone, and it lasted fifteen minutes. At 10:29 a.m., there was a call from a different customer asking about a quote to fix a leaking roof, and it lasted eight minutes. At 1:12 p.m., there was a second call from the defendant's cell phone, and it lasted four minutes. At 3:00 p.m., he got a call from his girlfriend, and it went straight to voice mail."

"Were there any outgoing calls from Butch Redding's phone on the day of the attack on Cayo Costa?"

"Yes," Detective Dagle looked at his notes. "At 6:40 p.m., he made a twelve-minute phone call to his son in Georgia."

Frank looked at Judge McDaniel. "No further questions, Your Honor."

Judge McDaniel looked at the jury. "We're going to break for lunch at this point, so be back here by one o'clock."

After the jury and spectators cleared out of the courtroom, Beth walked up to the bar dividing the courtroom and smiled at Frank. "Would you like to go get some lunch?"

Frank walked to the bar and held Beth's hand. "No, but thanks. I brought an apple, so I'm just gonna stay here in court and eat it while I prep for the afternoon. But I'll be ravenous by the end of the day, so I'd like to take you to dinner."

Beth smiled and said playfully, "You've got a date, lover boy."

Frank leaned forward and gave Beth a kiss on the cheek and squeezed her hand. "See you later."

Beth walked out of the courtroom and headed toward the elevators. She saw Debby, the court reporter, stepping on to an elevator and debated whether to wait for another elevator or introduce herself. She decided on the latter and walked quickly to the elevator, catching the door as it was closing. She stepped in and saw that Debby was the only person in the elevator.

Beth smiled at her and stuck out her hand. "Hi—I'm Beth Mancini."

The elevator door closed as Debby shook her hand warmly. "I know, I heard in court. But it's nice to meet you outside of the courtroom. I'm Debby Wilson."

There was an uneasy silence for a few seconds as the elevator went down, but Beth ventured forward. "I didn't know until last night that you and Frank used to date."

"Frankie and I used to date a long time ago," Debby said fondly. "He's a really nice guy, and I think you two make a great couple."

"Thanks. Are you dating anyone now?"

"Yes," Debby gushed, "I've been dating a doctor for about two years. Next month he's taking me to Paris for a week, and I'm hoping he proposes there."

The elevator door opened and they both stepped off.

Beth's eyes sparkled and she said cheerfully, "I hope it's the trip of a lifetime for you."

Chapter 22

Judge McDaniel looked at Charley. "Mr. Kline, do you have any questions for the witness?"

Charley stood up. "I do, Your Honor."

Charley walked to the podium with his notes and looked at Detective Dagle over the rim of his reading glasses. "Good afternoon, sir."

Detective Dagle nodded. "Good afternoon."

"Did I hear you right earlier, when you said you took Dr. Jacoby to jail in his robe?" "Yes, I did."

Charley held out his hands. "Why didn't you allow him to change into normal clothes?"

Detective Dagle sat up in his chair. "He was being disruptive, sir."

"Isn't it a fact, there's no regulation that prohibits you from allowing an arrestee to change out of his robe and into normal clothes before being taken to jail?"

"There's no regulation. However, because he was being disruptive, I was worried about my safety."

Charlie chuckled quietly for a few seconds. "Detective, are you telling this jury that a muscle-bound young man like you, with a gun and a taser, was worried about a skinny, middle-aged man in a silk robe with no weapon?"

There were a few snickers in the courtroom and Detective Dagle's face flushed with embarrassment. "Sir, I wasn't scared, but we're taught to avoid situations that might turn violent. I was worried he might try to fight me to avoid arrest."

Charley nodded for a second with a smirk on his face. "Are you sure it wasn't retaliation for Dr. Jacoby saying, 'What the fuck are you talking about? If you arrest me, I'll sue you for false arrest and have you fired. I'm calling my lawyer.'?"

"Absolutely not," Detective Dagle said firmly.

Charley removed his reading glasses and cocked his left eyebrow. "Sir, you knew that when you arrested Dr. Jacoby, he was going to be put in a holding cell with all the other male arrestees that day, didn't you?"

"Yes, that's protocol."

"Wouldn't you agree with me that a middle-aged man in a blue silk robe might get harassed when he was put in a holding cell with dozens of hardened criminals?"

Detective Dagle shifted uncomfortably in his seat. "I hadn't thought about that, sir."

"You knew that one of the alleged victims was this prosecutor's girlfriend, didn't you?" Charley said and pointed at Frank.

Frank felt his face flush, but he knew there was nothing he could do.

"I knew that, but it didn't influence my decision," Detective Dagle said irritably.

Charley nodded and smirked as he put his reading glasses back on. "So, if I understand you correctly, you're telling this jury that you used your judgment when you decided to keep Dr. Jacoby in his robe?"

Detective Dagle considered the question before answering. "Yes."

"In your judgment," Charley asked sarcastically, "how should an innocent man act when he's arrested for a crime he didn't commit?"

"Objection, argumentative," Frank boomed as he stood up.

Judge McDaniel nodded. "Sustained. Move along, Mr. Kline."

Charley looked at Detective Dagle and asked loudly, "Isn't it true you arrested Dr. Jacoby with zero physical evidence against him?"

Detective Dagle shifted in his seat and tried to think of an answer that wouldn't help Charley. After a few seconds, he said, "I arrested Mr. Jacoby based on the statements of the witnesses about the perpetrator saying he was sent there by Mr. Jacoby and his actions during the mediation."

Charley held his hands out to his side, palms up. "This is a yes or no question, Detective Dagle. Isn't it true you arrested Dr. Jacoby with zero physical evidence against him?"

"I arrested him based on all the evidence."

Charley looked at Judge McDaniel. "Your Honor, will you

instruct the witness to answer my question with a yes or a no?"

Judge McDaniel turned and looked at Detective Dagle. "Mr. Kline is going to ask you the question a third time, and I want you to answer it with a yes or a no."

Detective Dagle nodded. "Yes, Your Honor." Judge McDaniel looked at Charley and nodded.

Charley looked at Detective Dagle and enunciated each word slowly. "This is a yes or no question, Detective Dagle. Isn't it true you arrested Dr. Jacoby with zero physical evidence against him?"

"Yes," Detective Dagle said flatly.

There were a few murmurs in the courtroom, and Beth looked at the jurors. Two ladies in the back row looked at each other and raised their eyebrows. Beth looked at Frank and saw him squeezing the armrests on his chair as his shoulders tightened.

Charley talked slowly. "Sir, isn't it true your entire case depends on whether Butch Redding was truthful when he said, 'Your husband sent me to deliver a message to you and your lawyer—ya'll shoulda settled at mediation' to the women at the beach cottage?"

"Objection, argumentative," Frank said as he stood up. "Overruled. You can answer the question," Judge Mc-

Daniel said firmly.

Detective Dagle hadn't learned from his last verbal sparring with Charley. "Yes, that's true. But why would he lie about that?"

Charley had set another trap and Detective Dagle had taken the bait. Charley turned and looked at the jurors.

"That's a very good question. The jurors will have to answer that one."

"Objection, argumentative," Frank blurted out. "Sustained. Move along, Mr. Kline."

"Yes, Your Honor."

Beth noticed that one male juror on the front row nodded his head slightly, and she felt sick to her stomach.

"Detective, the next set of questions has to do with the phone records from Butch Redding. Isn't it true you said there was a twelve-minute call from a 7-11 to Butch Redding's phone at 5:12 p.m. on the day of mediation?"

Detective Dagle nodded. "Yes, that's true."

"Isn't it a fact that the 7-11 the call came from is on the corner of McGregor Boulevard and Cypress Lake Drive?"

"Yes, that's true.

"Do you know that 7-11 is less than a half mile from the condo that Karen Jacoby is renting?"

"I have no idea if that is true," Detective Dagle said dismissively.

"Did you know that Karen Jacoby fills her car up with gas from that same 7-11 on a regular basis, according to her credit card records?"

"Objection, relevance," Frank pleaded.

"Overruled," Judge McDaniel said and glared at Frank.

Charley smiled at Detective Dagle. "You can answer the question."

"I have no idea. You'll have to ask her."

"Oh, I will, sir; you can count on that. Let me ask you another question. Did you know this same 7-11 is about half-way between Karen's rented condo and her gym?"

Detective Dagle didn't want to prolong Charley's antics. "No, I didn't know," he said contritely.

"Did you get Dr. Jacoby's phone records for the past year that showed he called Butch Redding between two and five times per week?"

"I only got the phone records for those two days."

"Sir, isn't it true that Butch Redding was the handyman that worked on Dr. Jacoby's riverfront house and his beach cottage on Cayo Costa?"

"Yes, that's true. He was also friends with him and went to the gun range with him. We verified that with people at the range."

"Sir, are you aware how many times Butch Redding was alone with Karen Jacoby, at the riverfront house and the beach cottage when he was working on repairs?"

"Mrs. Jacoby denied ever being alone with Butch Redding."

"Do you have any proof of this, other than Karen Jacoby's word?"

Detective Dagle leaned forward and put his elbows on the counter as he spoke loudly into the microphone, "The word of a rape victim is good enough for me."

Charley looked at Judge McDaniel. "Objection, nonresponsive."

Judge McDaniel nodded. "Sustained. Just answer the question, Detective Dagle."

Detective Dagle leaned back in his chair in frustration. "Just her word."

"Isn't it a fact, your case boils down to the credibility of Karen Jacoby?"

Detective Dagle was fed up with word games. "Yes, that's true."

Charley turned and faced Judge McDaniel. "No further questions."

As Detective Dagle stepped off the witness stand, Judge McDaniel looked at Frank and said, "Call your next witness."

Frank looked at the assistant bailiff. "The State calls Dr. Rawlings."

The assistant bailiff walked to the witness room and opened the door. Dr. Rawlings walked to the front of the courtroom and was sworn in by the clerk. He was dressed in a black suit with a white shirt and gray tie. He sat down in the witness stand and faced Frank.

Frank looked at Dr. Rawlings. "Please give us your full name and where you work."

Dr. Rawlings cleared his throat. "My name is Dr. Alfred Forrest Rawlings the third, and I'm the coroner for Lee County, Florida."

"How long have you been a coroner, sir?"

"I was an assistant coroner in Miami right out of medical school for five years, and I've been the head coroner here in Lee County for twenty-one years."

"Dr. Rawlings, do you recall examining the body of Butch Redding in your office a few months ago?"

"I most certainly do. His cause of death was extraordinary—a spear through his neck. I've never examined a body with that cause of death before. When my assistant moved the body from Cayo Costa, he clipped the tip of the spear off, and pulled the base of the spear back through the neck and bagged the two items for evidence. He had to cut the spear so the body bag would close."

Beth saw a female juror on the back row put her hands to her mouth.

"Were you given a history about the cause of death?"

Dr. Rawlings nodded. "I was. The police report stated that the victim of the kidnapping broke free and shot Mr.

Redding while he was raping her friend."

"Objection, hearsay." Charley said as he stood up. Judge McDaniel shook his head. "Overruled. The doc-

tor can testify about hearsay because it was used in reaching his opinion."

Frank took a deep breath and looked back toward Dr.

Rawlings. "Was death instantaneous when the arrow entered the neck?"

Dr. Rawlings shook his head. "No. I examined the wound in the autopsy room, and it appeared the spear nicked the anterior side of the jugular vein but lodged in the neck. There would've been some seepage of blood from the neck, and Mr. Redding would've been in intense pain, but he would've been alive for a period of time from the initial wound. However, the police report stated there was a struggle, and one of the victims pulled on the spear. At this point, the seal was broken, and the decedent would've rapidly lost blood. He would've been unconscious within five seconds and expired in less than a minute."

Beth felt clammy as she recalled the life-or-death struggle she had with Butch. She remembered the bullet burning through her hair, and how she felt as she fell to the ground. She remembered looking up at the blood spurting through the air from Butch's neck, and wondering if he'd fire his gun at her again. A chill ran through her body.

"Do you have an opinion about the cause of death of Butch Redding?"

"I do. The cause of death was the cutting of his jugular vein by the spear and the subsequent struggle."

"Is this consistent with the facts of the case that were listed in the police report?"

"Yes."

"No further questions."

Judge McDaniel looked at Charley. "Cross-examination?"

Charley stood up. "Yes, Your Honor."

Charley walked to the podium and looked at Dr. Rawlings over his reading glasses. "Good afternoon, doctor."

"Good afternoon."

"Sir, isn't it true you stated the cause of death is consistent with the facts that were in the police report?"

"I did."

"Sir, I'd like to give you another hypothetical series of facts, and I'd like you to answer if that's consistent with the cause of death."

"Okay."

"Objection, may we approach?" Frank asked. "Everyone approach," Judge McDaniel said and then

looked over his desk at the jury. "More white noise." After everyone assumed their place at sidebar, Judge

McDaniel looked at Frank. "Grounds for your objection?" "Your Honor, my objection is relevance. Any hypothetical series of facts isn't relevant to the evidence that has been presented."

Judge McDaniel looked at Charley. "Your response, Mr. Kline?"

"I have two points," Charley said. "The first one is that there was no need for Dr. Rawlings to testify. This isn't a homicide case where the state is required to prove that the victim is dead, and the defendant caused his death. This is a conspiracy case, and the State only has to prove an agreement between the defendant and Butch Redding to commit kidnapping and rape. The only reason the State put Dr.

Rawlings on the stand is to try to boost the credibility of Ms. Mancini.

"The second reason is the State has opened the door by asking Dr. Rawlings if the cause of death is consistent

with their version of events. I'm attempting to ask the same thing—is the cause of death consistent with our theory of what happened?"

Judge McDaniel scratched his beard and leaned back in his chair. After a few seconds of contemplation, he looked at Frank. "I'm overruling your objection. I think both of Mr. Kline's points are valid, so I'm going to allow it."

Frank started to argue with Judge McDaniel, but he knew

he'd lose, and the jurors would think he was trying to hide something from them. He turned abruptly and walked back to his table. Charley returned to the podium and looked at Debby to make sure her machine was ready. When she nodded at Charley, he looked at Dr. Rawlings.

"Sir, I'd like to give you another hypothetical series of facts, and I'd like you to answer if that's consistent with the cause of death."

"Okay."

"Is the cause of death consistent with Mrs. Jacoby hiring Butch Redding, who is her secret lover, to set up an attack on her, without Ms. Mancini knowing about it, and Ms. Mancini breaking free from being tied up, confronting Mr. Redding, and killing him with a spear fired from a speargun?"

Beth wanted to yell at Charley and slap him across the face. Beth looked at Frank and expected him to jump up and object, but he didn't. His face was red, and he was squeezing the armrests, but he didn't stand up. She looked at Dr. Rawlings, who had a smirk on his face and shook his head slowly.

Dr. Rawlings said sarcastically, "I'll play your game, counselor. Yes, it's possible, but highly unlikely."

Charley pointed at Dr. Rawlings and shouted, "This is no game. This woman is trying to steal fifty million dollars from my client and put him in prison for a crime he didn't commit!"

Frank jumped to his feet. "Objection. Move to strike!" Judge McDaniel stood up and banged his gavel three times. He looked at the head bailiff and said firmly, "Take the jury to the jury room."

Judge McDaniel glared at Charley, but Charley didn't look away. Beth looked at Frank, and his hands were shaking at his side. Beth looked at Debby; she had a look of fear in her eyes. Stan had a smile on his face for the first time since the trial started. The jurors looked back over their shoulders at Charley as they went through the jury room door. The head bailiff shut the door after they were all inside and nodded at Judge McDaniel.

Judge McDaniel sat down and took a deep breath. "Mr. Kline, that was not a question; it was an argument to the jurors, and you know that's highly improper. Tell me why I shouldn't hold you in contempt of court and put you in jail!"

Charley pointed at Dr. Rawlings. "Your Honor, I admit that was improper. But the State's witness, Dr. Rawlings, who has testified in different courts for over twenty-five years and knows how he's supposed to answer questions, made a condescending remark about my client's defense, and I lost my temper. I simply couldn't let Dr. Rawlings' comment go unchallenged. I'll gladly go to jail if you'll sentence Dr. Rawlings to the same amount of jail time."

Judge McDaniel turned and looked at Dr. Rawlings. "I might take Mr. Kline up on his offer, and sentence both of you to thirty days jail."

Dr. Rawlings' face turned crimson, and he shifted in his chair. After a few seconds of uneasy silence in the courtroom, Dr. Rawlings said sheepishly, "I'm sorry, Your Honor. It won't happen again."

Judge McDaniel glared at Dr. Rawlings for a few seconds and then at Charley. He shook his head in disgust and turned to the head bailiff. "Bring the jurors back in."

The head bailiff knocked on the door and opened it. He told the jurors that Judge McDaniel was ready for them, and they walked timidly into the courtroom. They quickly sat down and looked up at Judge McDaniel quizzically.

Judge McDaniel said to the jurors, "Ladies and gentlemen, I'm striking Mr. Kline's last comment from the record. I'm instructing you to disregard the statement."

Judge McDaniel looked at Charley. "Mr. Kline, please ask your prior question," he turned and looked at Dr. Rawlings. "And the witness shall answer the question truthfully."

Charley looked at Dr. Rawlings and asked slowly, "Is the cause of death consistent with Mrs. Jacoby hiring Butch Redding, who is her secret lover, to set up an attack on her, without Ms. Mancini knowing about it, and Ms. Mancini breaking free from being tied up, confronting Mr. Redding, and killing him with a spear fired from a spear gun?"

Dr. Rawlings answered meekly, "Yes." "No further questions, Your Honor."

As Dr. Rawlings stepped off the witness stand, Judge McDaniel looked at Frank and said, "Call your next witness."

Frank looked at the assistant bailiff. "The State calls Dr.

Shara Lance."

The assistant bailiff walked to the witness room and opened the door. Dr. Lance walked to the front of the courtroom with a folder in her hand and was sworn in by the clerk. She was dressed in a dark blue dress and matching shoes. Her salt and pepper hair was cut in a short bob, and she wore no makeup. She sat down in the witness stand and smiled at Frank.

"Please tell us your full name and where you work." Dr. Lance leaned forward and spoke into the microphone. "My name is Shara Jessica Lance, and I'm an emergency room doctor at Lee Memorial Hospital."

"How long have you been a doctor?"

"I've been a licensed physician for seventeen years." "As an emergency room doctor, do you treat rape victims?"

Dr. Lance nodded. "I do. The first thing we do is to check for any acute trauma and stabilize the patient. After that, we do a rape exam, which is required procedure, and use a rape kit to look for evidence."

"Do you recall examining a rape victim, Karen Jacoby, about two months ago in the emergency room?"

"Objection to the term 'rape victim'." "Sustained."

Frank nodded and took a deep breath. "Do you recall examining an *alleged* rape victim, Karen Jacoby, about two months ago in the emergency room?"

"I do."

"Could you tell the jury the results of your examination?"

"I brought a copy of her medical records." Dr. Lance turned to Judge McDaniel and held up her folder. "May I refer to the records while testifying?"

Judge McDaniel nodded. "Yes, you may."

Dr. Lance looked through the records for a second and looked up to Frank. "There was some bruising around the wrists and ankles. This is consistent with the patient's history of being tied up during the rape."

"Objection to the word 'rape'."

"Sustained," Judge McDaniel said and turned to Dr. Lance, "Please use the term '*alleged rape*' in your testimony."

"Yes, Your Honor."

Frank waited for Dr. Lance to face him and asked, "Was

the bruising on the hands and ankles consistent with someone struggling while having their extremities tied to the four corners of a bed?"

"Yes, most definitely."

Beth looked at the jurors and every one of them was glaring at Stan.

"Did you do anything to treat the ankles and wrists?" "The nurse had already cleaned the injured area and the skin hadn't been compromised, so there was nothing else to do but prescribe bed rest and plenty of fluids."

"Did you begin the rape examination after this?" "I did."

"Did you find any trauma to Mrs. Jacoby's vagina?" "I did a thorough exam and, fortunately, there was no

scratching or tearing to the vagina."

"Were you able to collect any DNA or trace samples?" "There was no DNA present, which was consistent with the history from the patient that ejaculation never occurred because her friend killed the attacker with a spear gun.

There were no trace samples of carpet, clothing or hair present."

Frank looked at Judge McDaniel. "No further questions."

Judge McDaniel looked at Charley. "Cross-examination?"

Charley walked confidently to the podium and looked at Dr. Lance.

"Good afternoon, doctor." "Hello."

"Isn't it a fact that the majority of rape exams show some tearing and/or bruising to the vagina?"

Dr. Lance sat back in her chair and considered her answer for a few seconds. "Some rape exams show trauma to the vagina and some don't."

Charley was getting irritated. "Doctor, this is a yes or no question. Isn't it a fact that the majority of rape exams show some tearing and/or bruising to the vagina?"

"If you define majority as more than fifty-one percent, then yes, I would agree that the majority of rape exams do show some tearing and/or bruising to the vagina."

Charley shook his head in frustration. "Let me ask it a different way, doctor. Wouldn't you agree that at least sixty-seven percent of rape exams show some type of tearing and/or bruising to the vagina?"

Dr. Lance didn't like the question, but she had to answer truthfully. "Yes, I would agree with that."

Charley hesitated and let the jury digest the answer.

After a few seconds, he continued. "Isn't it true that the reason a vagina is torn and/or bruised during a rape is a lack of lubrication?"

Dr. Lance nodded. "That's one reason. Another reason for trauma is the violence of the attack beyond the actual sexual act. Some rapists use weapons to injure the vagina before or after penetration."

Charley was annoyed that Dr. Rawlings was trying to divert the point of his question. "Let me ask it a different way, doctor. Wouldn't you agree that if a woman isn't lubricated during a rape, there's a much greater likelihood of tearing or bruising to the vagina?"

"Yes, I'd agree with that."

"Isn't it true when you examined Karen Jacoby, there was no tearing or bruising of the vagina?"

"Yes."

"Wouldn't you agree with me that a logical explanation for this," Charley said, "is that Karen Jacoby's vagina was lubricated during the sexual act?"

Frank jumped to his feet. "Objection."

Judge McDaniel shook his head. "Overruled."

Charley looked at Dr. Lance. "You can answer the question."

Dr. Lance leaned forward to the microphone. "Sir, sometimes during a rape, a woman has involuntary lubrication based on penetration. The younger the woman, the more likely she will have involuntary lubrication."

Charley snorted disdainfully. "Doctor, could you tell the jury which course in medical school taught you that?"

Dr. Lance straightened up in her chair and said indignantly, "I can't recall any course in medical school going into that much detail about rape cases. However, based on my experience, I'm certain that is what happens in some rape cases."

"Doctor, wouldn't you agree that if a woman is consenting to sex, and she's lubricated, then there shouldn't be any tearing or

176

bruising to the vagina?"

"Yes, I would agree with that."

"Doctor, isn't it just as likely that Mrs. Jacoby was consenting to sex and was lubricated, as if she was raped and had involuntary lubrication?"

Dr. Lance shook her head forcefully and said firmly, "No, that's not true. She was tied up!"

Charley asked loudly, "Isn't it possible she staged her attack?"

"Why would she do that?"

Charley looked at the jury for a few seconds and then turned toward Judge McDaniel. "Your Honor, could you instruct the witness to answer my question?"

Judge McDaniel looked at Dr. Lance. "Please answer the question."

Dr. Lance was dismissive. "Anything is possible." "Doctor, I want to narrow my question. Based solely on your examination of Karen Jacoby's vagina, was there any evidence of an unwanted sexual encounter?"

Dr. Lance shook her head and answered sarcastically, "Based on the restrictions of your question, the answer is no."

Charley looked at Judge McDaniel and said politely, "No further questions."

Judge McDaniel looked at the jurors. "We're going to break for the night. Remember, don't watch the news on the TV, or surf the internet, or read the paper. I'll see you tomorrow morning at nine."

* * * * * *

Frank and Beth walked together into the Veranda and immediately smelled the welcoming aroma of freshly cooked steak with sautéed onions. It was a balmy night with a steady wind, so they asked to be seated outside in the courtyard by the goldfish pond. Frank was quiet and looked across the rippling pond at the bamboo shoots that went thirty feet in the air. Beth knew Frank was exhausted, so she sat quietly and watched the goldfish.

The waitress walked up to the table. "Good evening. Can I bring you drinks?"

Frank nodded. "Scotch on the rocks." Beth said, "A gin and

tonic would be nice."

After the waitress walked away, Frank asked, "How did the jury react to all the fireworks today?"

"I don't know," Beth said and shrugged her shoulders. "Some of the time they seemed interested in Charley's bullshit theory, and other times they glared at Stan."

Frank cracked his knuckles. "I told you Charley was good at trials."

Beth nodded. "He has a certain charm about him, but surely the jury can see it's all a smokescreen."

Frank shook his head. "He doesn't have to convince them he's right; he's just got to create reasonable doubt."

The waitress brought their drinks to the table and set them down. They both took a healthy pull on their drinks. The waitress smiled and said cheerfully, "You must've been ready for a drink."

"If you only knew," Frank said wearily.

The waitress said, "Let me give you our specials tonight. The soup of the day is butternut squash, and the entrée is bronzed grouper with rice and glazed carrots."

Beth said enthusiastically, "I'll take the grouper special." Frank nodded. "I'll have the same and another drink."

The waitress walked away, and Beth asked quietly, "How are you doing?"

Frank leaned back in his chair. "I'm second-guessing my decision to prosecute this case. I took the case because I wanted everything done right, and I wanted justice for you and Karen. And now, me being on the case is part of their defense. I should've seen this coming from Charley."

"Honey, I'm sure the jury can see this for what it is—a desperate attempt to divert their attention from the evidence."

"I hope so. I was so angry today, that it was hard for me to focus," Frank said and drained his glass. "Of course, keeping me off-balanced and angry is one of Charley's strategies."

Beth reached out and held Frank's hand. "There's one secret weapon that you have, that Charley doesn't." "What's that?"

Beth smiled and said coyly, "The magical pixie dust I'm giving you tonight in bed."

Chapter 23

Beth opened the newspaper at her breakfast table and read the headline: *DEFENDANT'S PHONE RECORDS CONNECT HIM TO RAPIST*. It was the third day of the trial, and the newspaper article chronicled the highlights of the trial. Beth was irritated because the article focused on the defense version of events and how there was no physical evidence in the case. Beth wondered how many jurors were reading the paper that morning over their breakfast, contrary to Judge McDaniel's instructions.

Beth ate half of her banana and set it down because her stomach was turning after reading the article. Beth knew that some rape victims failed to report the crime because they feared the legal process. Now she understood it personally, and she was only a witness to a rape. When she was in Frank's bed the night before, he had told her Karen was the State's last witness at trial. She wondered how Karen felt, knowing that she was going to testify today. Because of court rules, Beth hadn't been able to talk to Karen since the trial had started.

Bella and Gracie rubbed up against Beth's legs looking for attention. Beth picked them both up and cradled them to her chest. They both held their heads next to Beth's neck and purred loudly. Beth thought of all her other divorce clients she'd put on hold during the trial and felt guilty. After court was over today, she would go to her office and return all their phone messages before she left for the night.

* * * * * *

Beth walked into the crowded elevator at the courthouse and squeezed into the last space on the right side. As the door closed, she glanced across the elevator and saw Stan and Charley against the far wall. Charley gave her a polite nod, but Stan glared at her. She looked to the back of the elevator and saw two male jurors looking at her. She gave them a polite nod and looked up at the ceiling of the elevator. It was the slowest and most uncomfortable elevator ride of Beth's life.

* * * * * *

"All rise. Judge Tom McDaniel is presiding over this court," the head bailiff announced.

Judge McDaniel walked in and sat down. "Please be seated."

After everyone settled down, Judge McDaniel looked at Frank. "Call your next witness."

Frank stood up and announced, "The State calls Karen Jacoby."

The assistant bailiff walked to the witness room and opened the door. Karen walked into the courtroom, and everyone stared in silence as she walked up the aisle. She was wearing a red dress with matching red four-inch heels and her nails were freshly painted matching red. Her blond hair was pulled back in a tight ponytail, showcasing her bright red lipstick and perfect makeup. She walked to the front of the courtroom and was sworn in by the clerk. She sat down in the witness stand and glared at Stan for a few seconds.

Frank was uncertain if he should be pleased or deeply concerned about her bold choice of color. Beth looked at the jurors, and they were all intensely focused on Karen.

"Please give us your full name." "My name is Karen Lynn Jacoby." "How do you know the defendant?"

Karen stared at Stan for a second before she said blandly, "He's my husband."

"Are you in the process of getting divorced?" "Yes," Karen said forcefully.

"Do you know Beth Mancini?"

Karen looked at Beth and smiled. "I do. Beth is my divorce attorney and friend."

"Let me direct you back to this past spring. Do you remember the unsuccessful divorce mediation on your case?" "I most certainly do."

"After the unsuccessful mediation, did you invite Ms.

Mancini to spend the weekend at the beach cottage that you and your husband own?"

Karen nodded. "Yes, I did. It was my week to be at the cottage."

Frank lifted his left hand and pointed toward the jury. "Can you tell the jury how you and your husband have divided time at your beach cottage during the divorce?"

Karen looked at the jury. "Our attorneys worked out an agreement to alternate weeks at the cottage while the divorce was pending."

"Did you tell anyone that Ms. Mancini was spending the weekend with you at your beach cottage?"

Karen shook her head. "No one except the workers at the marina, because they helped us load the boat."

"Did you and Ms. Mancini arrive at your beach cottage around noon on a Friday?"

Karen cocked her head to her left and thought for a second. "By the time we drove to the marina and took the boat out, it was sometime around noon when we arrived."

"What did you do after you got to the beach cottage?" "We unloaded our luggage and supplies first. We then turned on the electrical system and the water pump. After that, we went for a swim in the Gulf of Mexico and relaxed a bit."

"Did you and Ms. Mancini take your boat to a nearby island restaurant to eat dinner?"

Karen nodded. "We drove to Cabbage Key for dinner."

Frank cleared his throat and raised his voice. "When you returned, did you find a stranger waiting for you inside your cottage?"

Karen sat up in her chair. "When we walked in the front door, I saw a man dressed in black and wearing a clown mask sitting on the couch. He said, 'I've been waiting for both of you.' He had a handgun and was pointing it at us."

"What did you do?"

"I stopped in my tracks." "What happened next?"

Karen glared at Stan for a second and looked back at Frank. "He stood up and said, 'Your husband sent me to deliver a message to you and your lawyer—you all should've settled at mediation.'"

Beth watched every juror turn and stare at Stan. Frank

waited and let everyone in the courtroom savor

Karen's words before he asked, "How did you feel?"

Karen took a deep breath and lowered her voice. "I was scared like I've never been scared before in my life."

Karen brought her right hand to her mouth and looked down. Beth noticed her hand was quivering.

Frank waited until Karen looked up at him and asked gently, "What happened next?"

"He pointed the gun at us and told us to walk upstairs to the guest bedroom."

"What did you and Ms. Mancini do?"

"We walked upstairs and sat on the bed, exactly like he told us to. And then he told me to go sit in the corner on top of my hands, so I did."

"What happened next?"

Karen looked at Beth for a second and bit her lower lip. "He told Beth to lay face down on the bed, and he tied her up with fishing leader. After that, he pointed the gun at me and told me to go in the other bedroom."

"What did you think was going to happen?"

Karen shook her head slowly. "I wasn't sure, so I didn't move until he pointed the gun at Beth and he..." Karen's voice cracked, and she stopped speaking as a tear ran down her left cheek. She wiped the tear away with a handkerchief she pulled from her purse and took a deep breath before continuing. "He told me he would shoot Beth if I didn't go with him to the other bedroom, so I went."

Frank waited a second for Karen to gain her composure. "What happened in the other room?"

Karen glared at Stan for a second and looked back at Frank before answering. "He told me to take off my clothes and lie on the bed, so I did. He put his gun on the nightstand and he tied my wrists and ankles to the four corner posts on the bed with fishing leader. And then," Karen's voice trailed off and she put her face in her hands. After a few seconds, she looked up and said firmly, "he stroked my right breast, and I spat on him."

Frank hesitated to let the jury picture the scene. He lowered his voice and asked, "What happened next?"

Karen cleared her throat and said matter-of-factly, "He

slapped me and said, 'Blondie, we can do this the easy way or the hard way. How do you want it?'"

Beth looked at the jurors and they had all leaned forward to hear Karen. Beth looked over at Stan and he was glaring at Karen, while Charley was furiously writing on a notepad.

Frank asked, "What happened next?"

Karen sat back in her chair and said somberly, "He took off his clothes and raped me."

Frank hesitated and looked over at Stan, hoping the jury would follow his lead. Beth noticed that the male jurors were staring at Stan, but the females were staring at Karen. Frank had told Beth in his experience female jurors were more critical of a rape victim's testimony than male jurors. Beth felt the bile in her stomach churning and became lightheaded for a few seconds.

Frank asked, "How long was it before Ms. Mancini escaped and confronted the rapist?"

Karen shook her head and said quietly. "I don't know."
"What did you hear Ms. Mancini say to the rapist from

the doorway?"

"I heard her say, 'Don't move or I'll shoot!', but I couldn't see her because he was on top of me."

"What happened next?"

Karen leaned back in her chair. "I felt him slide off me and lean back on his knees. I saw him reach for his gun on the nightstand and I saw something go through his neck, but I didn't know what it was. He fell to the ground, and I heard him thrashing around and I looked at Beth in the doorway. That's when I saw her holding the spear gun and realized she shot him with a spear. And then I looked over and saw him reaching for his gun, so I yelled 'no' to warn Beth, and she tackled him. They started fighting, and then I heard the gun shot. I thought that . . ." Karen's voice cracked, and she hesitated, "I thought he'd shot Beth, so I yelled to see if she was okay, and she answered."

Karen started to cry, and Judge McDaniel passed her a box of Kleenex. Karen thanked him and set the box down next to the microphone and wiped her eyes with a Kleenex since her handkerchief was damp.

Frank waited for Karen to regain her composure. "What happened next?"

"I told Beth to cut me loose, and she ran to the kitchen and got a knife. She cut me loose and I grabbed her and held on. She put a sheet around me and called 911."

Frank hesitated and let the jurors digest her testimony.

"After Ms. Mancini called 911, did you ask her to take the clown mask off of the rapist?"

Karen nodded. "I did. She crawled over the bed and pulled it off his face and turned on the overhead light. That's when I realized it was Stan's handyman, Butch."

"Did you know Butch's last name at that time?"

Karen shook her head. "I just knew him as Butch. He worked as Stan's handyman fixing things at our house on the river and the beach cottage. Stan told me they both liked to shoot their guns together at the firing range, so I guess they became friends."

"You now know that his full name was Butch Redding?" Karen nodded. "Yes."

"Had you and Mr. Redding ever had a conversation before that night?"

Karen shook her head slowly. "Not really. I saw him working at the house a few times as I was going to school, and we'd say hello. But that was it."

"Were you and Mr. Redding ever alone together at your river house or the beach cottage?"

Karen shook her head vigorously. "Of course not." "Mrs. Jacoby, I'm required to ask you the next two questions to prove a crime occurred at the beach cottage, so please don't be offended." Frank took a deep breath. "Did you invite Butch Redding to your beach cottage the night he attacked and raped you?"

"I most certainly did not," Karen said indignantly. "Did you consent to sex with Butch Redding?" "No!"

Frank looked up at Judge McDaniel. "No further questions."

Judge McDaniel looked at the jurors. "This is a good time to break for lunch. I'll see you back here at one o'clock."

* * * * * *

Beth walked up to Frank at the bar after everyone had left

the courtroom. She touched his hand and said gently, "I think she did great on the stand."

"I thought she was very believable," Frank said hesitantly, "but I can't believe she wore that solid red outfit today.

She didn't look like a pitiful rape victim trying to recover from a trauma."

Beth put her hands on her hip and raised her voice. "Why does that matter? Just because she's a confident woman that dresses nicely, she is somehow unbelievable?"

Frank held his hands up in front of him as if he was surrendering. "Slow down, honey. I'm just saying you never know how jurors will react to someone that's dressed up so impeccably. I'd dare say that outfit probably cost more than what some of the women on that jury make in a month."

"Why does that matter?" Beth asked angrily.

"It shouldn't, but you never know what the jury is thinking," Frank said gently.

Beth took a deep breath and tried to calm down. "Do you want to go get some lunch?"

Frank shook his head. "No, but thanks. I brought a Diet Coke and a granola bar in my briefcase. I'm just gonna sit here and prepare for the afternoon."

Chapter 24

Judge McDaniel looked at Charley. "Mr. Kline, do you have any questions for the witness?"

Charley stood up. "I most certainly do."

Charley walked to the podium with his notes and glared at Karen. "Are you ready to answer some questions, Mrs. Jacoby?"

Karen nodded and said indignantly, "Of course." "Isn't it a fact that Butch Redding was often at your riverfront house and your beach cottage?"

"I wouldn't say often, I would say occasionally I saw him at the riverfront house, but I was never at the beach cottage when he was there."

Charley pulled a piece of paper from his notes and held it up. "Would you like to see the ledger from your husband's accountant that shows Butch Redding was paid over $50,000 last year to fix problems at the riverfront house and the beach cottage?"

Karen shrugged. "I don't know what my husband paid him. My husband was always at home, so I'm sure he saw him a lot. However, I rarely saw Mr. Redding."

"Isn't it a fact that your husband took seven golfing vacations last year while you stayed home and taught?"

"I didn't keep count, but that sounds about right." "Isn't it a fact that while your husband was out of town on golf vacations, you had an affair with Butch Redding?" Karen raised her voice. "That's a lie!"

Charley cocked his left eyebrow and gave her a smirk because he was ready to draw first blood. "Isn't it a fact that while your husband was out of town on a golf vacation, you had an affair with a fireman named Steve Busbee?"

Frank stood up. "Objection, relevance."

Judge McDaniel beckoned Frank and Charley to the bench and then looked at the jurors. "We're going to have a sidebar conference. Please enjoy the white noise."

After everyone had assumed their position at sidebar, Judge McDaniel looked at Charley. "How are her affairs relevant to this case?"

Charley answered, "Your Honor, bias of a witness is always relevant. I submit to you that if Mrs. Jacoby is having affairs, she is unhappy in her marriage, and therefore, she is more likely to stage this rape to have the pre-nup voided and get more money from her husband in the divorce."

Judge McDaniel looked at Frank, "Your response?"

Frank was flustered. "Your Honor, Mr. Kline is trying to attack the morality of Mrs. Jacoby to make her look bad in front of the jury. Any affair she might have had is not relevant to the issues in this case. She was obviously getting divorced from the defendant."

Judge McDaniel stroked his beard for a second and considered his ruling. "I'm going to allow this line of questioning. However, Mr. Kline, we don't need to know about intimate details of any affairs. Do I make myself clear?"

"Yes, Your Honor," Charley said and returned to the podium.

Judge McDaniel glanced at Debby and gave her a small smile to let her know of his continued interest in her. She quickly glanced down and began moving her machine back to its stand. Judge McDaniel sat back in his chair in frustration.

After they had returned to their places, Charley looked at Karen. "Isn't it a fact that while your husband was out of town on a golf vacation, you had an affair with a fireman named Steve Busbee?"

Karen shifted in her chair before answering. "Yes, but only because he had two affairs before. And the last one was with my cousin!"

There were a few murmurs in the courtroom and Beth looked at the jury. All the jurors were stone-faced and staring at Karen intently. Beth looked over at Stan. He was glaring at Karen and rocking in his chair.

"Isn't it true the affair lasted a month before your husband found out about it?"

Karen answered flatly, "Yes."

"Isn't it true your husband found out about the affair when he came home early from his golfing vacation and found you having sex with Mr. Busbee?"

Karen answered flatly, "Yes."

There were louder murmurs in the courtroom and Beth looked at the jury. All the jurors were looking at Karen with disapproving looks. Beth looked over at Stan, who was looking down at his table in embarrassment.

"Isn't it true your husband jumped on Mr. Busbee and started hitting him with a jewelry box that had a $200,000 diamond and emerald necklace in it?"

"I didn't know how much it cost," Karen answered. "But yes, he hit Steve with it, and Steve hit him back and knocked him out."

"Isn't it a fact that your husband had a broken nose and was taken to the hospital by ambulance?"

"Yes."

Charley held up his right pointer finger. "By the way, whatever happened to the necklace that was in the jewelry box?"

Karen said indignantly, "The next day Stan left a note on the kitchen island telling me he was divorcing me and to move out of the house within three days. So, I put the necklace with my other jewelry and packed it for moving."

Charley was incredulous. "You kept the necklace?"

"Yes," Karen said evenly.

Charley asked sarcastically, "What did you think it was—a happy divorce gift?"

Frank stood up. "Objection, argumentative." "Sustained. Move along, Mr. Kline," Judge McDaniel said.

Charley nodded at Judge McDaniel and then turned back to Karen. "How many affairs have you had during your marriage?"

Karen considered her answer for a second. "Do you mean before, or since he filed for divorce?"

Charley shook his head slowly. "I guess we've got to do a Bill Clinton analysis of defining the word 'affair,'" Charley chuckled quietly for a second. "I will define the word 'affair' as you having any sexual relationship with any man, other than your husband, between the day of your marriage and today." Charley pointed his right pointer finger at Karen. "So, again I will ask you—how many affairs have you had during your marriage?"

Karen leaned back in her chair and took a deep breath. "I had the affair with Steve before Stan filed for divorce. Steve and I have since ended our relationship, and I'm now dating Tim

Bonnoyer, a teacher I work with."

Charley wasn't done. "Are you telling this jury that you have only had two affairs during your marriage?"

Karen was irritated. "Yes."

"Are you as certain about that as you are about the rest of your testimony?"

"Absolutely," Karen said firmly.

Charley smiled and waited a few seconds because he wanted the jury to remember her answer when he called a certain witness.

"Isn't it a fact that Butch Redding said, 'I've been waiting for both of you' when you walked in the beach cottage after dinner at Cabbage Key with Ms. Mancini?"

"Yes."

"How did Mr. Redding know Beth was going to be at the beach cottage?"

Karen shrugged. "I have no idea."

"Isn't it a fact you told Mr. Redding that Ms. Mancini was going to be at the beach cottage with you?"

"No, that's a lie!"

"Isn't it true you told Mr. Redding you were taking Ms. Mancini to Cabbage Key for dinner and that he should be waiting when you returned?"

"Objection, asked and answered," Frank said as he stood up.

Judge McDaniel looked at Charley. "Sustained. Mr. Kline, please move along."

Charley looked at Karen. "Isn't it true there was no forced entry at the beach cottage?"

"Yes."

"Did you give him a key?"

"I did not. Stan must've given him a key when he told him to attack us."

"Isn't it possible Butch had a key because he was Stan's handyman?"

"That's possible," Karen said.

"Isn't it true you yelled 'no' after Butch was shot?"

Karen sat back in her chair. "I yelled 'no' because Butch had grabbed his gun from the nightstand to shoot Beth after she shot

190

him with a spear."

Charley was getting frustrated. "This is a yes or no question. Isn't it true you yelled 'no' after Butch was shot?"

Karen nodded her head and said dismissively, "Yes." "Isn't it true, you yelled 'no' after Butch was shot and your plan wasn't working?"

"No, that's not true," Karen blurted out.

Charley snickered and shook his head before he asked, "You've heard the phrase from Shakespeare 'thou doth protest too much,' haven't you?"

"I have, and I've also heard the phrase from Shakespeare, 'the first thing we do is kill all the lawyers,'" Karen quipped.

There was laughter in the courtroom, and Judge McDaniel banged his gavel. "There will be order in my courtroom. Mrs. Jacoby, I don't want any more gratuitous comments, and Mr. Kline, please ask proper questions. Now move along."

Charley looked at Karen. "Isn't it true after Mr. Redding was shot and Ms. Mancini called 911, you were alone in the bathroom for fifteen minutes?"

"Yes."

"Isn't it true you wanted to be alone so you could formulate a story to tell Ms. Mancini and the police?"

"That's a lie. I was alone because I'd just been raped, and I wanted privacy!" Karen shouted.

"Isn't it true after you came out of the bathroom, Ms. Mancini asked you if you wanted to talk about it, and you said 'no'?"

"That's true. I didn't want to talk about all the details of how I was raped."

"Isn't it true you were quiet in the rocker for another fifteen minutes until the police arrived?"

Karen took a deep breath and tried to regain her composure. "Yes, that's true."

"Isn't it true you wanted more time to formulate the story you were going to tell the police?"

Karen leaned forward and spoke into the microphone. "No, it's not true, damn it, and I'm tired of your bullshit!"

Judge McDaniel banged his gavel and glared at Karen. "There will be no profanity in my courtroom. Do you understand?

Karen answered meekly, "Yes, I'm sorry."

Frank stood up. "Your Honor, is it possible to take an afternoon break?"

Judge McDaniel nodded. "That's a great idea. We're in recess for fifteen minutes."

Chapter 25

"All rise. Judge Tom McDaniel is presiding over this court," the head bailiff announced. Judge McDaniel walked in and sat down. "Please be seated."

After everyone sat down, Judge McDaniel looked at Charley. "You may continue cross-examination of the witness."

Charley looked at Karen. "Isn't it true that during mediation, you and Ms. Mancini went to lunch at the Veranda?"

"Yes."

"During lunch, didn't Ms. Mancini's boyfriend, Frank Powers, come to your table?"

Frank exploded from his chair. "Objection!"

Judge McDaniel looked at the jury and shook his head apologetically. "More white noise."

Two of the jurors snickered quietly.

Judge McDaniel beckoned the attorneys to the sidebar. Once everyone walked forward to the bench and lined up at sidebar, Judge McDaniel looked at Charley and asked, "How is this relevant?"

Charley said adamantly, "Your Honor, it's relevant because it shows Mrs. Jacoby had knowledge that her lawyer's boyfriend was a senior prosecutor at the State Attorney's Office, and that if her lawyer was a victim of a crime, her case would get extra special attention. This goes to the defense theory that Mrs. Jacoby staged her rape to get an advantage in the divorce case."

Frank's face was crimson, and his voice was quivering with anger. "Your Honor, this is slanderous. You can't let him get away with this!"

Judge McDaniel shook his head. "I disagree, Mr. Powers. This is relevant to the defense case, and it shows bias. The jury will have to decide what weight to give it."

Returning to his position, Charley looked at Karen and asked, "During lunch, didn't Ms. Mancini's boyfriend, Frank Powers, come to your table?"

"Yes," Karen said flatly.

"Isn't it true after he returned to his table, Ms. Mancini told you he was a senior prosecutor that handled serious cases?"

"Yes."

"Isn't it true that you invited Ms. Mancini to your staged rape so she would be a believable witness and her boyfriend would vigorously prosecute your case?"

Beth couldn't believe that Frank wasn't objecting, and she squeezed her hands into fists in anger. Beth looked at the jurors. They all had stone-faced expressions as they waited for Karen to answer.

"That's preposterous! No, it's not true."

Charley put his reading glasses on and looked down at his notes. He let the jurors consider his questions and Karen's answers for a few seconds.

"Did you read the police report when your husband was arrested?"

"Yes."

"Isn't it true that a knife was found in Mr. Redding's pocket when the police searched his body?"

"Yes, that's true."

Charley pulled a piece of paper from his notes and held it up. "Are you aware that the pocketknife that was found in his pocket cost over $1,200?"

"I wasn't aware," Karen answered blandly.

Charley nodded. "It seems that the case of this pocketknife is made from walrus tusks. Scrimshaw is cut into the case by very skilled craftsmen, which is why it costs so much. Are you aware that the only place that sells this pocketknife within one hundred miles of Ft. Myers is Sally's Collectables on Sanibel?"

Karen shrugged. "I have no idea if that's true."

"Do you think a handyman spent $1,200 for a pocketknife?"

Karen was flustered. "I have no idea who bought it."

"I took your picture to the owner of Sally's Collectables, and she recognized you as one of her customers. Do you ever shop at Sally's Collectables?"

Karen nodded and answered evenly. "I go there occasionally."

"Isn't it a fact that you bought this pocketknife as a gift for

Butch Redding?"

"No, it's not," Karen said loudly.

Charley hesitated and nodded slowly. "I asked the owner if you bought a pocketknife from her shop. Do you know what her answer was?"

Karen considered her answer for a second. "I didn't buy a pocketknife there."

"Her answer was she didn't remember," Charley said and waited a second before he continued. "I guess you got lucky she didn't remember."

"Objection, argumentative!" Frank said as he stood up. "Sustained. Move along now, Mr. Kline," Judge Mc-
Daniel said sternly.

"Are you aware I subpoenaed your bank records and credit card records?"

Karen said icily, "Yes."

"Isn't it a fact you withdrew $1,500 cash from your bank at 3:50 p.m. on the day of mediation?"

"Yes."

"Isn't it a fact that you get your gas at a 7-11 near your rented condo?" "Yes."

"Are you aware that a phone call was made from the pay phone at this 7-11 to Butch Redding at 5:12 p.m. on the day of mediation?

"I have no idea," Karen said dismissively.

"Isn't it a fact you used this pay phone because you didn't want any calls from your cell phone traced to Butch Redding's phone?"

"No, that's not true," Karen said angrily.

Charley put his reading glasses back on and looked down at his notes for a second before he looked back at Karen. "Are you a member of Mensa?"

Karen shifted in her seat. "I am, but what does that have to do with this case?"

"Isn't it true that to be invited to join Mensa, you have to score in the top two percent of IQ tests?"

"That's true, but what does that have to do with this case?"

"Isn't it a fact you were asked to join Mensa when you were fifteen?"

"That's true, but what does that have to do with this case?"

"Isn't it true that you got an academic scholarship to Florida State because of your high SAT scores and that you were a member of Mensa?"

"Yes, I got an academic scholarship to Florida State."

"You're a pretty smart woman, aren't you, Mrs. Jacoby?"

Karen glared at Charley before she answered. "Yes."

Charley let her answer echo around the courtroom for a few seconds before his next question.

"Isn't it a fact, you signed a pre-nuptial agreement with your husband before you married?"

"Yes."

"Your husband was represented by Ralph Purvey, wasn't he?"

"Yes."

"Isn't it true he prepared the first draft of the pre-nuptial and presented it to you for review?"

"Yes."

"Didn't he tell you that you should get your own legal advice?"

"Yes."

"But you represented yourself instead, correct?"

"Yes."

"Isn't it true you made Mr. Purvey add one clause to the pre-nuptial before you would sign it?"

Karen was irritated. "Yes."

"Isn't it a fact that the clause added was that the pre-nuptial was invalid if your husband was convicted of a violent crime against you?"

Karen shifted in her chair before answering. "I have been friends with women who were victims of domestic violence, and I wanted to protect myself in case it ever happened to me. And now, seven years later, my fears have come true."

Charley pointed at Karen. "Isn't it true you thought you were smart enough to be your own lawyer?"

"Yes, but you don't have to be that smart to be a lawyer," Karen said.

There were a few laughs in the courtroom, and even Judge McDaniel smiled. Charley was irritated but didn't object. He forced himself to smile at Karen before he said, "You think pretty well when you're being questioned. You're able to come up with a sarcastic answer. Don't you think that shows you have superior cognitive ability?"

Karen sat back in her chair and considered her answer momentarily. "I suppose so," she said carefully.

Charley smirked and slowly shook his head. "Isn't it true that your Mensa brain concocted a way to get out of the pre-nup if your marriage failed?"

Frank flew to his feet. "Objection!" "Sustained," Judge McDaniel said sternly. Charley said, "No further questions."

Judge McDaniel looked at Frank. "Call your next witness."

"The State rests, Your Honor," Frank said.

Judge McDaniel cleared his throat and looked toward the jurors. "We're going to break for the night. Remember not to watch the news on the TV, or surf the internet, or read the paper. I'll see you tomorrow morning at nine, and we'll start the defense case."

After the jurors left the courtroom, Karen quickly walked off the witness stand and didn't look at anyone as she left the courtroom. Beth started to follow her but thought better of it. Beth pulled her cell phone out of her purse and texted Karen that she'd see her in court tomorrow, and they could sit together on the front row.

Chapter 26

Beth opened the newspaper at her breakfast table and read the headline: *STATE RESTS IN TROPHY WIFE RAPE CASE*. It was the fourth day of the trial, and the newspaper article focused on Karen's testimony. Bella and Gracie jumped on the breakfast table and lay on the newspaper for attention. Beth picked them both up and held them to her chest while she finished the article.

Beth was pleased the article quoted experts from the rape crisis center criticizing Charley for attacking a rape victim. In the newspaper article, the reporter quoted Charley's opening statement where he stated there were going to be three witnesses for the defense. Charley had promised in his opening statement there was going to be a lawyer as an expert witness about the value of a civil lawsuit and that Stan would testify, but the reporter noted the third witness wasn't named. Based on how the trial had unfolded so far, Beth had a bad feeling about this unknown witness.

Now that Karen had testified, she could come to the courtroom and watch the rest of the trial. Beth was anxious to talk to her because they hadn't seen each other for a week.

If the jury returned a guilty verdict, then the pre-nuptial would be declared invalid, so Judge Sanchez had continued the divorce case until the criminal case was over.

* * * * * *

Beth saw Karen walk in the back of the courtroom and motioned for her to sit next to her on the front row. Karen was dressed in a turquoise blue dress and white pumps. She made her way forward, and a few of the courtroom spectators whispered to each other and pointed. Beth looked at Stan and saw him staring at Karen with laser darts as she walked forward. Stan tapped Charley's shoulder, and he turned around and saw Karen sitting down next to Beth. He looked at Stan and shrugged his shoulders before he looked back at his notes.

Beth reached out and held Karen's hand. She asked sympathetically, "How are you doing?"

Karen smiled. "I'm fine. Yesterday was a little rough, but I can't wait for Stan to testify today. He's such an arrogant prick, I'm sure Frank will tear him to shreds on cross-examination."

Beth nodded. "I guarantee it."

The door behind the bench opened, and Judge McDaniel walked in.

"All rise. Judge Tom McDaniel is presiding over this court," the head bailiff announced.

Judge McDaniel sat down and said politely, "Please be seated."

After everyone sat down, Judge McDaniel looked at Charley. "Call your first witness."

Charley stood up and announced, "The Defense calls Duke Godfrey."

The assistant bailiff walked to the witness room and opened the door. Duke walked into the courtroom, and Frank looked at him curiously as he walked up the aisle, trying to remember his connection to the case. Duke was wearing a white Columbia fishing shirt with blue jeans and topsiders. He walked to the front of the courtroom and was sworn in by the clerk. He sat down in the witness stand and faced Charley.

"Please give us your full name."

"My name is Duke Ellington Godfrey."

Judge McDaniel and most of the courtroom chuckled quietly.

Duke looked at Charley and shrugged. "My mama was a jazz fan."

Charley didn't miss a beat. "Son, your mama has good taste."

"Thanks," Duke said quietly.

Charley cleared his throat. "How do you know Stan and Karen Jacoby?"

"I've been their fishing guide for the past four years."

"What did you do for a living before you were a fishing guide?"

"I was in the Marines for eight years and was honorably discharged."

Beth noticed his long wavy black hair and decided he had

let it grow after eight years of the jarhead look. Duke was about six feet tall and wiry, like a basketball point guard. He was tan all over, except for the skin around his eyes that was apparently covered everyday with sunglasses, giving him a raccoon look.

"How did you meet Dr. Jacoby?"

"I had won two tarpon tournaments in a row up at Boca Grande, and Dr. Jacoby was waiting at my boat one morning at the dock. He said he wanted to charter me, and I asked which day and he said for the next two months." Duke smiled. "We bonded."

Charley smiled. "Did he charter you for the next two months?"

"Yes, he did. God love 'im," Duke said sincerely.

Stan actually chuckled for the first time at the trial, along with Judge McDaniel and the jurors. Beth didn't know what to think, but she knew it wasn't good if Stan and Judge McDaniel were happy with the small talk of the first witness for the defense. Beth glanced over at Karen, and she looked uncomfortable.

"Son, let me ask you a question. Did Dr. Jacoby and Karen like the same type of fishing?"

"No, sir," Duke said as he shook his head. "Dr. Jacoby liked tarpon fishing, and Karen liked fishing the back waters for snook and redfish."

"You're aware that Karen is divorcing Dr. Jacoby, aren't you sir?"

Duke shifted in his seat. "Yes, sir. Karen has told me she's gettin' a divorce."

"Have you ever been married before, Mr. Godfrey?" Duke shook his head slowly and said uneasily, "Naw, I'm not really the marrying type."

Charley had hired a private investigator to find out if Duke and Karen had been sleeping together. The private investigator had followed Duke to his favorite bar the previous two weeks looking for information. The private investigator had paid $1,000 to two bartenders, on different nights, at Duke's favorite bar for information on Duke's love life. The low down had been the same from each bartender—Duke was a player. Duke had never specifically admitted to an affair with Karen, but he'd made the comment to one bartender that rich women need love too. Charley was ready to gamble with Duke's honesty and his knowledge of

Karen's lust for healthy, young men.

"Isn't it a fact, that when the police interviewed you after the incident on Cayo Costa, you told them, 'Karen said to pick them up at eight, but they might've slept late so just come up to the cottage for coffee'?"

Duke nodded. "Yes, that's what she told me."

"So, she trusted you enough to come to the cottage early in the morning, even though she might've been walking around in her nighties?"

Duke shrugged. "I guess so."

"Now, Duke, isn't it true that you would meet delivery drivers at Four Winds Marina to bring supplies to the beach cottage with your boat?"

"Yes, sir. Dr. Jacoby paid me to do that on a regular basis."

"Isn't it true that Karen was at the beach cottage sometimes when you made deliveries?"

Duke shifted in his seat. "Sometimes, she was there. Sometimes Dr. Jacoby was there. Sometimes no one was there, but I had a key."

"Isn't it true, that while the divorce has been pending, you've taken Karen fishing alone?"

Duke nodded. "Yes, sir. She liked to fish, and in the past few months she'd go to the cottage by herself sometimes, and she'd pay me to take her fishing."

"Isn't it true that when just you and Karen went fishing on your boat, she'd wear her bikini?"

Duke blushed and shrugged apologetically. "On nice days, sometimes she'd wear a bikini."

Beth glanced over at Karen and noticed she was nervously tapping her nails on the bench. Beth looked at the jurors and saw two male jurors looking at Karen. Beth then looked at Stan and saw he was cracking his knuckles underneath the table, frowning. Beth also turned to Frank and he was rolling his neck sitting at his table, clearly uncomfortable where this testimony was heading.

"Now, Duke, you served our country proudly when you were in the Marines, didn't you?"

"Yes sir, I did," Duke said proudly.

"When you entered the Marines, you took an oath to honor the constitution, didn't you?"

"Yes sir, I did."

"When you took your oath, did you mean it?" "Of course I did," Duke said indignantly.

"Isn't it true that you fought to preserve our constitution and our right to fair trials?"

"Yes, sir."

"Isn't it true, a fair trial requires that witnesses honor oaths they've taken?"

Duke nodded. "Yes, sir."

"So, son, wouldn't you agree that if you dishonor your oath to tell the truth here today, you dishonor the Marines?"

"Yes, sir!"

"When you took an oath this morning to tell the truth, did you mean it?"

"Yes, sir!"

Charley took a handkerchief from his left front pants pocket and cleaned his glasses, taking time to let everyone in the courtroom focus on him. After a few seconds, he asked forcefully, "I'm asking you a question, as a veteran, and someone that has taken an oath, did you have an affair with Karen Jacoby in the past six months?"

Duke looked down for a few seconds and then looked at Judge McDaniel. "Do I have to answer this question?"

Judge McDaniel nodded and said solemnly. "You have to answer truthfully."

Duke was defeated and took a deep breath before he said quietly, "Yes."

There were murmurs throughout the courtroom as Charley turned around and stared at Karen. She was looking at her feet, and Beth had shut her eyes. Stan was smiling like he'd won the lottery.

Charley turned toward Judge McDaniel and said solemnly, "No further questions, Your Honor."

Charley walked slowly to his table as he shook his head in disgust. He patted Stan on the back before he sat down. Beth looked up and saw all the jurors glaring at Karen.

Frank stood up shakily and said quietly, "No questions, Your Honor."

Judge McDaniel looked at Charley. "Call your next witness."

Charley stood up and announced, "The Defense calls Patrick Benning."

The assistant bailiff walked to the witness room and opened the door. Patrick walked into the courtroom. He was wearing a blue suit, with a starched white shirt, and a diagonally striped green and blue tie. He walked to the front of the courtroom and was sworn in by the clerk. He sat down in the witness stand and faced Charley.

"Please give us your full name."

"My name is Patrick Landon Benning."

Charley held his left hand toward the jurors. "Could you tell us your educational background?"

Patrick nodded. "I received my B.A. in history from Georgetown, and I got my law degree from Yale."

"How long have you been practicing law in Florida?" "I've been practicing twenty-six years here in Ft. Myers,

and I have my own firm."

"What is your primary area of practice?"

"I specialize in civil litigation regarding personal injury claims and intentional torts. I represent plaintiffs about 90% of the time, but sometimes I represent defendants."

"Have you ever handled civil battery cases?" "I have."

"Could you please explain the different types of damages in civil battery cases?"

Patrick nodded and looked at the jurors. "The first type of damages is out-of-pocket expenses, such as medical bills or lost wages, and the loss of bodily functions and scarring. The second type of damages in civil battery cases is punitive damages and they're fact sensitive, based on the financial strength of the defendant. A jury is instructed by the judge to consider the net worth of a defendant, and to award an amount of money that will punish the defendant and discourage him from doing the same type of conduct in the future."

"Has Dr. Jacoby hired you as an expert witness for his case?"

Patrick nodded. "He has."

"Are you familiar with the allegations against Dr. Jacoby?"

"I certainly am."

"As you know, Dr. Jacoby denies the criminal charges

against him. But, if Dr. Jacoby was convicted of these charges, could his wife file a civil battery case against him after that?"

"Yes, she could, and she'd potentially have a very valuable lawsuit against her husband. The civil jury could award her actual damages and punitive damages, if they believed her."

"Could the jury award damages even if he wasn't the person that touched her?"

Patrick nodded. "If the person that touched her did so at his direction, then he is just as liable as if he did it, according to Florida law."

"Are you aware of Dr. Jacoby's net worth?"

"I have reviewed his financial affidavit, and he's worth slightly over fifty million dollars."

Beth looked at the jurors. They were all stone-faced.

Charley held his hands out to his side in a questioning manner. "How much money could a civil jury award to his wife for punitive damages?"

Patrick scratched his chin for a few seconds. "A civil jury has very broad powers when awarding punitive damages. The jury would be told his net worth, and they could award all it to the wife if they thought it was warranted."

Charley stared at Karen for a few seconds before he faced Judge McDaniel. "I have no further questions, Your Honor."

Judge McDaniel looked at Frank. "Do you have any questions?"

"Just one," Frank said as he walked to the podium.

When he reached the podium, he pointed at Stan. "How much money has the defendant paid you for your testimony?"

Patrick shifted in his seat and said uncomfortably, "My fee includes my time reviewing his case and testifying here today."

"How much?" Frank asked loudly.

"Fifty-thousand dollars," Patrick said unapologetically.

There were murmurs through the courtroom, and Judge McDaniel looked sideways at Patrick. Beth looked at the jurors and they all sat back in their chairs with smirks on their faces and crossed their arms. Charley sat up straight and grimaced for the first time during the trial.

Frank shook his head in disgust. "I don't have any other questions."

As Frank walked back to his table, Judge McDaniel looked at Charley. "Call your next witness."

Charley stood up and announced, "The Defense calls Dr. Stan Jacoby."

There was silence in the courtroom. Judge McDaniel sat back in his chair and stroked his beard. Frank turned toward Stan and sized up his prey. Beth noticed every juror watching Stan as he slowly stood up at the defense table. Stan was wearing a perfectly pressed dark green suit with a custom tailored, white starched shirt, and a pure silk yellow tie with small white dots inside black circles.

Judge McDaniel looked at the clerk and said dutifully, "Please swear him in."

The clerk swore him in as he stood at the defense table.

Judge McDaniel motioned to the witness stand, and Stan walked around the defense table. After he settled in the witness chair, he looked up at Judge McDaniel and stated, "I'm ready."

Charley had prepared for this theatric moment. "Dr. Jacoby, you're aware that the United States Constitution states that you don't have to testify, aren't you?"

Stan nodded solemnly. "I am aware."

"But here you are," Charley held his left hand out toward the jury, "prepared to tell the truth to rebut your wife's lies."

"Objection!" Frank yelled.

"Sustained!" Judge McDaniel said furiously.

The jurors shifted in their seats based on the intensity of the exchange. Charley had anticipated Judge McDaniel's wrath, but he knew it was a pivotal moment at trial and was ready for the obligatory censure.

"Bailiff, escort the jury to their room," Judge McDaniel said forcefully as he stared bug-eyed at Charley. The jurors quickly scurried to their room before Judge McDaniel called lightening down from the heavens to strike down Charley.

Debby shifted in her seat directly under Judge McDaniel's bench, and avoided looking at anyone in the courtroom because she recognized his angry tone of voice. Frank wasn't sure what to do, so he sat down and waited in eager anticipation for Judge McDaniel's words.

After the jury room door shut, the head bailiff turned and nodded. Judge McDaniel looked at Charley and blared, "You have pushed my patience, Mr. Kline. When this trial is over, I'm holding a contempt of court hearing, and I'll

decide how much jail time I'm going to give you based on your intentional violation of the rules of this court." Judge McDaniel shook his right pointer finger at Charley. "At this time, you're on notice of my view of your actions. If you want to keep adding to the amount of jail time you're getting, keep it up!"

The courtroom was silent, and everyone stared at Charley, but he looked back at Judge McDaniel unrepentantly and said, "Your Honor, I mean no disrespect to this court. However, I have an ethical obligation to my client to vigorously represent him. I've been forced to sit here and listen to lies told about my client, and I've not been able to respond until now. Therefore, I think my questions are proper."

Judge McDaniel leaned back in his chair and stared at the ceiling while he considered his response. Frank turned toward Beth and shrugged slightly. Everyone else in the courtroom was scared to breathe.

Judge McDaniel finally looked down at Charley and took a deep breath before he spoke. "Mr. Kline, your actions are wrong, and I'll deal with you in the future. However, the defendant has the right to testify, and he shouldn't be penalized for his counsel being a horse's ass! Therefore, I'm ordering you to follow the rules of this court from now on. You haven't done that to this point, and you'll suffer consequences in the future for your actions. Do I make myself clear?"

Charley nodded. "Yes, Your Honor."

Judge McDaniel looked at his head bailiff and said bitterly, "Bring the jury in."

The head bailiff knocked on the jury door and gently opened it. He asked the jurors to return and held the door open as they hesitantly walked back in and sat down. Frank caught Beth's eye and slowly shook his head in disgust.

Judge McDaniel looked at Charley and said matter-of-factly, "Please continue."

"Yes, Your Honor," Charley said respectfully. "Dr. Jacoby, could you tell the jury where you were born?"

Stan looked at the jurors. "I was born in Akron, Ohio, and we moved to Ft. Myers when I was seven."

"What did your parents do for a living?"

"They were both schoolteachers in the public school system here in Lee County."

"Are you an only child?" "Yes."

"Could you tell the jury your educational background after high school?"

Stan nodded. "I went to Maryland and got my undergraduate degree in chemistry there. After that, I went to the University of Florida and got my dentistry degree."

"Did you marry your first wife while you were in dentistry school?"

"I did. We amicably divorced after four years of marriage."

"How long did you practice dentistry here in Ft. Myers?"

"I was a dentist for eleven years before I retired."

"Dr. Jacoby, could you tell the jury how you were able to retire so early?"

"Both of my parents died in a plane wreck, and I inherited some money. My stockbroker convinced me to invest in a new startup internet company called Google."

There were a few jealous snickers in the courtroom.

Stan continued his answer. "I was lucky. The company took off, and my stock increased exponentially. I was able to retire early."

Beth saw two female jurors on the back row look at each other sideways and cock their eyebrows.

Charley turned and looked at Karen sitting on the front row. He turned back to Stan and asked, "When did you first meet your current wife, Karen Jacoby?"

"I met her at an art auction for a charity. She was with her old boyfriend, and a mutual friend introduced us."

Charley hesitated. "Dr. Jacoby, do you remember how the mutual friend introduced you to Karen Jacoby?"

"I do," he said and sighed. "At the time, I didn't think much of it. But now, years later when I find myself in this situation, it was a very significant introduction."

"What were the exact words your friend used when he introduced you to Karen Jacoby?"

Stan straightened up in his chair and said bitterly, "Karen, this is my friend Stan Jacoby. He got lucky and invested in Google

208

when it was new. All he does now is sit around and count his money."

The courtroom was silent, and Stan glared at Karen for a few seconds before Charley asked his next question.

"Did you and Karen hit if off that night?"

Stan sat back in his chair and took a deep breath. "I was immediately attracted to her because she's beautiful. But she was there with her boyfriend, so it was hard to talk to her much. But I saw her staring at me the whole evening. I found out which school she taught at from our mutual friend and sent her three dozen red roses to her classroom the next day. On the card, I had the florist put my cell number and asked her to call me. She did, and we got to know each other with phone calls. We met for coffee a few times, and I convinced her to break up with her boyfriend and we started dating."

"How long was it until you married her?"

"We married six months after we met at the art auction." "Why did you marry her?"

Stan closed his eyes for a second and then said solemnly, "I loved her."

Beth was livid with Stan's act and wondered how many times he and Charley had practiced this dog and pony show.

She looked over at the jurors and they were all stone-faced as they watched Stan.

"Why did you have your wife sign a pre-nuptial?"

"I wanted to protect myself in case of divorce. I was retired, and I valued my financial security. I was concerned that she might get bored with me as I got older, that she would want to get a younger boyfriend. As it turns out, my fears were justified."

"Did you know she had boyfriends during the marriage?"

Stan shook his head adamantly. "Not until I came home early from a trip and walked in on her having sex in our bedroom. Before that, I had no idea she had a boyfriend. And now I know she's had at least three other boyfriends."

Charley held his hands out to his side in a questioning manner. "Which three men are you talking about?"

"I heard my wife testify about the teacher she's dating now, and earlier today, I found out she's screwing our fishing guide." Stan's face was red, and he glared at Karen. "And she had to be doing Butch to get him to help her with the staged rape."

"Objection."

"Sustained. Move along, Mr. Kline," Judge McDaniel said firmly.

Charley nodded. "Tell the jury how you met Butch Redding."

Stan took a deep breath and leaned back in his chair. "I met Butch at my neighbor's house. He was redoing the gutters, and I noticed how meticulous he was in his work. He was on time every day and took only thirty minutes for lunch. One day I went over and introduced myself and asked if he could do some work at my house.

"I liked his work, so I kept him on retainer. I trusted him, so I gave him keys to my house and the beach cottage. He had a small johnboat, so he was able to get back and forth to the island whenever something broke. Once I filed for divorce, Karen and I alternated weeks at the beach cottage. Karen would always text me when something broke at the beach cottage, and I'd send Butch out to fix it. He never complained, and now I know why!"

Charley hesitated before he asked the next question and let the jury consider the opportunity Butch and Karen had for an affair on an isolated island.

"Dr. Jacoby, did you ever show Mr. Redding where the Tunnel of Love was located in the mangroves near your beach cottage?"

"I did not," Stan said indignantly. "Why would I show a man where couples go to have sex?"

Charley walked back to his table and grabbed an eight-by-ten-inch exhibit. He looked at Judge McDaniel and said, "May I freely approach the witness, Your Honor?"

Judge McDaniel nodded. "Yes, you may."

"I'm showing you Defense Exhibit 1, Dr. Jacoby. Do you recognize this?"

Stan nodded. "I do. It's a picture from Google maps showing the Tunnel of Love that I printed out. It's real easy on Google maps. You type in 'Cayo Costa Island' and when it comes up, you expand the map until you can see 'Murdock Bayou' on the southern part of the island. The Tunnel of Love opens up at 'Murdock Bayou' and runs northwest through the island and ends right before it hits the Gulf of Mexico."

Charley looked at Judge McDaniel. "I move to enter Defense Exhibit 1 into evidence."

Judge McDaniel looked briefly at the map and admitted it.

Charley said, "Your Honor, I'd like to publish this to the jury."

Judge McDaniel nodded and looked at his head bailiff. "Please show this to the jury." He then looked at the jury. "Just like last time, please look briefly at the exhibit and pass it to the next juror when you're done. You'll have time during deliberations to study it more fully."

It took the jury about a minute for all six to look at the exhibit.

Charley turned back toward Stan. "Do you have any idea why Butch Redding parked his boat in the Tunnel of Love the night your wife and Ms. Mancini were tied up by him in the cottage?"

Stan shook his head. "Karen must've showed him the Tunnel of Love and told him to park his boat there to hide it from Ms. Mancini."

Charley hesitated momentarily and let Stan's comment echo around the courtroom before he asked, "Did you and Butch enjoy shooting together at the gun range?"

Stan nodded. "Yes. One day when he was working at the house, he saw me cleaning my guns after shooting at the range. He mentioned he liked to shoot, so we started going together to the range about once a month."

"Was your wife ever alone with Butch at your riverfront estate or the Cayo Costa beach cottage?"

"All the time," Stan said bitterly. "I would travel on golf vacations at least seven times a year. There was always stuff breaking or something needing maintenance, so Butch went to the house and beach cottage all the time. If I was out of town or playing golf at the club, he'd be there alone with Karen. I trusted her, so I didn't think anything of it.

And like I said earlier, once the divorce started, I'd send him out to Cayo Costa to fix stuff at the cottage whenever Karen texted me. Karen was alone with him on the island, and I can only guess what they were doing."

"Objection, speculation," Frank said as he stood up.

"Sustained," Judge McDaniel said and looked at Stan.

"Mr. Jacoby, I don't want you to speculate about things. I only want you to testify about what you saw and heard. Do you understand?"

Stan nodded. "Yes, Your Honor."

Charley asked, "Did you pay Butch Redding to kidnap and rape your wife?"

"I did not," Stan said indignantly.

"Did you pay Butch Redding to kidnap your wife's divorce attorney?"

Stan looked at Beth and shook his head. "No, I didn't." "Do you remember your mediation?"

"I do. It wasn't one of my finer moments." "Did you yell and curse at Beth Mancini?"

"I did. It was wrong, but my temper took over. I'm sorry it happened."

Beth was sick of this dog and pony show. The questions and answers were so obviously rehearsed that the jury had to see this farce for what it was.

"Let's go back to before you married Karen. Did your attorney, Ralph Purvey, prepare a pre-nuptial at your request?"

"He did."

"Did he advise you that Karen should get her own attorney?"

Stan nodded. "He told me I had to pay for an attorney for her, and I agreed. I asked Karen to get her own attorney, but she insisted she didn't need one. She told me she'd sign it if I'd add the clause about the pre-nup being voided if she was a victim of domestic violence. I agreed because I knew I'd never do anything to her. Mr. Purvey added the clause, and she signed it. I didn't think anything of it until all this happened. I guess she's a lot smarter than me."

"Objection," Frank said as he stood up.

"Sustained," Judge McDaniel said and looked over at Stan. "Mr. Jacoby, no more gratuitous comments."

Stan looked down. "Yes, Your Honor."

Charley waited for Stan to look up. "Did you call Butch twice on the day your wife and Ms. Mancini were tied up by him at the beach house?"

"I did."

212

"What were you talking about?"

"I had some tiles that were cracked in one of my bathrooms at the river house, and we talked about the materials and how much it would cost. He was going to Home Depot for another project, and he told me to call him back later after he'd priced the job out."

"Did you tell him that Ms. Mancini was going to be with your wife at the beach cottage for the weekend?"

Stan shook his head. "No, I had no idea she was going to be there."

"When did you find out that Butch Redding was killed at your beach cottage?"

"When I read about it in Sunday's paper. The article didn't say anything about Karen and Ms. Mancini being tied up. The article just stated there was a domestic dispute and that Butch had been killed. I tried to call Karen all day on Sunday, but the calls went straight to voice mail."

"What happened the next day at your house around four p.m.?"

Stan sat up in his chair. "I heard the doorbell and walked to the front door. I looked out the sidelight and saw a man in a wrinkled blue sports jacket and two uniformed deputies behind him. I answered the door, and the man in the wrinkled jacket told me I was under arrest. I asked him what for, and he told me to turn around to be cuffed. I asked him what he was talking about, and he became irritated."

"Did you use profanity?"

"I'm sure I did, but I can't recall exactly what I said because I was very angry."

"You now know that the man in the wrinkled sports jacket was Detective Dagle?"

"I do."

"Did you hear him testify earlier in the trial?"

"I did, and he was wearing a much nicer jacket." "Do you agree with everything he testified about?" "Ninety percent of what he said is accurate."

Charley held his hands out to his side in a questioning manner. "What is inaccurate?"

Stan sat up in his seat. "I'd just gotten out of the shower, and I was in my robe. When he handcuffed me and I realized I was actually being arrested, I asked him if I could change out of my robe and put on clothes. He told me no, it'd be easier for his homeboys at the jail to get at my hemorrhoids. I cursed him and told him I'd get him fired, and he laughed at me."

Charley put on his reading glasses and looked at his notes as he let the jurors consider Detective Dagle's manners. Beth looked at the jurors and saw one man on the front row shaking his head uncomfortably. Frank was concerned because the testimony about the robe rang true to his seasoned ears. He also knew from his experience that jurors detested policemen that abused their powers.

"Did Detective Dagle ever tell you what you were being arrested for?"

"Finally," Stan said disgustedly, "on the ride to the jail. He told me I was being arrested for conspiracy to commit kidnapping and rape. I asked him kidnapping and rape of whom, and he just laughed. He told me I knew and to stop playing dumb."

"What did you do next?"

Stan shook his head slowly. "I went crazy in the back of his car. I was yelling and cursing and kicking the windows. I felt like a caged animal, and I knew I hadn't done anything wrong. It was a nightmare. And he laughed at me the whole time."

Charley's tone softened. "What happened at the jail?" "I was fingerprinted, and my mug shot was taken. And then they put me in the holding cell with everybody else that had been arrested that day."

Charley hesitated. "Were you still in your robe?" Stan nodded and said quietly, "I was."

Charley asked, "What happened?"

Frank stood up and said, "Objection, there's no relevance to this question."

Judge McDaniel shook his head. "Overruled. I want to know what happened."

Charley said gently, "Stan, you can answer the question."

Stan took a deep breath and said uneasily, "There were about twenty-five younger guys in there, and they were all muscle-bound and had tattoos. They started whistling and grabbing their crotches. They called me fresh meat, pretty boy, and rump roast. And then one of them grabbed my robe and pulled it off and everyone laughed. And…"

Stan looked down and put his face in his hands. After a few seconds, he looked up and his face was pale, but he took a deep breath and continued, "And then I laid on the floor in a fetal position and listened to everybody laughing. One prisoner kicked me, and that's when the guards came to the door with their tasers and told everyone to backup. They opened the door and threw me a jumpsuit and I quickly put it on. I sat on one of the cold steel benches and couldn't sleep because I was scared of what might happen to me if I let my guard down. I waited there until the next morning when the judge set bail. It was the worst night of my life."

Charley waited a few seconds and let everyone in the courtroom consider Stan's ordeal at the jail. "Dr. Jacoby, I have one last question for you. Why have you pled not guilty to the charges against you?"

Stan looked at the jury. "Because I didn't do what I've been accused of," Stan said firmly. "I've been framed for this crime by my wife because she wants my money!"

"No further questions, Your Honor."

Judge McDaniel banged his gavel. "We'll recess for lunch until one o'clock."

Chapter 27

Frank, Beth, and Karen were sitting in the back of the main dining room at the Veranda, looking at menus. Frank had requested a quiet table in the back for privacy. Frank and Beth knew what they were going to order, but they looked at the menu to avoid talking to Karen about Duke's testimony. Karen also knew what she was going to order, but she looked at the menu as she tweaked her forthcoming apology about Duke in her mind.

The waitress walked up and looked at Beth. "What can I get for you today?"

Beth sat her menu down. "I'll have the mandarin orange salad with chicken and honey mustard dressing. Iced tea to drink, please."

The waitress looked at Karen. "What can I get for you, ma'am?"

"A Caesar salad and a dirty martini," Karen said quietly. The waitress looked at Frank. "And you, sir?"

Frank smiled at the waitress. "A bowl of the black beans and rice with iced tea."

The waitress picked up the menus and walked away, leaving everyone awkwardly quiet for a few seconds. They all listened to the lunchtime buzz drifting through the tables as they waited for someone to speak.

"I have to apologize," Karen said finally. "I didn't think my fling with Duke was anybody's business. I didn't think it would come up at trial. I'm sorry."

Beth leaned forward and said irritably, "Don't you remember when I went with you to Frank's office last week to prepare for trial, and he told you to tell him everything?"

Karen nodded and looked down.

Frank shook his head and said pensively, "If we had brought it up on direct, it wouldn't had been so bad. You were separated from Stan and going through a divorce, and nobody cares who you're sleeping with now. But, by you denying under oath that you were sleeping with anybody else, you are now a proven liar.

And Charley will bring that up during closing argument, I guarantee it."

Karen nodded and started to tear up. "Excuse me for a minute. I've got to go to the ladies' room."

Karen stood up and walked to the other side of the dining room and entered the bathroom. Beth and Frank looked at each other and sighed. Beth reached for Frank's hand and held his fingers tenderly. The waitress brought their iced teas to the table, and they both picked up their glasses and took a long drink. Frank leaned back in his chair and looked at the ceiling in frustration.

Beth finally spoke. "What do you think?"

Frank shrugged his shoulders and said quietly, "Unless I can make Stan look bad on the stand this afternoon, we've lost."

Chapter 28

"All rise. Judge Tom McDaniel is presiding over this court," the head bailiff announced.

Judge McDaniel walked in and sat down. "Please be seated."

After everyone sat down, Judge McDaniel looked at Frank. "Mr. Powers, you may cross-examine the witness."

Frank walked to the podium with his notes and asked loudly, "How long were you sleeping with your mistress before your wife found out?"

"Objection, relevance," Charley said as he stood up. Judge McDaniel shook his head. "Overruled, Mr. Kline.

You've opened the door by inquiring about Mrs. Jacoby's affairs. What's good for the goose is good for the gander, so I'm going to let the State question him about his affairs, also."

For the first time during the trial, Charley had made a miscalculation and wasn't sure what to say, so he quietly sat down. He hoped Stan would keep his cool, but he knew better.

Frank asked loudly, "How long were you sleeping with your mistress before your wife found out?"

Stan shifted in his seat and answered matter-of-factly. "Tami and I dated about two months before Karen found out."

"Isn't it true you never told your wife you were having an affair during the two months?"

Stan shrugged. "I don't know any husband that tells his wife about his affairs."

"Isn't it true you were dishonest for two months before your wife found out about your affair?"

Charley stood up and blared out, "Objection, improper characterization."

"Overruled," Judge McDaniel said firmly. "Sit down, Mr. Kline."

Frank pointed at Stan. "Mr. Jacoby, I'm going to ask you again. Isn't it true you were dishonest for two months before your wife found out about your affair?"

"Mr. Powers," Stan said condescendingly, "you will address me as Dr. Jacoby."

Frank was tired of Stan's obnoxious behavior and looked at Judge McDaniel. "Objection, Your Honor. May we approach?"

Judge McDaniel nodded and looked at the jury. "More white noise while we address the legal issues."

Everyone assumed his and her place at sidebar, and Frank said, "Your Honor, there is no legal reason that I'm required to address him as *doctor*. In fact, the custom in every courtroom in this building is to address the witness by his or her surname. I'm objecting to the defendant requiring me to call him doctor."

Judge McDaniel held up his hand to Charley before he spoke. "Mr. Kline, I don't need to hear any argument, because Mr. Powers is correct." Judge McDaniel turned and looked at Stan as he said firmly, "No one in my courtroom is required to call you *doctor* Jacoby. They are only required to address you as *mister* Jacoby. If your lawyer wants to call you *doctor* Jacoby, he can, but no one else must. Do I make myself clear, *mister* Jacoby?"

Stan leaned back in his chair and glared at Judge McDaniel. "I understand," Stan said irritably.

"You may ask you question, Mr. Powers," Judge McDaniel said.

After everyone returned to their places, Frank asked, "Mr. Jacoby, I'm going to ask you for the third time, isn't it true you were dishonest for two months before your wife found out about your affair?"

Stan's face was red. He was fed up with Frank and Judge McDaniel, so he was ready for payback. He'd paid a private investigator $20,000 to thoroughly research Frank's background in preparation for trial and was ready to flaunt his knowledge.

Stan answered sarcastically, "I was as honest as your mother was when she was screwing your father's lawyer while he was in prison."

Frank's face turned pale and he squeezed the podium.

Beth could see his hands shaking and saw the veins popping out in his forehead. She saw pure hatred in Frank's eyes and was taken aback—she'd never seen Frank like that before.

"Take the jury out," Judge McDaniel bellowed.

The head bailiff opened the jury room and motioned for the jury to enter. The jurors scurried to the sanctuary of their room before the fireworks exploded in the courtroom. Frank felt his head pounding and was dizzy with adrenaline, so he sat down at his table. Charley had warned Stan not to interject Frank's embarrassing background into his answers, but Stan didn't care about courtroom etiquette; he just wanted to be acquitted, and he was certain it would help. Once all the jurors were in the jury room, the head bailiff shut the door and nodded at Judge McDaniel.

"Mr. Jacoby," Judge McDaniel seethed, "I'm warning you not to add information to a question because you think it's cute. You'll only answer the question that is asked of you in a very respectful manner. If you make another gratuitous comment, you'll find yourself back in that holding cell that you have such fond memories of. Now, do I make myself clear?"

Stan nodded his head and answered curtly, "Yes." Judge McDaniel sat up in his chair and pointed at Stan.

"I'm still not sure you understand me, Mr. Jacoby. If you do it again, I'll hold you in contempt of court and sentence you to six months in jail. You've already testified that you don't do well in jail, so you better consider your answers to Mr.

Powers' questions before you respond. Now again, do you understand me?"

Stan was seething inside from this public dressing down, but he pulled himself together and said quietly, "Yes."

Judge McDaniel looked at his head bailiff and said wearily, "Bring the jury back in."

The head bailiff knocked quietly on the jury door and opened it. He informed them the judge was ready to resume the trial and they all walked back in. Once they sat down, Judge McDaniel looked at Frank and nodded toward him.

Frank walked to the podium and glared at Stan. "Your first affair was with a woman named Tami, wasn't it?"

"Yes," Stan said evenly. "What's Tami's last name?"

"That's none of your business!" Stan said irritably. Judge McDaniel banged his gavel and said forcefully,

"Answer the question, Mr. Jacoby."

Stan considered his response for a few seconds and said smugly, "Smith."

Charley looked down in frustration and shook his head slowly. All the good things he'd done so far in the trial were being forgotten because of Stan's bulbous ego.

Frank pointed at Stan and asked sarcastically, "Does lying come easy for you, Mr. Jacoby?"

Stan sat back in his chair and said evenly, "I'm not lying. That's her name."

Frank shrugged his shoulders. "Where does she live?" "I don't know. She moved back to Canada."

"Where did she live in Ft. Myers when you were having an affair?"

Stan hesitated for a second as he made up his lie. "I don't know. We always met in a hotel because she was married."

Frank looked skeptically at Stan and shook his head. "Let's move to your second affair. Isn't it true you slept with your wife's cousin on the day your wife buried her mother?"

Stan glared at Frank and realized there was no way around the truth. He answered quietly, "Yes."

"Isn't it true that your wife had her affair with the fireman after your two affairs?"

"Yes."

"Isn't it true you filed for divorce the day after you found out about your wife's affair with the fireman?"

"Yes," Stan muttered.

"Why is it all right for you to have affairs and not your wife?"

Stan shifted in his chair before he answered. "I made my mistakes, but I apologized to my wife and tried to make it better. Once I saw her in bed with another man, I stopped trusting her, so I filed for divorce."

Frank held his hands out to his side in a questioning manner. "Your wife found you in bed with her cousin and she gave you another chance, didn't she?"

Stan shook his head. "Not really. She was very distant after that."

Frank shook his right pointer finger at Stan and raised his voice. "Isn't it true you believe in double standards for husbands and wives?"

"No, I don't. It was a different situation," Stan said

condescendingly.

Beth looked at the jurors, and they were all rolling their eyes at Stan's answer.

Frank shook his head in doubt. "Let's switch topics to the mediation on the divorce case. Do you remember yelling at your wife's attorney, Ms. Mancini?"

"I do, and I apologize for that," Stan said matter-offactly.

"Isn't it true you never apologized before today?" "Well," Stan said slowly, "my attorney advised me not to say anything before today because you would try and use it against me."

Frank shook his head in disgust. "How many times did you and your attorney practice your questions and answers before today?"

"Objection, attorney-client privilege," Charley pleaded as he stood up.

"Overruled. You need to answer the question, Mr. Jacoby," Judge McDaniel said sternly.

Stan shrugged his shoulders. "We never practiced exact questions and answers. He just told me the types of questions he would ask and the types of questions you would ask to try and make me look bad."

Frank raised his voice. "How many times did you meet to talk about the types of questions?"

Stan scratched his head for a second. "We met every day the week before the trial started. We would spend about two hours every day analyzing the evidence and talking about the types of questions."

Charley took a deep breath and looked at the ceiling in frustration. It was one of Charley's favorite tricks he learned from his criminal law professor in law school. When Abraham Lincoln was a criminal defense lawyer before he was president, he developed a trick when the evidence was against him. He'd look up at the cathedral ceiling in the old courtrooms and stare at a spot and hoped the jury would look up there, purely out of curiosity. Of course, if jurors focused on the spot, they couldn't hear the damaging testimony against the defendant, and they wouldn't convict.

Frank held his hands out to his side and asked sarcastically,

"How do you think your performance is going so far?"

"Objection, argumentative," Charley said as he stood up. "Sustained. Move along, Mr. Powers."

Frank took a deep breath. "After mediation had ended, isn't it true you said to Mrs. Barnes, 'You know what? It would've been cheaper to hire a different prostitute every month. I would've had variety, and they would've been thrilled with the money. And, most importantly, I wouldn't have had to listen to any bullshit'?"

Stan hadn't anticipated the question and his shoulders slumped slightly as he manufactured his answer. Beth looked at the jurors, and all the females had their arms crossed and were frowning. Charley sat back in his chair and hoped Stan wouldn't be flippant.

Stan said angrily, "I said it because I felt Karen had acted like a prostitute with me. I loved her, but she used me for my money."

Frank pointed at Stan. "Didn't you use her for her looks and set the price at $250,000?"

"I did not," Stan said indignantly. "I loved her, and she flushed our marriage down the toilet when she started sleeping with that Neanderthal fireman."

Frank looked down at his notes as Stan's ridiculous answer echoed around the courtroom.

After a few seconds, Frank asked, "Isn't it true that shortly after mediation ended, your lawyer called you and told you the trial had been continued because the judge's daughter had been in a car accident?"

Stan nodded. "Yes, that's true. He told me the trial had been continued because the judge's daughter was in intensive care at a Gainesville hospital."

"Mr. Jacoby, isn't it true that after mediation failed, and after your lawyer told you the trial had been continued, you went to your bank the next day?"

"Yes, that's true. When I need money, I go to the bank," Stan said flippantly.

Frank pointed at Stan. "You withdrew $5,000 cash from your account the day after mediation failed. What did you use the cash for?"

"I like to gamble. Some weeks, I go out on the gambling

boat at Ft. Myers Beach. Some weeks, I go to the dog track in Bonita Springs. That day, I went to the dog track."

"Was anyone with you?"

"No," Stan said as he shook his head. "I was by myself."

"Of course you were," Frank said sarcastically. "Did you win or lose?"

"I lost $2,500," Stan said matter-of-factly.

Frank nodded for a few seconds. "That's very convenient. Do you have an answer for everything?"

Stan pointed his finger at Frank. "I have answered all your questions. When you tell the truth, you don't have to remember your lies!"

"That's a very good point, Mr. Jacoby. Let me ask you about the two phone calls you made to Butch Redding on the day he tied up your wife and raped her."

Stan waved his right pointer back and forth. "That's not exactly right. He tied up my wife so it would be consistent with rape. And he tied up your girlfriend, so you'd be blinded by her naive belief in her client. How does it feel to be used, Mr. Powers?"

Judge McDaniel banged his gavel. "Mr. Jacoby, you will refrain from gratuitous comments and from asking questions. Your job is to answer questions. Do I make myself clear?"

Stan sat up in his chair and took a deep breath. "I'm telling the truth. What's wrong with that?"

Judge McDaniel banged his gavel three times before he said loudly, "Just answer the questions!"

Frank waited a few seconds and let everyone settle down. He looked at Stan and asked, "Why did you call Mr. Redding twice that day?"

"I testified already that I was asking about the price of fixing some broken tiles in my bathroom, and I wanted it priced out."

Frank asked sarcastically, "Are you telling this jury that a man that's worth 50 million dollars cares about pricing on a small repair job in his bathroom?"

Stan sat back in his chair and cleared his throat. "Just because I'm rich doesn't mean I can't be frugal."

Frank shrugged his shoulders and announced sarcastically, "I think we've heard enough from Mr. Jacoby. No further questions,

Your Honor."

"Call your next witness, Mr. Kline," Judge McDaniel boomed.

Charley stood up and said quietly, "The defense rests, Your Honor."

Judge McDaniel looked at the jury. "We'll take a fifteen-minute break and then start closing arguments."

Chapter 29

Frank swiveled on his chair and watched Charley and Stan walk out of the courtroom for a bathroom break before closing arguments started. He knew from past experiences that he should wait for them to return because there is nothing more awkward than to be in a bathroom with your opponent during trial. Frank turned his head and looked at Beth and Karen.

Beth walked to the bar and said quietly, "You were spectacular, honey."

Karen stayed seated while Frank stood up and walked toward the bar. When he reached the bar, he held Beth's fingers gently and said, "I tried my best, but he was pretty adamant with his answers. I hope his temper showed through and the jury can see he got angry and paid Butch for this attack."

Karen said disdainfully, "His answers were so rehearsed, but you caught him off guard with the questions about his double standards. You certainly pushed his buttons and showed he's the king of justification."

Frank looked in Beth's eyes for a few seconds before he spoke quietly. "I just hope I can tie it up together in closing."

Beth lifted Frank's right hand up and gave it a quick kiss. "A little bit of pixie dust never hurt."

* * * * * *

"All rise. Judge Tom McDaniel is presiding over this court," the head bailiff announced.

Judge McDaniel walked in and sat down. "Please be seated."

After everyone sat down, Judge McDaniel looked at the jurors. "Ladies and gentlemen, the State goes first with their argument and then the defense. After the defense lawyer has made his argument, the State is permitted to have a rebuttal argument." Judge McDaniel turned to Frank and said, "You may proceed with closing arguments, Mr. Powers."

Frank walked to the podium and set down his notes. He was dressed in a black suit with a white shirt and his power red tie. The stress of the trial had gotten to him. He had dark circles under his eyes and a small fever blister was forming on his lower lip. He looked at every juror momentarily before he spoke.

"Ladies and gentlemen, I'd like to thank you for your time and attention during this trial. It's been a long week for all us, and I want you to know that the State Attorney's

Office appreciates your dedication and service. Our judicial system depends on jurors to hear difficult cases and return fair verdicts."

Frank looked down at his notes and cleared his throat. "Ladies and gentlemen, I'd like to start with a simple question. Why did this attack happen? The attack happened because this man," Frank turned and pointed at Stan, "was angry that he couldn't bully his wife and her attorney into a divorce settlement. He's a rich man that tried to use his money to punish his wife and her attorney because they didn't accept his offer at mediation.

"We know that on the day of the rape, Stan Jacoby and Butch Redding talked twice on their cell phones to each other. Mr. Jacoby's plan was to hire his trusted handyman to tie up his wife and her attorney at gunpoint at their secluded beach cottage. And after they were tied up, he wanted his wife raped by a masked clown to further humiliate her. He knew there'd be no way to identify the rapist because of the mask, and he'd deny he had anything to do with the attack. He paid his trusted handyman $2,500 up front and was going to pay him another $2,500 after the rape. That's the reason he withdrew $5,000 from his account on the day of the rape. There'd be an investigation, but he knew there'd be no way to connect the masked rapist to him, so he wouldn't be arrested. After that, the divorce case would settle to his satisfaction, and he would win.

"However, he didn't count on the intelligence, perseverance, and courage of Beth Mancini. We all heard how Ms. Mancini foiled Mr. Jacoby's plan by her quick thinking and her actions."

Frank turned and looked at Beth for a second on the front row and smiled.

"Mr. Kline has tried to make it an issue that Beth Mancini is my girlfriend. Ladies and gentlemen, this is nothing but a smoke screen, and I'd ask that you look at the evidence in the case and not listen to Mr. Kline's wild conspiracy theories. The evidence is that Mr. Jacoby was extremely angry during mediation at his wife and her lawyer, Ms. Mancini. He cursed Ms. Mancini and abruptly ended mediation when it didn't settle. He knew his wife loved going to the beach cottage and that it was her weekend to be there. During the divorce, I'm sure he'd talked to Butch Redding at the shooting range about his wife's divorce lawyer and how they were friendly. And you know what? I bet he didn't have anything good to say about Ms. Mancini and described her to Butch Redding. Mr. Jacoby had correctly assumed Ms.

Mancini would accompany his wife to the beach cottage for the weekend when the divorce trial was continued at the last minute.

"That's the reason Butch Redding said, 'I've been waiting for both of you. Your husband sent me to deliver a message to you and your lawyer—you all should've settled

at mediation.' Butch Redding pointed his gun at them and forced them upstairs. Ladies and gentlemen, listen to the definition of kidnapping that Judge McDaniel will give you. He'll tell you that force, or threat of force, to move people against their will is required to prove kidnapping. And that's exactly what happened here. Once they were forced upstairs at gunpoint they were tied up, and Mrs. Jacoby was raped by Butch Redding. The judge will instruct you that a conspiracy is an agreement between two parties. In this case, there was an agreement that Stan Jacoby would pay Butch Redding to kidnap his wife and her attorney. And there was a further agreement that Butch Redding should rape his wife after she was tied up."

Frank pointed at Stan, "Mr. Jacoby paid Butch Redding to attack his wife and her divorce lawyer. Mr. Redding received his just reward for his actions, and now I'm asking you to give Mr. Jacoby his just reward—a guilty verdict on all counts."

Frank took a deep breath before his finished his argument. "Ladies and gentlemen, if it walks like a duck, and flies like a duck, and quacks like a duck, it's a duck! Don't let Mr. Kline manipulate your deliberations with his wild conspiracy theories. Please look at the evidence and return a guilty verdict. Thank you for your attention."

Frank walked back to his table and sat down.

Judge McDaniel looked at Charley. "Mr. Kline, you may proceed."

Charley walked confidently to the podium with his notes and looked at the jurors over his reading glasses. He was wearing a tan suit with a light blue shirt and striped green tie, but his rattlesnake boots made the outfit. Stan watched from the defense table. Sweat was running down his back as he cracked his knuckles. Beth reached over and held Karen's hand as she said a silent prayer for a guilty verdict.

Charley held his hands out in front of him in a defensive posture and said sarcastically, "Ladies and gentlemen, don't let me manipulate you with wild conspiracy theories."

Beth noticed that one female juror on the back row smiled slightly, but the other jurors were stone-faced.

Charley continued, "I'm not going to talk about conspiracy theories here this afternoon. I'm going to talk about the facts, and you, Ladies and gentlemen, will have to decide if the State has proven their allegations against Dr. Jacoby. And remember, the burden of proof in criminal cases is proof beyond a reasonable doubt. When you're in the jury room and you think *maybe* the State has proven the case, then the correct verdict is not guilty. If you are in the jury room and you think the State has *probably* proven the case, then the correct verdict is not guilty. You have to *know* that the State has proven their case beyond *all* reasonable doubt before you can convict. Judge McDaniel will instruct you on the definition of reasonable doubt and the burden of proof on this case. I'd ask that you listen very closely to his instructions."

Charley took a deep breath and continued. "I want to point out different facts that have been established during this trial. At the end of my argument, I'll tell you what I think all these facts mean. Of course, you'll have to make your own assessment of these facts during deliberations. The first fact I'd like to point out is that Karen Jacoby, the State's star witness, lied under oath about her affair with Duke Godfrey. Mrs. Jacoby has been proven to be a liar, and when this trial is over, she should be prosecuted for perjury. I'm sure Mrs. Jacoby will say it was only a little white lie and it doesn't really matter."

230

Charley shook his head and shifted his weight on his feet before he continued. "Lying a little bit under oath is like being a little bit pregnant. You either are, or you aren't. Plain and simple, you tell the truth or you're a liar."

Charley turned and stared at Karen for a second and shook his head in disgust. Beth felt Karen's hand start to sweat and gently squeezed her hand for support. Charley turned and pointed at Frank. "If this prosecutor is intellectually honest, during jury deliberations he'll go back to his office and file charges against Karen Jacoby for perjury."

"Objection!" Frank roared as he jumped to his feet. "Sustained. Move along Mr. Kline, and I'd suggest you remember our prior conversation."

Charley put on his reading glasses and looked at his notes for a second as he collected his thoughts.

"The next fact I'd like to talk about is Dr. Shara Lance's testimony about the examination of Karen Jacoby at the hospital. If you remember, she said there was no tearing or bruising to Mrs. Jacoby's vagina. And then I asked her, 'Wouldn't you agree that at least 67% of rape exams show some type of tearing and/or bruising to the vagina?' Dr.

Lance agreed with this question and opined that one reason for this is there might've been involuntary lubrication. I got her to agree that another possibility is that Mrs. Jacoby was consenting to the sexual act, and that was the reason for lubrication. Ladies and gentlemen, I'm asking you to consider this fact, along with all the other facts in this case. I don't take joy in bringing up this salacious fact, but I'd be a delinquent lawyer if I didn't bring this up for your consideration.

"The next fact I'd like to talk about is that Mrs. Jacoby knew her secret lover, Duke Godfrey, was coming the next morning to pick them up for a day of fishing. And remember what Duke Godfrey testified to: 'Karen said to pick them up at eight, but they might've slept late so just come up to the cottage for coffee.' Mrs. Jacoby knew he'd find them tied up the next morning and cut them loose. Of course, they'd be bruised and dehydrated and there'd be great pictures the prosecutor could show you of their injuries. However,

Mrs. Jacoby's plan didn't work, and Butch Redding is dead

because he was greedy and under her spell."

Charley held up his right pointer finger. "I'd like to make this point: Ms. Mancini is an innocent victim of this staged rape, because Mrs. Jacoby wanted a witness to back up her story. I'm truly sorry that she was tied up during this staged attack and her survival instincts took over, causing her to kill Butch Redding with a spear gun"

Charley walked over to his table and took a drink of water. Beth wanted to jump across the bar and beat Charley with his rattlesnake boots for what he'd just said. Karen had shifted in her seat and had her arms crossed in front of her chest in anger. Frank cracked his neck and looked at the ceiling while Charley grandstanded.

Charley returned to the podium and looked at his notes. "The next fact I'd like to talk about is the pocketknife that was found in Butch Redding's pocket. This unique knife cost $1,200, and the only place that sells it within 100 miles of Ft. Myers is Sally's Collectables on Sanibel Island. Mrs. Jacoby admits she shops at this store but denies she bought the knife for Butch Redding as a gift. I think we can all agree that a handyman wouldn't spend $1,200 for a knife. So, let's talk about the possibilities of how he ended up with this knife in his pocket on the day he died."

Charley hesitated and shrugged his shoulders. "I guess one explanation is that he bought it at a garage sale for a few dollars. Another explanation is someone else gave it to him as a gift. However," Charley raised his right pointer finger and cocked his left eyebrow, "a third possibility is that Mrs. Jacoby bought it and gave it to him as a gift because he was her lover. She knew she needed him for her staged rape and she used gifts, money, and sex to get him to agree to the plan."

Beth looked over at Karen and her eyes were bulging out in anger. Karen leaned over and whispered desperately, "Can't you do something to stop this bullshit?"

Beth leaned into her ear and whispered back. "I'm sorry. They're allowed to make their arguments to the jury."

Charley continued, "The next fact I'd like to talk about is the phone call made to Butch Redding's cell phone from the 7-11 on the corner of Cypress Drive and McGregor Boulevard on the day before the attack. We know this is the 7-11 near Mrs. Jacoby's rented

232

condo and the gym that she works out at. We also know she goes there on a regular basis to fill up with gas. She knew there was a pay phone at this 7-11 and there'd be no way to trace the call to her. She already had some cash in her wallet and went to the bank to get more cash. After the call, she went over to Butch Redding's house and gave him cash. We know that because her bank records prove that. I'm sure she promised him a lot more cash after the pre-nup was set aside, and she sued her husband for civil battery."

Charley turned and stared at Karen as he shook his head.

"The next fact I'd like to talk about is how Butch Redding knew that Ms. Mancini was going to be at the beach cottage. Dr. Jacoby told you he didn't know Ms. Mancini was going to the beach cottage with his wife. Mrs. Jacoby denies telling Butch Redding that Ms. Mancini was going to be there. The prosecutor realizes this is a weak part of his case because he tried to gloss over it. He said Dr. Jacoby correctly assumed Ms. Mancini would be there and told Butch Redding. There's no proof of this assumption, so the prosecutor glosses over this weakness by asking you to assume Dr. Jacoby guessed Ms. Mancini would be there.

"Ladies and gentlemen, I want you to listen very closely to the instructions Judge McDaniel will read to you. I guarantee you that he won't say you can assume facts. He'll instruct you that the State has to prove their allegations with evidence. And they haven't done this, so you should return a not guilty verdict. Before the trial started, you took an oath to follow the law. You saw Mrs. Jacoby take an oath to tell the truth and you saw her not honor that oath." Charley shook his head in disgust. "Don't be like Mrs. Jacoby."

Charley looked down at his notes for a second before he continued.

"I'm going to play devil's advocate for a second, and I want you to assume the State's theory is correct. Assume Dr. Jacoby paid Butch Redding to kidnap his wife and her lawyer. If so, that means that there were only two possibilities about how Butch Redding's attack on Mrs. Jacoby and Ms. Mancini would end.

"The first possibility is that after the rape, he'd kill them and leave them. The problem with this possibility is that there's no reason to wear a clown mask to conceal his identity if he's going to kill them.

"The second possibility is that after he ties them up and

233

rapes Mrs. Jacoby, he leaves them tied up so they can't call the police, and Butch Redding can escape back to Pine Island and drive home undetected. And then the next morning, Duke Godfrey would come to take them fishing and discover them tied up. He'd call 911 and the police would investigate. At that point, do you think Mrs. Jacoby and her lawyer would want to settle the divorce case? You've met Karen Jacoby and Beth Mancini. Do they seem like shrinking violets to you? Of course not. They'd be mad as hell, and the divorce case would go to trial. There'd be nothing for Dr.

Jacoby to gain financially by hiring Butch Redding to kidnap and rape his wife and her lawyer and leave them alive."

Charley walked over to his table and took another drink of water. He returned to the podium and said quietly, "Of course, there's a third possibility."

Charley raised his voice. "The third possibility is that Mrs. Jacoby used her Mensa brain to plan this staged rape to get the pre-nup set aside because Dr. Jacoby would be convicted of a violent crime against her. Of course, then she could file a civil battery case against him and take the rest of his money while he rots in prison. Mrs. Jacoby uses her sexuality as a weapon, and it's more deadly than a spear gun."

Charley took a deep breath before he continued. "Ladies and gentlemen, I've pointed out some of the holes in the State's case that show reasonable doubt. You might see more holes in the State's case during deliberations, so I'd ask that you discuss them with your fellow jurors. I'm asking you to return a not guilty verdict because the State's case smells like rotten eggs."

Charley returned to his table and looked up at Judge McDaniel. "The defense rests, Your Honor."

Judge McDaniel looked at Frank. "Mr. Powers, a brief rebuttal argument?"

Frank stood up. "Yes, Your Honor"

Frank walked to the podium without any notes and looked at the jury for a few seconds before he began. "Ladies and gentlemen, this is my last time to talk to you before you begin deliberations, so I'd ask that you pay close attention. We have a very simple case here. We have a rich, arrogant man that wanted to humiliate his wife because she dared to challenge him in court about his pre-nuptial agreement. When he couldn't bully her into

234

accepting the divorce settlement that he thought was proper, he wanted revenge.

"So, he decided to hire his trusted handyman and shooting buddy, Butch Redding, to extract his revenge. As a bonus, Mrs. Jacoby's divorce lawyer was at the beach cottage with her. You heard Butch Redding, while wearing a clown mask to conceal his identity, tied them both up and said, 'Your husband sent me to deliver a message to you and your lawyer—ya'll shoulda settled at mediation.'

"However, Mr. Jacoby underestimated Ms. Mancini's survival instincts, and she killed Butch Redding with the spear gun when he went for his gun. And ever since then, Mr. Jacoby has used his money to try and get away with his crime. He spent $50,000 for his so-called expert witness, Patrick Benning, to try and confuse you. And God only knows how much he's paid Charley Kline to try and throw mud on the evidence to confuse you. However, I don't think that you're the type of jurors that will let a rich man buy a not guilty verdict. The State is asking that you return a guilty verdict. Thank you for your time."

Judge McDaniel looked at the jury. "We're going to take a fifteen-minute break and then I'll instruct you on the law in this case. After jury instructions, you'll retire to begin your deliberations."

Chapter 30

It was four-thirty p.m. and Judge McDaniel had just finished his instructions on the law. He looked up at the jurors and said, "The first thing you should do when you retire to the jury room is to pick a jury foreman, and it can be a man or a woman. Once you've decided on a verdict, the jury foreman should check the correct spot on the verdict form and sign it. After that, knock on the jury door and let my bailiff know you've reached a verdict." Judge McDaniel shifted in his seat and smiled. "On a lighter note, I have ordered a pepperoni pizza and a vegetarian pizza for your dinner. When they arrive, the bailiff will bring them and sodas to you. At this time, you may retire to the jury room."

The jurors stood up and walked slowly to the jury room. After the door shut, the head bailiff looked at Judge McDaniel and nodded. Judge McDaniel turned toward Charley and said sternly, "Now that the jury is deliberating, I'm going to hold a contempt hearing against you, Mr. Kline."

Everyone in the courtroom sat up in their chairs and looked at Charley. Stan slid his chair a few inches away from Charley.

Charley stood up uncertainly and said, "Your Honor, I'd ask that you hold the contempt hearing after the trial is over."

Judge McDaniel shook his head vigorously. "No, I'm holding the hearing right now before the verdict is returned. I don't want any claims that I'm mad over the verdict and that I'm taking it out on you. I'm making the finding that you intentionally violated the rules of evidence and the rules of procedure by your improper questions and comments during the trial. I warned you, but you continued your actions, so I'm finding you guilty of contempt of court."

Charley sat down and closed his eyes as he concentrated on his precarious position.

Judge McDaniel stared at Charley for a few seconds and then turned to Frank, "Mr. Powers, does the State have a recommendation on the sentence I should impose?"

Frank was more concerned about the verdict than Charley's

sentence. He stood up and said solemnly, "Your Honor, the State is pleased that you've found Mr. Kline guilty of contempt. As you know, I objected repeatedly during the trial to Mr. Kline's questions and comments. I think your sentence should involve some jail time because a fine would just be a slap on the wrist, and Mr. Kline won't change his tactics in future trials."

Judge McDaniel turned to Charley and asked tantalizingly, "How much jail time do you think I should give you, Mr. Kline?"

Charley stood up and said unrepentantly, "Your Honor, I defended my client with every ounce of strength I had and used every technique I know to make the State's witnesses look bad because I believe my client is innocent of these charges. So, in answer to your question, I think you should give me as much jail time as you think is appropriate under these circumstances."

Judge McDaniel sat back in his chair and stroked his beard for a few seconds. "Mr. Kline, I'm sentencing you to ten days in jail. Once the verdict is returned and the jury has been escorted from the courtroom, the assistant bailiff will escort you from the courtroom to jail to begin serving your sentence. I suggest while the jury is deliberating, you rearrange your work schedule and notify your family where you'll be spending the next ten days."

Judge McDaniel banged his gavel and said, "Court is in recess until we have a verdict."

* * * * * *

When Beth and Karen walked outside of the courtroom while the jury was deliberating, all the reporters were lined up and the camera lights came on. One reporter shouted out, "How does it feel to be accused of staging your own rape?

A second reporter shouted out, "How many affairs did you have during your marriage?"

A third reporter shouted out, "How much money are you getting in your divorce?"

Beth held up her hands and said, "We have no comment. Please leave us alone."

Beth and Karen scurried to the elevators to get away from the reporters and the cameras. The elevator door shut, and they cherished their silence as the elevator went to the ground floor. Beth and Karen walked outside of the courthouse and on to the plaza to get some fresh air and privacy. They walked to the far end of the plaza and sat down on an empty bench.

"Finally," Beth said irritably, "we're away from those vultures."

Karen shook her head. "They have no shame."

"We can stay out here and wait if you want. I told Frank to call me on my cell when they have a verdict."

"That sounds like a great idea," Karen said wearily.

* * * * * *

"All rise. Judge Tom McDaniel is presiding over this court," the head bailiff announced.

Judge McDaniel walked in and sat down. "Please be seated."

After everyone sat down, Judge McDaniel said, "The bailiff has informed me that the jury has a verdict. I'm going to bring the jury in and review the verdict, then the clerk will publish the verdict. I want no loud reaction to the verdict here in court. If there's an outburst, I'll hold that person in contempt of court and send them to jail. If you can't control yourself, you need to leave the courtroom at this time."

Judge McDaniel looked around the crowded courtroom to see if anyone wanted to leave, but no one moved. Judge McDaniel looked at his head bailiff, "Bring in the jury."

Beth looked at her watch. It was eight p.m., so the jury had deliberated for three and a half hours. Karen reached over and grabbed Beth's hand, squeezing it tightly. Frank, Charley, and Stan stood up at their respective tables as the jurors entered the courtroom. The jurors were aware everyone in the courtroom was looking at them for some indication of the verdict, so they looked down to avoid everyone's stares.

After they sat down, Judge McDaniel looked at a female juror on the first row that was holding the verdict form. "Mrs. Resh, it appears you've been chosen as foreman. Has the jury reached a verdict?"

Mrs. Resh said quietly, "We have, Your Honor." "Please

hand it to the bailiff."

The head bailiff retrieved the verdict form and gave it to Judge McDaniel. He looked it over for a few seconds and handed it to his clerk. "Please publish the verdict, Madame Clerk."

The clerk stood up and read, "The State of Florida versus Stan Jacoby. The jury finds the defendant not guilty." There was a rush of air that moved through the courtroom as everyone gasped. All the spectators in the courtroom whispered their opinions of the verdict as they stood up. Beth felt the blood running out of her face and her ears were ringing. She looked over at Karen and she had her face in her hands. Stan hugged Charley, who was smiling from ear to ear and looking sideways at Judge McDaniel.

Judge McDaniel nodded politely at the jurors and said sincerely, "Ladies and gentlemen, I'd like to thank you for your jury service. My bailiff will escort you to the elevator and walk with you to the parking garage. As jurors you have the absolute right to not talk about your decision to anyone. However, if you wish to speak to the media, or anyone else about your jury service, you may. Have a good night."

Judge McDaniel's head bailiff escorted the jury out of the courtroom and after the door shut, Judge McDaniel turned to Stan. "Mr. Jacoby, you've been found not guilty by a jury of your peers. You are free to leave the courtroom." Judge McDaniel turned his gaze to Charley. "However, Mr. Kline, you're remanded to custody to begin serving your sentence."

Charley shook Stan's hand and Stan walked out of the courtroom quickly before Judge McDaniel changed his mind. The assistant bailiff walked up to Charley and said apologetically, "I've got to put handcuffs on you, sir."

"No problem, son. I know you're just doing your job."

Charley put his hands behind his back, and the assistant bailiff gently cuffed him. The clicks of the cameras were loud and the lights from the news cameras lit up the courtroom. Charley followed the bailiff to the side door of the courtroom that led to a secure hallway with a holding cell. As the bailiff opened the door, Charley turned and smiled at the photographers and news cameras that were filming.

As he walked through the door, Charley turned around and gave Judge McDaniel a small smile. Judge McDaniel's back stiffened in anger, but he knew there was nothing he could do over a smile.

After the door from the court room shut, the bailiff asked incredulously, "Why are you smiling?"

"Son," Charley said happily, "you can't buy this kind of publicity."

Chapter 31

Judge McDaniel banged his gavel. "Court is adjourned."

As Judge McDaniel walked off the bench, the second assistant bailiff watched the action from the side of the courtroom. Frank stood up and walked to the bar with the glare of the lights from the news cameras in his face. All the reporters surged toward Frank and blurted out questions, but he held up his hand and they stayed back a few feet and stopped asking questions. Beth stood up unsteadily and met Frank at the bar, but Karen stayed seated, her face down in her hands.

Frank leaned forward and whispered in Beth's ear, "Stay here in the courtroom. I'm going to ask the bailiff to take you and Karen down the back elevator to avoid the media.

Just wait here until I leave the courtroom, and the media will follow me out."

Beth nodded and sat down next to Karen, between her and the cameras. Beth put her left arm around Karen's back and pulled her close, shielding her from the lights of the camera and the rude reporters' questions. She could feel Karen shaking and heard her weeping. Beth felt numb.

Frank walked up to the bailiff standing on the side of the courtroom and spoke to him quietly. The bailiff nodded and Frank walked back to his table and gathered all his notes and put them in his briefcase. He walked outside of the bar with his briefcase and all the reporters surged forward.

One reporter blurted out, "Are you going to prosecute Karen Jacoby for perjury?"

A second reporter held a microphone in his face and asked, "Do you think it hurt your case that you're sleeping with one of the main witnesses?"

"Are you going to apologize to Stan Jacoby for prosecuting him?" a third reporter asked sarcastically.

Frank kept walking as he said evenly, "I'll answer all your questions outside."

The pack of reporters followed him outside the courtroom

like hammerhead sharks tracking a bleeding tarpon. After Frank's tormenters followed him out of the courtroom, there was no one left in the audience area but Karen and Beth. The bailiff quickly walked to the back of the courtroom and locked the door.

The bailiff walked up to Beth and said gently, "If both of you follow me, you can avoid the cameras."

"Thank you," Beth said.

Karen stood up and walked unsteadily with Beth to the door behind the judge's bench. The bailiff opened the door to the hallway that led to the judge's elevators and motioned for them to follow. They walked down the hallway in silence and the bailiff used his key to unlock the signal on the elevator and hit the down button. When the elevator arrived, everyone got on and rode down in awkward silence without looking at each other. On the ground level, the bailiff led Beth and Karen down a long hallway to a fire door that opened to an outside sidewalk. Karen started weeping and sniffling as they approached the fire door.

"Thanks," Beth said quietly as the bailiff held open the door.

"Good night, ladies," the bailiff said as he closed the door securely.

After the door shut, Karen wiped her tears away and took a deep breath. She asked flatly, "What happens now?"

Beth considered her answer for a few seconds. "We file a notice of trial with Judge Sanchez and get the divorce back on the trial docket. Of course, we can still file a civil battery suit against Stan. Remember the O.J. Simpson cases? He was found not guilty at trial, but a civil jury awarded millions to the victims' families. We can use this civil battery suit as a tool to try to get you a better settlement in the divorce."

Karen said irritably, "Whatever you think is best, but I need a drink right now. I'm calling some of my friends to meet me out."

Beth nodded. "I understand. I'm a little thirsty myself, and I'm sure Frank will be drinking tonight."

They turned and walked to the parking garage in silence.

Chapter 32

Beth was sitting in her overstuffed recliner at home, listening to classical music and drinking Merlot, when her cell phone rang with Frank's special ring tone. She answered quickly. "Hi, honey. How are you doing?"

"Not good," Frank said wearily. "I spent thirty minutes answering all the reporters' questions without losing my temper. I held it together pretty well until I walked out of the courthouse and saw one of the TV reporters interviewing the jury foreman. As I walked by, I heard her say that the jury was disturbed that I stayed on the case when I was dating you, so it's going to be all over the news. Everyone's going to be a Monday morning quarterback at the courthouse. I'm taking tomorrow off so I don't have to deal with all the contrived condolences at work."

Bella and Gracie jumped on the recliner, and Beth petted them while she answered. "I'm sorry, I know you did your best. If Karen hadn't lied, I'm sure the verdict would've been different."

Frank sighed. "Her lie about her affair with Duke hurt us, but all Charley's bullshit confused the jury. I hope he enjoys his ten days in jail."

Beth softened her tone of voice. "I'm having a glass of wine and trying to relax. Do you want me to come over?"

Frank hesitated for a second. "Baby, I don't think I'll be good company tonight. I'm driving home right now to have a couple of belts of scotch before bed. I'm beat."

Beth answered compassionately, "I understand. I love you."

"I love you, too. Sleep tight and tomorrow night we'll go out."

"Sounds like a plan."

Beth ended the call and pulled Bella and Gracie up to her chest lovingly. They put their heads against her neck and purred softly as Beth closed her eyes and listened to the music.

* * * * * *

The next morning Beth opened the newspaper at her breakfast table and read the headline: *TROPHY WIFE DIES IN CAR WRECK AFTER NOT GUILTY VERDICT!*

Beth couldn't believe the headline and started to sweat, her stomach roiling. She quickly read the article and found out that Karen had lost control of her red SL550 Mercedes and hit a large palm tree. An eyewitness said Karen had passed him going at least seventy miles per hour on Mc-Gregor Boulevard. When she tried to pull back into the lane, she'd lost control of her car and it flipped over and went airborne before it hit the palm tree. The accident had happened at midnight about three blocks from Karen's rented condo. There was a picture of Karen's Mercedes upside down and wrapped around the palm tree with four firemen trying to use the Jaws of Life to free Karen from the wreckage, but they'd been unsuccessful. She was declared dead on the scene. Beth looked closely at the picture and could see Karen's bloody blond hair in the background. Beth pictured Karen's mangled and deformed body in the twisted metal, and she realized it would be a closed casket funeral.

The reporter cited an unnamed fireman at the scene who had said there was a half empty vodka bottle in the wreckage.

Beth's head started pounding and her vision narrowed.

She picked up her cell phone with trembling hands and called Frank with the news.

Chapter 33

Beth asked for the hostess at the Veranda to seat her at the same table she and Karen had sat at during mediation. Beth had the front page of the paper with her to show Frank, who was meeting her for lunch. The headline read: *HUSBAND BURIES TROPHY WIFE WITH UNUSUAL TOMBSTONE.*

The story recounted the two-week legal battle between Karen's father and Stan over who had the right to bury her and pick the tombstone. Karen's father had filed suit alleging that because there was a pending divorce, Stan had no right to the body, and since her father was the next of kin, he had the right to his daughter's body. The judge disagreed and cited precedent that gave a husband the absolute right to bury his wife and pick out her tombstone, so Stan had gotten custody of her body. Underneath the headline was a large color picture of Karen's grave and the tombstone that read: *Here lies Karen Jacoby. She was a lying gold digger that God struck down for her sins.*

Beth had researched the issue of what money Karen's estate was entitled to from the marriage. Because she was still married at the time of her death, the $250,000 she was due under the pre-nuptial was not available. She was a joint owner of the Cayo Costa beach cottage, so the property transferred totally to Stan upon her death. Beth found out that Karen had never taken Stan's name off her life insurance policy through the school board, and since he was still listed as the beneficiary, he got the $100,000 policy. Of course, Stan had told the newspaper reporter this, and it was in the story about Karen's tombstone. Beth was depressed and angry that Stan was publicly gloating over Karen's death and his acquittal. Beth missed Karen deeply and thought of the old saying: *Only the good die young.* Beth picked up her cloth napkin and wiped a single tear from her left eye.

Beth saw Frank walk in the front door of the Veranda and her spirits lifted. Frank had sent flowers every day since the trial ended to her office, with the simple message: *I love you. Frank.* Beth's secretary and receptionist were insanely jealous, and Beth enjoyed the attention.

She stood up and gave Frank a kiss on the lips when he walked up but was immediately concerned because his lips were cold and his face was pale.

"What's wrong?" Beth asked as she stepped back. They sat down and Frank stared at Beth for a few seconds and slowly shook his head.

Beth was perplexed and asked quietly, "What is it?" Frank took a deep breath before he spoke quietly. "During our investigation, we did a full background check on

Butch Redding. His ex-wife lives in their hometown of Macon, Georgia with their five-year-old son, Ralph. We shipped his body up there, and his family buried him in a closed casket ceremony because of the hole in his neck from the spear."

Beth leaned forward and arched her eyebrows quizzically. "And?"

Frank closed his eyes and rubbed them with his right thumb and pointer finger for a few seconds. He looked up and said gravely, "I just got a call about twenty minutes ago from a probate lawyer that prepared Karen's will a few months ago. This afternoon he's filing her probate case and her will with the court. He told me she left everything to Butch's son, Ralph."

Beth stared at Frank in disbelief and felt a chill run up her spine.

"Here's the worst part," Frank said somberly. "The will was prepared and signed by Karen a week after you killed Butch."

About the Author

John D. Mills is a fifth generation native of Ft. Myers, Florida. He grew up fishing the waters of Pine Island Sound and it's still his favorite hobby. He graduated from Mercer University in Macon, Georgia with a BBA in Finance and worked for Lee County Bank in Ft. Myers for five months. He returned to Macon and graduated from Mercer's law school in 1989.

He started his legal career as a prosecutor for the State Attorney's Office in Ft. Myers. In 1990, he began his private practice concentrating in Divorce and Criminal Defense.

Other thrillers by John D. Mills

Reasonable and Necessary

The Manatee Murders

The Objector Sworn Jury

The Hooker, the Dancer and the Nun

These and other John D. Mills thrillers are available at
www.pineislandsoundmysteries.com
and online retailers everywhere

Made in the USA
Columbia, SC
26 June 2021

40665855R00157